MAYA MYSUN
&
The World That Does Not Exist

PM Perry

Disclaimer

This book is a work of fiction. Any references to historical events, real people, or real places are used fictitiously. Other names, characters, places, and events are products of the author's imagination, and any resemblance to actual events or places or persons, living or dead, is entirely coincidental.

Acknowledgements

This book is dedicated to the three remarkable women in my life (my daughter, my wife, and my mum). Without their continued belief in my dream to write and their continued support, the creation of the Siantian & Konjiurian realms of Maya Mysun would not have been possible.

The science of magic & the magic of science.

TABLE OF CONTENTS

1

SILENT WITNESS

As Earth, the realm of science, continued the life of order, the magic realms beyond tipped into chaos.

Maya, woke abruptly on a clear night in London.

'Tommy that felt real, bewitchingly real,' she whispered to her pet tortoise in his vivarium across the window. Fully awake, she hugged her soft duvet. 'I was in these dark woods and I saw a portal appear; you know, a doorway to another world. It had an intense blue light with lightning sprouting from its edges, and it tore the woods before me. Don't worry, nothing happened to the woods; it was like a tear in a photograph, only it was a tear in the air. Through the tear I saw a chamber with a glowing fireplace. And then a wizard walked through!'

Vivid dreams were normal for Maya, but this felt like something else. Rubbing the goosebumps on her arms, she quietly sat up and swept her brown fringe back before leaning across to pluck Tommy from his world. Excited and frightened, she cuddled the small creature and looked through the gap between the curtains behind her to see if it was still night. Her heart sank to the bottom of her stomach when she saw the otherworldly grey sky. An ungodly hour, she thought, recalling what she'd read. It was a period of uncertainty, neither day nor night, when the dark arts were at their strongest.

'I've still got some time before our big day!' She sighed, giving Tommy another embrace before returning him to his pebbles. Maya and Jack, her not so-identical twin, were about to celebrate their thirteenth birthday. But that wasn't for a couple of hours, so she snuggled down with thoughts of presents floating in her mind. Comfortable, she gazed up at the glowing stars stuck on her ceiling and gave a quick glance to her fluffy toys before closing her eyes. It wasn't long before images of fantasy, of wizards, kings and magic rose in her mind. The images returned like a flash flood: slow at first, then quickening until she was swept into another world.

****

In her dream, Maya found the wizard at the edge of a small opening. He stood with a long staff in hand, studying a tall tower that rose over the woods, like a mushroom above grass. The blue portal was no more, but she didn't have time to ponder this for the wizard turned to her and said, 'Something's wrong! It's too dark. Stay here, keep an eye out, and leave at the sign of any trouble. Understand, old friend?'

Old friend? Maya looked around, wondering if he meant her, and noticed a small monkey standing quietly beside her. It was about half her height and frail, and it looked on with large, unblinking eyes.

'Do you understand, old friend? Don't follow. Leave if there is trouble.'

'But Hopper prefers to stay by your side, by Torackdan's side,' the monkey said feebly.

Maya stared wide-eyed – *a talking monkey?*

'I know you want to come along but something doesn't feel right. Best if you stay back. Understand?'

Seeing the monkey nod, the wizard began towards a wooden door at the foot of the tower. Maya hurried after him, turning back briefly to glance at the monkey, but by then it had disappeared into the nearby undergrowth. Exposed in the open with the fading light, Maya felt her stomach tighten.

When the wizard reached the door, he knocked loudly with his staff. Seconds passed without a response. The wizard was about to knock again when the heavy door creaked open and a bald, plump figure emerged from the darkness, carrying a dim lamp.

'Ebbelle!' said the wizard extending his hand.

'T-Torackdan!' Ignoring the gesture, the plump man scanned the woods over the wizard's shoulders, 'W-Where's your aide?'

His voice was scratchy and tense.

'Hopper's on another errand,' Torackdan said, withdrawing his hand.

'That is unfortunate; more company would have been welcomed.' He ushered the wizard in. Maya snuck in before Ebbelle shut the door.

Inside was an empty round hall with winding steps at its centre.

'Tell me, did you see anyone or anything strange out there?' Ebbelle asked.

'No! Why? What's the matter? Why the darkness?' Torackdan pointed at the faint lamp Ebbelle carried.

Good, good! This way then,' Ebbelle said, ignoring the questions. He led the way up the stone steps. At the top, he placed the lamp on an untidy desk covered with scrolls and books, and rummaged on a long wooden table, lifting various bottles and urns. Maya looked around in the grim light and found that the tower opened up into a deceptively large circular hall with two balconies facing each other and a window at the far side. Her eyes raced around, looking at all the pots, pans, flasks, and herbs that covered the furniture and hung from the walls.

Torackdan spoke: 'Allow me to brighten the place, light a few lamps'—

'No!' Ebbelle snapped returning with a bottle and two chalices.

'What's the matter? This isn't like you, Ebb.'

'It's to do with the boy! The prince.' He poured a dark liquid into the goblets.

'The lost prince?'

'Yes. Someone comes with news of him.'

'Is it genuine? How can you be sure?'

'You doubt me? Your friend?' Ebbelle handed him the drink.

'No! No, of course not.' Torackdan patted Ebbelle's shoulder and took a large sip. 'With so many false hopes, I have simply grown doubtful these past few years.'

Both men remained silent for few seconds, lost in their own thoughts. Maya compared the two men. Torackdan stood like a statue: staff in one hand, cup in the other. Silver armour gleamed on his left shoulder. Underneath it his rich blue robes were draped like a Roman toga. Ebbelle was shorter, bald and more simply dressed than the thin Torackdan, but each boasted a long white beard. Maya's attention was drawn to Torackdan; something about him captivated her more, but she couldn't decide what. It wasn't the heavy ornate collar chain under which he'd tucked his beard, nor the kindness of his face.

'I see you have your staff!' said Ebbelle. 'Good, I'll get mine as well. We might need them before this night is over.'

'Hopefully not! These are peaceful times. I nearly left Konjiur without it.'

Torackdan's staff was a single pole that twisted and curled at the top, where a large fist-sized crystal sat. Maya's gaze shifted from the pole to Torackdan's face and realised what captivated her: his eyes. They were two completely different shades of blue.

'Who comes?' Torackdan asked suddenly, moving away towards one of the balconies.

'Aldrr!'

'One of the enslaved warlords! A wraith! I've heard they're a growing menace.'

Disturbed by the mention of an undead spectre, Maya shut her eyes tight, trying hard to dispel the hooded image forming in her mind, and slowly the images vanished as she slipped into pure sleep.

****

Sometime later, as the sun climbed the sky, a police car took the winding country lanes away from London. At the back sat, a scruffy blonde boy in designers: a grey hoodie, blue jeans, and matching canvas trainers. He stared sneakily at the two officers from underneath his thick blonde mop, thinking *little and large – a perfect couple to dupe.* He was desperate to escape, not because he had something important to do but because he hated being confined and forced to do simple things that didn't interest him.

Today he had planned to visit the biggest library in London – The Big L, as he called it – to find books on myths, legends, and general folklore. He loved such mysterious things that science couldn't explain. He called them 'frontiers' and London was full of them. Having read all the books at his local Ls, he was forced to make a perilous trek to the Big L where he'd hoped its supply of good books would allow him to learn more about his latest interests – ghosts and otherworldly apparitions. He dreamt of one day explaining these myths and other inexplicable 'fantasy' things, and becoming famous.

Keen to get going, he'd made a schoolboy error by breaking his main rule: be invisible. It didn't mean actually being invisible – that was still in the realm of myth. For now he was content with doing things to simply blend in and not draw attention. He kicked himself for ignoring his inner voice and boarding an earlier train than he should have. For daydreaming, when he should have been walking alongside an unsuspecting adult as though he was their son. Two silly errors and one broken rule meant the ticket inspectors at Baker Street Station had stopped him for a routine check. The rest was history. The inspector had snapped his fingers and, as if by magic, David's freedom had vanished. He was taken into custody, handed over to the police and, after surprisingly quick routine paperwork, he was being transferred to some correctional facility outside London.

Pete, the smaller of the two officers, was driving, while the larger one, Bruce, tried for the umpteenth time to settle his big frame into a more comfortable position. His constant movement irritated David, who had more than once contemplated kicking the back of his seat. Settling down some thirty minutes into the journey, Bruce flicked through the boy's file and read it out loud.

'Aka, Wizard or Wiz; what'd you like?'

Seeing an opportunity for distraction, he jovially replied, 'David actually! That's only for mates.'

His trick seemed to work; Bruce gave him a steely look from the mirror on his sun visor. David returned a comically innocent stare. The officer looked away, choosing to be professional and diffuse the matter.

This was not the first time they'd met. The officer didn't recall, but David couldn't forget any of the sixteen officers he'd had a run-in with. He remembered how the security guards, at an expensive clothing store in Victoria Station, had handed him over to this mountain of muscle. On that occasion, David had got the better of him by escaping while being escorted to the car.

Muscles! That was a good nickname. Muscles had chased him through the crowded shopping centre, down the escalators to platform 15 and through the station, where it had been easy for David to give him a slip.

Now Muscles snickered, amused by something in the file. 'Wizard, always running away. Well, where we're taking you, you'll need all your tricks to get away. It's no holiday camp.'

David ignored this. 'I wanna go to the boys' room!' he wailed.

'This isn't a school trip. Hold it till the next services,' Muscles responded casually.

Spotting another opportunity, David smacked the officer's seat as if he found the statement funny.

Taken by surprise, Muscles turned back, annoyed, and stared into his blue gaze. 'Listen buddy, you trying to be a ...' But then he held his tongue and looked away.

David's plan was beginning to work: Muscles had given up using real names. With luck he may get his chance to bolt. Life as an orphan had taught him many things: how to survive, how to run and, above all else, how to get what he wanted with a smile. There was no need to get annoyed, ever. And he had all he wanted. The state had always provided the basics and the rest he had learnt to acquire or, as the well-off folks called it, steal.

Nevertheless, David always felt alone and empty. He couldn't quite place what he wanted. Perhaps that was why he kept running away, searching for his own elusive Holy Grail.

'... quite a file you have here,' Muscles began again. 'Being defiant, arguing. Trouble follows you like a shadow.' Just then, the smaller officer shot him a stern look.

David ignored him once more. 'Where'd ya say this holiday camp is?' He knew that, as a minor and a serial offender, he had been assigned to yet another institute, a private one this time. That's what the officer at the station had said: 'a private residential home'. That worried him.

'It's a specialised place to help your kind of case,' said the smaller officer. David dubbed him 'Tiny'.

7

Those words increased his worry. A specialised place? He knew that only meant one thing: a centre for behavioural disorders. But what did they mean his kind of case? What was that supposed to even mean? He couldn't understand why no one saw the simple answer: if they left him alone, he wouldn't continually need to escape. Would he? Anyway, Tiny, the cleverer one, had thrown a spanner in his plans with his stare. Muscles had gone cold and needed some warming up.

'I really neeeed to go ...' David said, watching the passing woods.

The officers looked at each other and exchanged some silent police code.

'At the next services, when we have a cuppa,' Muscles repeated carefully.

'Step on it then.'

Concerned about the mysterious place, David settled back, pretending to doze off. He needed to know more and hoped the two would let something slip. Tiny was first to start, after he had feigned sleep for about ten minutes.

'Mate, have you heard of this private centre – "Red Gate"?'

Muscles adjusted himself again. 'Nay, can't find it on the satnav either.'

David shrank further into the back seat. He wasn't really as bold and snarky as he pretended to be; that was simply his way of dealing with trouble. Now, he was troubled about the secretive home that didn't exist on the satnav. He told himself it was just a fancy name, but despite his best efforts, he wasn't at rest.

2

BIRTHDAY

Grand finales often have humble beginnings.

In London, Maya awoke to the sweet smell of Mum's baking –
a rich wisp of caramelised sugar – and the soft hum of her
parents chatting downstairs. She recalled her dream and got a
chill remembering how it felt. She wanted to speak to Jack
about that … Then she perked up as she realised what day it
was: their birthday, the first day of half-term break and
Saturday. It had her excited and worried at the same time.

But first she needed to search her room. Her warm brown
eyes snapped open and studied the sunlight filtering through the
gaps between the curtains. Next, she looked up and down all the
walls, concentrating on the corners and the edges, searching for
her nemesis: spiders. She didn't like them; they hunted her
favourite, the butterflies, and then there was the matter of their
appearance. She couldn't decide whether it was their shape,
colour or just how they moved, but she despised them. This
autumn was particularly bad. In a newspaper article entitled
'Spider Invasion!', an expert had theorised that the unusually
warm autumn meant they lived longer, fed for longer and were
seeking shelter in homes due to the change of season. Maya
wanted to be certain that there were none in her room, lurking to
spring on her when she got out of bed. Luckily she found her
room exactly as she expected it: neat, peaceful, and spider-free.

Satisfied, she climbed out of the bed, opened the curtains to
let the sunlight flood in and retrieved Tommy from his
vivarium. The miniature tortoise was least concerned and

continued chewing on a small piece of carrot. Maya raised him to her face to tell him about her dream. She loved confiding her secrets to him; he was a good listener.

'Tommy, I had more of that dream. It was so real – the wizards, the tower, the frightened little monkey. He spoke, fancy that. Imagine if you could speak? Should we tell Jack?' She paused for a second. 'I want to, but no, he doesn't believe in magic and will only laugh. He doesn't need to know.' She placed Tommy on the windowsill where he slowly headed towards the window as she turned towards the bookshelf and began to play the books like piano keys. 'Now, do you remember where I hid it? I think it was …' Her fingers jumped from book to book: from *Warrior Kings and Queens* to *Fairies & Butterflies* to *Modern Warlocks & Spells* and finally to *Mysterious Ancient Games*. 'Which one was it? Do you remember?' She pulled *Fairies & Butterflies* half out, then pushed it back. 'Ah, yes! It's this one.' She drew out *Modern Warlocks* and shook an envelope out from within. It was addressed to Jack.

'Ta-da! Quickly now, let's rush to wish him first.' She tied up her long brown curls. 'You know what? I should listen to Mum – mustn't read books on sorcery and witchcraft and magic at bedtime. She's right – they give me those scary dreams. But they're all so interesting. Dad says you should face your fears. Imagine facing a real witch or a dragon. That would be scary but great! And what about a unicorn or a griffin? Mmm.'

She looked around for her slippers. 'And think I am getting stronger? Jack didn't realise I had a scary dream. Otherwise he'd have sensed I was troubled and rushed in. He always does, but last night he didn't.'

Maya had barely finished speaking when there was a soft knock on the door, followed by a low, 'M^2?'

Hearing 'M-squared', Maya paused for a split second. She liked the way he called her by her nickname; it was different and brotherly.

'Jack!' She opened the door and threw her arms around the tall, well-built boy with short brown hair. Lost in his big frame, she felt even smaller and more fragile than she really was. Maya was quiet and shy and dreamt to be as brave and daring as her brother.

She stepped back and looked up into his kind brown gaze. 'Happy birthday, Jack, this is for you.' She gave him the card.

'Happy Birthday, M^2!' He handed her a pink envelope, but then his eyes narrowed. 'You OK?'

'Yes.' She nodded, wondering if he had sensed her nervousness at night.

Though they were starkly different, Maya and Jack shared a mysterious bond. Jack always sensed her unease, especially when Mark, the class bully, tried to taunt her. Being quiet, Maya was an easy victim for Mark, and he would repeat worn-out jokes in his annoying voice. He'd go on and on, dredging up anything he could find in his shallow little mind, with his favourite being a dig at their surname.

'Mysun! What's that? Is it like a sissy version of the Masons? If you are not good enough then, you can be a Mysun. Well? Say something Mysun. What's the matter? Protecting some secret, are we? Must be a Mysun secret; is it more important than a Freemason one? Well, is it? Is it?'

Maya could still hear his irritating voice ringing in her ear. She longed to stand up to him, but would lose her courage at the last second. Her mind would go into lockdown, and her silence would just feed Mark's cruelty until Jack pitched up.

Miraculously, her hero brother always appeared to spoil Mark's party. Unable to understand how Jack knew, Mark always concluded that it must be magic. He was joking, of course, but it happened to be the one bone of contention

11

between Maya and Jack. They had a running debate around magic and science. Jack preferred science and Maya magic. Jack would often say to her, 'M^2, the only real magic is the magic of science.' Maya would nod politely and ask him to explain how he always knew when she was troubled. Unable to explain, he'd simply shrug.

Despite their differences, Maya and Jack were close. Jack was always around to help her, and though it was something she had come to depend on, Maya longed to be bolder and braver. Reflecting on their closeness, she changed her mind and decided to share her dream.

'Jack I want to tell you something.'

'Knew it! I knew something was up. Is it one of those strange birthday events?'

'Oh, no! No. Not that; just a dream I had.'

'Oh, good! Got worried for a second.'

Inexplicable things happened on most of their birthdays. At first the Mysuns had tried to understand these strange occurrences, but over time they'd come to treat them as family secrets.

'I remember last year, when you made that ball disappear,' Jack said. 'How many days later did it appear? I still need to figure that out; there must be some logical, scientific explanation.'

Maya didn't respond. Instead, she slowly walked over to the window and lifted Tommy, who continued walking in the air, oblivious.

'Still not as good as your bullseye incident: you managed to hit three on your first attempt at archery.'

Jack laughed. 'That was weird! But not as much as our first birthday. I still can't believe what Mum says – that we began to walk just like that. I mean, how does that happen?'

Suddenly they heard a car being driven erratically, bouncing off speed bumps and screeching. Jack joined Maya by the window. She placed Tommy on the windowsill and together they looked out. A bright autumn morning was dawning.

A white van came into view from the bend up the road. They found it amusing until it stopped abruptly right in front of their driveway, kicking up the dunes of autumn leaves on the road. The leaves hadn't settled, and the van was still bouncing when the driver's door swung open with such force that it almost closed back on itself. Maya held her breath as a large girl in black t-shirt wriggled out. Once outside, she stood facing the pavilion across the road, straightening her long locks while seemingly admiring the same view they had moments earlier.

'And here we go!' Jack said. 'That isn't normal, is it? Look at that snake tattoo on her arm.'

The girl turned and stared straight at their window. She was only a teenager.

Maya's heart was drumming. 'She can't see inside, can she?' she asked, pulling Tommy back.

'No! Not through the nets,' said Jack. 'Sure looks familiar; I've seen that tattoo of a curled up snake somewhere.'

The girl left the van door open, darted to their front door, shoved something through the letterbox and rushed back. It all happened too fast for either to react. Back at the van, she stared at their window once more, until the front door opened. Startled, she jumped into the van in one swift movement and sped away without closing the door. The vehicle bounced over bumps, swerving a little before she pulled the door shut and disappeared down the road.

'Now that was strange,' said Maya.

'Yes, that qualifies as odd. Let's find out what it was all about.' He headed for the door but stopped to say, 'Oh, you were describing your dream?'

Maya shook her head. 'Later. This looks important.'

'Great!' Jack was already on the landing.

'Tommy, remind me to tell him,' she said, placing the tortoise back in his vivarium. Maya checked her hair again and stepped out of her room. Jack was already downstairs. She stopped outside his room and peeked inside. It was neat. Everything had a place: the posters of historical heroes, the models of the ancient weapons and various sporting things. She wondered how his collection would change today. Where would the presents go? Would they cause a big chain reaction like last year? What would survive in the end was anyone's guess. The model katana should; the helmet, possibly; the warrior poster, no; the long bow, definitely – that was his prized possession.

'Come on, not dreaming already?' Jack ran up and handed her a beige envelope. 'Here, it's for you. Dad said to open it downstairs. Even he found that delivery weird.'

Following Jack downstairs, Maya spotted a red emblem on the back of the envelope and entered their open-plan living room wearing a confused look.

Mum, Dad and Jack were waiting anxiously.

'Isn't it strange how she fled?' said Dad. 'Bizarre! I hope it's not a prank. Do you want me to open that, M^2?'

'It's fine, Dad.' She pointed at the fancy 'M' within a red circle. 'It's from my magic club.'

Mum and Dad sighed, lost interest and began to fuss over them. Dad gave Jack a firm handshake and a hug.

'Happy birthday, Maya,' Mum said, holding both her hands out.

Wondering what lay inside the envelope other than the usual monthly journal, Maya gave Mum a hug. She was eager to see but knew that it would have to wait. Family time was one of the many Mysun rituals, and today was no different. Maya knew Jack was eager to open one particular present: a reflex bow. He kept glancing at the sideboard where it lay but, like her, he resisted. Dad always liked family to come first, and often said that was the real gift. They joked, laughed and chatted for some time. Dad took some photos, and Jack even forced the family into taking a selfie. He wanted that to be the next addition to the framed photos on the lounge wall, proudly displaying how they'd all changed in the past thirteen years.

The Mysuns lived in a mansion in a peaceful suburb south of the Thames. They were quiet – the type that blended in and never stood out. Their home was cosy. Mr and Mrs Mysun both worked from home and the attic was their office. Mr Mysun was a game and toy inventor, making the twins the envy of all the kids in their school. His office was a treasure trove, an Aladdin's cave where any child could lose himself among weird and wonderful prototypes of toys and games. Mr Mysun was a slim man of average height who always dressed casually in jeans with polo t-shirts. Mrs Mysun, an interior designer, was always elegantly dressed in silky blouses and high-waist trousers.

After the day's greetings, Mum and Dad set up breakfast, allowing Maya and Jack to finally open their presents.

'Who's up for my special?' Dad asked, reaching for the porridge container.

'Me!' Jack said, carefully unwrapping the bow. 'Wow! I can't wait to use this.'

Mrs Mysun looked up briefly; she was whisking something near the hob. 'Wait till you try this new egg recipe,' she said.

Maya ignored her gifts and opened the envelope. It was a letter.

'What does it say?' Mum asked a few minutes later.

Maya didn't respond.

'Everything OK?' Dad asked.

Picking up on their concern, Jack came over with the bow.

Maya pointed at a big box on the kitchen counter. 'Is that the cake?' she asked, trying to divert their attention.

Mum nodded. 'What does the letter say?'

Maya said nothing and simply passed it to Mum, who read it aloud.

Dear Maya,

Happy birthday from the Magik Club!

I hope this letter finds you well. Now that you are 13 years old, I've upgraded your membership from beginner to apprentice. Congratulations! As a student, you will receive more information on:

- *discovering your magical abilities,*
- *improving your magikdom (the place where your magik is the strongest) and*
- *most importantly, protecting yourself against vile magik.*

Congratulations and good luck on your magikal journey.

From

Magik Club
PS: Note that vile magik is expected to be strong today! Be safe in your magikdom. If you must venture out, be swift and attentive, mindful of the fact that vile magik is unforgiving.

'An apprentice, wow! That's a nice surprise. So what does that mean?' Mum asked.

'Oh, better access to the club's website. I can read more on things I like. But most importantly, I'll get to do practicals.'

'Now that's what I've been waiting for,' said Jack. 'Finally we can see if there are any explanations or if it's all just tricks.'

She gave him a quick look. He was trying to help by changing her mood, but she was worried about the last part of the letter.

'There's a warning,' she said timidly. 'Maybe it's not a good idea to go out today?' A cautionary note on their birthday surely wasn't a coincidence. She hoped it wasn't the start of one of those strange events that happened today.

'Maya ...' Dad began. He paused, considering his words. 'Yes, the way it was delivered was odd but we can't live in fear. It wasn't nearly as peculiar as the other occurrences. I think if we continue as planned you'll see it's nothing really.' Normally the Mysuns took all strange events seriously, but Dad didn't seem to think this qualified.

'I agree with your dad,' said Mum. 'It's nothing to worry about.' She hesitated. 'But if it makes you feel better I suppose we could go tomorrow.'

Jack was smiling back at her, but she knew he'd be disappointed if they didn't go out today. He was always eager to view the mythical weapons at the Museum of Myths and Mysticism. His favourite was an exhibit of a large broken bow. He didn't believe the bow was magical or that it had any powers, but it captivated him for long periods nevertheless. The sign said it was a functional bow but, based on its size and weight, Jack couldn't logically see how it could even be lifted, let alone used in battle; people weren't strong or big enough. The conundrum appealed to his imagination.

'Perhaps Maya and I could stay back on our own,' Mum suggested. 'And you two could have a boys' day out.'

Dad wouldn't approve of them splitting up on such an important day. It wasn't just their birthday; it was their first day as teenagers. Slowly she looked at him; he was studying the letter once more.

'I don't mind if we do something at home, as long as it's not colouring fancy designs on fairies' wings,' Jack said, laughing. Maya knew he was trying to help.

The decision came down to her. She was worried about the warning but didn't want to disappoint Jack and Dad. Visiting the museum on their birthday was another Mysun ritual. She didn't want to break it so, putting on a brave face, she said, 'I saw an email about a visiting exhibit called the Scribe being unveiled today. It'd be nice to see that. And of course my fav'—

'Yes, I saw that mail too,' Jack interrupted her. 'It's a stone tablet, and articles say such stones held important inscriptions and were hidden away, mostly as foundation stones of important buildings, although sometimes in plain sight.' Jack paused for a second and grinned. 'It might be even more important than your favourite, that book.'

Maya shrugged, secretly hoping the tablet wasn't any better than the book. 'I read the blogs and the chats. Still, I'll be the judge when we get there.'

And, just like that it was settled: they were going to the museum.

Mum gave Maya a quick hug and a grin. 'Right. Would you like some breakfast?'

Maya nodded but secretly she was still worried. 'Can we squeeze in a movie night?' she asked. Perhaps she could at least get them to return home earlier.

Dad smiled. 'I don't mind, as long as you are OK with missing dinner at this new restaurant we planned to visit.'

'I am happy with that. Jack?'

Seeing Jack nod, Dad said, 'Great; lunch at the museum café and a takeaway tonight.'

With everything settled, they sat down to enjoy their breakfast. Maya and Jack ate quickly so they had enough time to open their presents. Jack received a science set and some video games. Maya received an ancient board game, a book on ancient myths and a jewellery box with a dragon design on it. Seeing the presents lifted her mood and soon they were all chatting and laughing again. Eventually Dad reminded them of the time, and the children headed to their rooms to get ready.

Upstairs in her room with the TV blasting children's programmes, Maya hurried around, trying to decide what to wear for their special day. Mum had suggested a pretty dress but she wasn't so sure.

As she tried out different outfits, she told Tommy about the letter from the magik club. He continued to chew obliviously, staring at the TV. A news break had started, and a reporter was questioning the meteorology experts about the approaching storm, dubbed 'the storm of the decade'.

'Consider the wind direction,' one expert said dismissively. 'It won't make landfall.'

Another quickly snapped in reply, 'No, it will change; it always does. It will hit the west coast by this afternoon with a high probability of arriving in London this evening.'

The experts argued until finally the presenter brought the debate to a close. 'As you can see, our experts remain divided over what will happen. Will the storm of the decade materialise or not? Either way, it's best if you stay indoors this evening.'

Maya turned and stared at the TV and then at the letter. Were the storm and the warning in the letter linked?

She tied her hair up. 'How do I look?' she asked, giving an unenthusiastic twirl. Despite Mum's request, she had settled on jeans, a T-shirt and a hooded jacket. 'I know, I know, Mum wanted a dress, but this is so comfortable. I'm sure she'll understand. Besides, it's better in the rain.' She acknowledged the response Tommy did not give and continued to speak her mind. 'We must return early. That storm and this warning aren't a coincidence. Protect the letter, Tommy.'

She switched the TV off and headed downstairs just as Dad called out, 'Guys! We have ten minutes before our train. We need to get going.'

3

THE OUTPOST & THE GATE

All is not what it seems.

It was mid-morning by the time the Mysuns emerged from the underground station in London. They had caught a train and a couple of tubes and now hurried down the main road that ran around a larger, more popular British museum before turning into one of the smaller streets. This part of London had an antiquated feel that lingered in the air. It always excited the twins and today was no different.

Stepping onto the cobbled lane, the Mysuns slowed and then stopped right in the middle of the ancient road itself. This was another Mysun ritual: standing at that spot and taking in all the sights before progressing. The road was not like the others. It wasn't pedestrianised, and yet for some unknown reason vehicles were rarely seen on it. Shoppers were happily crossing and strolling up and down as they browsed the shops. No one actually used the pavements because they never ran the entire length of the street. Where they did appear, they were hijacked by tables and pot plants, which gave the place its cosy, traditional feel.

The cobblestones always looked wet and reflected vague images of the buildings and the sky. To Maya, it wasn't a road but a magical waterway leading to the museum. At the top, the road turned right and disappeared around a church with a single light-brown spire that housed a clock tower and bore a flag Maya did not recognise. Closest to them on their right was a coffee shop with small wrought iron tables and chairs, all neatly arranged on a good-sized terrace fenced off by iron railings. Directly opposite the coffee shop was an authentic tavern with a blackboard advertising the dish of the day, and immediately below the sign were pots of shrubs and shaped bushes. A little further up were some steps leading into another part of the roadhouse.

In between the church, the café and the roadhouse were a number of shops, each with a wooden plaque bearing its name. Maya knew them all. And the museum was around the bend, after the church.

Maya looked into the shops as the Mysuns made their way up the road, but she was too distracted to take much notice of anything. She hadn't had a chance to tell Jack about her dream and grew increasingly worried that more strange events might occur before the day was up.

Passing the church, they sighted the entrance to the museum. It was small and unassuming, like the shops, with a simple black door and a small board outside which read 'Museum of Myths and Mysticism'.

Immediately inside was an open space housing a ticket booth, metal detector and furniture for guards and stewards. A narrow white corridor led to the various galleries inside. It was minimalist and ordinary in design.

The Mysuns were lifelong patrons of the museum, so as soon as they entered, the stewards ushered them through the clinical corridor, past the main gallery with all the popular artefacts and straight to the ancient text section. Today, this part was cordoned off for the unveiling of the Scribe.

The ancient building beyond the clinically white corridor always had an immense effect on the twins. It was a huge hall made from sand-brown stone with a large dome-shaped skylight that gave it a stately appearance. Stepping onto the polished wooden floor always brightened both of them. It was Maya's favourite place after home.

Jack, however, seemed distant. Something had his attention. Maya was about to enquire when he shook his head twice and said, 'Nah! That's just silly.'

She looked around to see what he might be talking about but found nothing except a security guard, and by then they had arrived at the Hall of Ancient Texts.

It was one of the smaller galleries, with two levels. All the guests, including many patrons like them, and specially invited experts and speakers, were on the lower level. A couple of guards stood on the upper balcony.

'So many experts – it must be important, Jack,' whispered Maya, seeing all the elderly gentlemen and ladies around.

Still distracted, all Jack said was, 'Come on, M^2, we're late. Let's get to the front.' He wove through all the guests to where a few other children stood. 'Excuse me, excuse me.' Maya followed his lead.

An expert in a dark, well-worn blazer and a greying moustache began to address the gathering. Other guests, many in similar or tweed attire, huddled together to listen. Maya only caught snippets of his speech '... like Egyptians ... you will see strange old symbols ... yet to be deciphered.' She was searching for her favourite relic, the *Book of No Words*, but the new and yet to be unveiled artefact stood in its place.

Where have they moved you to, No Words? Maya wondered. *I hope it's not a sign.*

The audience clapped and the speaker said, 'We now request that Professor Phang unveil what we have all been waiting for: the Scribe.' Maya turned in time to see an elderly figure in a tweed blazer cut a ribbon and pull the silky cover draped over the new artefact away. At first sight, the Scribe didn't strike Maya as much as the book had. It was a dark inscribed stone about the size of an A4 pad.

The audience applauded again and there were a few camera flashes. Several minutes later, with the official opening concluded, everyone began to talk and stepped forward for a closer look at the new jewel of the text gallery.

Maya was excited by the chance to learn about this new stone but disappointed at not seeing *No Words*. She searched for it, slipping through the spaces between the talking adults, when Jack tugged her sleeve and said, 'Come, let's get closer!'

They got within a couple of feet from the stone tablet. Normally that would be enough for Maya, but there was something about the Scribe that pulled her closer. She continued to edge towards the cabinet and was soon standing centimetres from the glass. There was a caption below but it didn't provide any further information. Her eyes traced the edges of the flat stone and were drawn towards the inscriptions. What story did they have to tell?

She reached out to touch the cabinet when a golden glow sparked up in the first symbol and moved across and down the tablet. Alarmed, she looked up and found herself in the wizard's circular room from her dream, surrounded by scrolls, books, bottles and urns.

****

Something was wrong. Torackdan and Ebbelle were tensed, watching as something rose from up the stairs. In the dim light, Maya couldn't quite make out what it was. To her it looked like darkness itself was rising. Then a part of the shadow broke free and floated up. As the dense black mist took shape, Maya realised what she was seeing: an undead spectre – a phantom – was forming. It continually shifted within itself, like hundreds of tangling snakes. Slowly, an apparition hooded in a dark medieval robe appeared.

'A wraith!' Ebbelle whispered.

'Aldrr!' said Torackdan.

There was no face within the black hood, just an abyss both disturbing and intriguing. Maya stared, unable to turn away. Aldrr hovered, rising and falling like a boat in gentle surf. From behind it came the sound of slow, deliberate steps and another figure came into view, wearing a dark green cape and carrying a staff. The face was hidden by a hood, but Maya was relieved to see that the person was about her own height and petite too.

Aldrr spoke: 'The Master Konjurer of Konjiur, Torackdan, himself!' Its voice was a shriek, filled with menace. 'Ebbelle the Wanderer, my master shall be pleased with your efforts.'

Torackdan turned to Ebbelle. 'I was right to suspect something, but never this! How could you, you traitor?'

'Old friend—'

'No friend would commit such treachery!'

'Pay heed, Torackdan, the defender of Konjiur. I have seen what this boy before us can do. He is a Hiertan, a changer of hearts.'

'Another lie! There hasn't been a Hiertan for centuries.'

'Perhaps, but his powers grow. You would be wise to change your alliances. Let go of your responsibilities and join us. If not, you will be made to surrender by force.'

'Coward! I'd rather die for a cause than live for nothing,' Torackdan said, retreating towards the balcony.

Ebbelle flicked his staff and the doors slammed shut. Two more bangs followed: the window and the other balcony. Trapped, Torackdan stood defiantly with his staff poised.

'Wizard,' hissed Aldrr, 'meet the boy you seek! He serves our master now. Join us, yield your staff, Tabioak, to our master's command and you shall be spared. What's your answer? Willing or not, Tabioak shall serve us.'

'Boy!' cried Torackdan, ignoring Aldrr. 'They've poisoned your mind with lies; come with me. Let me take you to your parents.' He stepped towards him, but the boy flicked his arm and hurled the long table at the wizard. Torackdan raised Tabioak and deflected the table into the wall behind him.

A bright green light erupted and a beast of jade-coloured flames emerged from the boy's staff. A moment later gusts of wind blew from Torackdan's Staff and snuffed out the flaming creature before it could launch a fireball. Pleased, Maya turned towards Torackdan but found him kneeling on the floor with Ebbelle standing over him, holding his staff like a club. Tabioak lay on the floor a short distance away.

'Forgive me, my friend, but you should have said yes ...' Ebbelle said.

'Master will be pleased ...' Aldrr began, when someone burst into the tower. A hulking beast-like soldier hurried up the stairs towards them.

'My Lord,' he said in flat, heavy voice, 'we encountered Vorsulgha's men escaping with this one!'

Two more soldiers came up and tossed something across the floor towards Tabioak. It was the small monkey.

'So Vorsulgha, the commander of Vykrutz has revealed his true face, the traitor,' said Aldrr. 'Seize Tabioak and finish the Konjurer.'

He had only just stopped speaking when the monkey leapt up, grabbed the Tabioak and scuttled towards Torackdan. Maya looked on transfixed, her heart thumping.

'There, there!' Torackdan said to the creature. 'Now listen to me ...' A translucent, cream-coloured sphere appeared around them. Ebbelle shot something at them but it bounced off.

'Protection spell,' Aldrr hissed. 'Quickly now.'

Ebbelle aimed his staff, and the Hiertan turned his open palm to the sphere. Inside it, a blue light and a lightning flashed as a portal opened. Good – they were escaping. Maya smiled until she noticed the Hiertan closing in. The sphere began to fade slowly. Eventually it disappeared, leaving an exhausted Torackdan surrounded by enemies.

'Where's that puny ball of fur?' screamed Aldrr.

'He's jumped to another world with the staff!' cried Ebbelle.

'Master won't be pleased.' Aldrr turned towards the Hiertan, already kneeling over Torackdan. 'My Prince, find out where the monkey goes. I'll hunt it down.'

The Hiertan removed his glove and reached out. Torackdan grabbed his hand. The Hiertan flinched and then the wizard stopped moving, lay back and faded into nothingness.

Confused, Maya looked around until she heard Torackdan's calm voice.

'In loss lies victory ...'

'In loss lies victory?' Aldrr wailed. 'Hiertan, what did he mean? What were his thoughts? Tell me his aide hasn't returned to Konjiur?'

The cloaked warrior turned and pushed his hood back. What stared at Maya shocked her: it was her own face, smirking. Shaken, she snapped her gaze away but still heard a voice just like hers say, 'He told the monkey to go to Siantia and find the Konjurer's kind there.

Confused and scared, Maya stepped back and found herself in the museum, standing before the Scribe.

****

'Done?' Jack asked, gently elbowing her.

Dazed, Maya slowly turned to see if anyone had noticed her daydreaming. Mum, Dad and the others were all busy socialising. She turned towards the tablet: it was as expected, without any glow.

'Come, let's go see our favourites,' Jack said, and led the way from the new exhibit.

Maya followed, mind in turmoil, skin tingling with gooseflesh; how could she be part of the vision? How could she be the villain? Was this one of those strange events? They shouldn't have come; she should have forced them to stay safe at home.

She wanted to sit Jack down and tell him about Aldrr, Torackdan, the staff, and the monkey who had fled to a place called Siantia. Jack was more logical and scientific than her, so he'd be able to figure out if the vision was connected to them or why she'd seen it near the Scribe. Most of all, Maya wanted to ask if he'd seen the Scribe glow too.

If only they could go home immediately and talk safely in her magikdom, but that wasn't possible. They'd just got to the museum, and Jack would be eager to see the massive bow that fascinated him. Talking would just have to wait, so she prayed that the vision was meaningless.

Pushing all troubling thoughts and questions to the back of her mind, she focused on finding *No Words*. It was a black leather-bound book the size of a pocket diary. It was nothing fancy, but she liked it because it was an enigma. As the name implied, it didn't have any written words inside; each page was blank and yet it was supposed to hold the wisdom of all its previous owners, all of whom were wizards. Maya had spent hours on the Internet researching but discovered nothing more, except that a wizard simply had to ask it a question and it would present the answer based on all the past owners' experience. *It's like the original cyberspace*, she'd thought. *Or conjur-space, rather.*

After conferring briefly, the Mysun family left the Scribe and headed in different directions. Maya stayed in the ancient text gallery with Mum, while Jack and Dad headed to the weapons gallery to view the broken bow.

****

In the countryside, after passing several signposts, Muscles and Tiny were fast losing their patience and wondering if the Red Gate Centre even existed. They had been driving through unusually thick woods for some time when Muscles decided to contact base, but the radio produced nothing but static.

'Try the mobile?' Tiny suggested.

'Look!' Muscles pointed. 'Another sign.'

Tiny slowed, switched on full beams and spotted a faded wooden plaque that read 'Red Gate Centre'.

Little and Large looked at each other and then at the arrow pointing down a short dirt trail. Tiny stopped the car at the trail; it led to a dark Gothic gate with broken fence on both its sides.

'Not that red then,' said Muscles.

At the back of the car, David peeked at the grim gate, sat up and said, 'That doesn't look right. You can't leave me here.' It was another act; he was playing on their emotions as he plotted his escape.

Tiny cringed ever so slightly as he turned onto the muddy trail to idle in front of the gate, and David suspected he didn't like getting the car dirty. Neither of the officer responded to his complaint, not that David had expected them to.

When the gate remained closed, Muscles opened his door to investigate but stopped after seeing the slushy mud below. He turned and looked at Tiny for a second when David cut in again.

'Listen, I don't mind being sent elsewhere.'

'Unlikely, buddy,' said Tiny sternly.

'No intercom or camera!' said Muscles. He turned towards the dark slush and prepared to put his left foot out, readying himself as though he were jumping off a plane. The sight was funny but David didn't laugh; he had his own worries. His chances of escaping were fast vanishing. Eventually, Muscles set his foot down and mumbled as it sank into the sludge. He muttered to himself in annoyance as he slowly hopscotched to the gate and tried to push it open. It didn't budge.

'Officer! Listen, this ain't right; take me back. Take me to a normal place, not some haunted house in the sticks.' He used his best pitiful voice but Tiny didn't respond.

Outside, Muscles shouted that he was going to look around. He was striding towards a gap in the fence when the gate silently swung open. Muscles' face contorted in frustration. David curbed the urge to laugh for he needed the officers to listen. In the hustle to get moving, they forgot about the gate, but David wondered how it had opened. Was someone watching?

Past the gate, the track narrowed and the officers struggled with the car. After a while, they emerged from the woods and the car rolled to a halt.

Muscles leaned forward, his mouth wide open. David followed his gaze.

'What is that?' asked Tiny.

'Now that's Red,' said Muscles, ever so slowly.

On the next hill, some distance away, sat a colossal fortress with a huge red gate at its centre. High walls snaked away on either side and quickly disappeared behind tall conifers.

Muscles, was the first to recover. 'It's a prison, buddy.'

Tiny shot his partner a stern look. 'I don't think so, David,' he said casually. 'Looks like some sort of forgotten fort or something. You'll be staying in a castle, now; that's cool, right?'

Uneasy with the building before him, David latched onto Muscles words. 'Ya can't take me to a prison.'

'Easy, buddy. It's a castle of some sort. Look carefully,' Tiny said, trying to diffuse his partner's comment.

'I don't see no castle. That's prison walls. Ya can't fool me.'

'It's not a prison. It's perhaps a little like the Great Wall of China. And that in the middle is the main entrance – that massive drawbridge,' Tiny said, steering the car down the dirt trail towards the structure.

David didn't respond. He was making mental notes of the route: the steep drive down from the woods, the rusty red bridge halfway down, which was wide enough for only one car to pass, and then an equally steep climb to the structure. He was planning his escape route: where he could hide, what could be a challenge and how he could overcome it.

Past the precarious bridge, David felt the dirt trail turn into a paved road. Somehow, on the paving, calm replaced his fear. The closer they went, the more intimidating the building became but the calmer David felt.

Tiny stopped the car some distance from the drawbridge, and they sat pondering about the place for a moment.

'How can this be unheard of?' Tiny asked. 'I mean, us coppers should 'ave heard of it? Right? Just look at it – it's our very own Gothic Great Wall of China.'

Muscles was in a trance. David noted the height and the thickness of the gate, the stately buildings with tall rectangular windows on either side, the soaring walls, the dense woods and the ornate sculptures. Strangely, the sculptures at the top were facing inside and away from them.

'Listen, buddy,' said Muscles, 'you must have heard about this on the streets, yeah?'

David gave a quick shake of his head, and the officers got out of the car to talk. He was pleased they hadn't heeded his earlier plea and hoped they would leave him here. He didn't want to leave anymore; his heart wasn't racing, he wasn't sweating and there were no butterflies in his stomach. All his life, David had chosen to be led by his sixth sense, which he'd associated with the dowsing technique that allowed people to find water. Many called it hocus-pocus, but it had served him well, leading him away from trouble. Now it was pulling him towards the Red Gate Centre. It looked alien and intimidating but he trusted his feeling; it would be fine at this mysterious place.

A loud bang woke him from his thoughts and then came the noise of a large chain moving. David imagined an anchor falling slowly and saw the massive drawbridge begin to drop.

Muscles opened the car door for David while Tiny retrieved his whole world from the boot: a frayed, half-full rucksack. He emerged from the car to find a hooded figure in brown robes coming into view as the bridge fell.

A Jedi? David smiled to himself. The bridge thudded to the ground, dust rose and little vibrations ran beneath his feet, but David wasn't concerned.

'Dropping off,' Muscles called out over the noise. 'Arranged earlier today,' he added, when he didn't receive a response.

'We'll come inside to make sure it's OK,' Tiny reassured David. 'If it's dodgy, you can come back with us. Alright, mate?'

'Welcome, Officers,' said the hooded figure after an awkward pause. His voice was clear and calm, which David liked instantly.

'A fortress no one knows about with funny monks. What next? Dragons?' Muscles muttered as he walked David towards the drawbridge. Tiny wasn't amused and shot his partner another disapproving stare.

Stepping onto the foot-thick drawbridge, the officers introduced themselves and then David.

'I am Shikshi Laksha,' said the monk.

'Sorry, shik …?' asked Muscles.

'Laksha. Just Laksha is fine. Shikshi is a form of address like mister or brother. It means 'learner'. Come this way!' With that, Laksha lead them into the tunnel.

The sudden change from bright sunlight to darkness temporarily blinded them.

'Trust your other senses,' said Laksha soothingly. 'Soon your night vision will develop.'

The massive entrance was more like a long, damp tunnel, for it ran the width of the big buildings on either side. The exit was some distance away, bright and blinding. As Laksha had said, David's night vision soon kicked in and he found that the tunnel was bare and old. Minutes later, they emerged on the other side, on a stone platform, high above the ground.

'Welcome to Red Gate! Only a few have had the privilege of admiring this view,' Laksha said.

David and the officers were stunned into silence with the valley before them. Behind them stood the high gate with stately buildings on either side, but beyond the huge stone platform they stood on, wide steps curved a winding path down a steep slope towards the open grassland with a narrow lake and a solitary oriental building on its bank. On either side of the lake, grassland led to thick woods, and to their right, behind the woods, were snow-capped mountains.

Scratching his head, Muscles asked, 'Where did those mountains come from? I don't remember seeing them from the car?'

'What is this place?' asked Tiny. 'What is that building down there? And why are these walls snaking around on both sides like the Great Wall of China?' He pointed at the wall in the distance dividing the landscape into two.

'Everyone has questions!' said Laksha, smiling. 'This is the Red Gate Centre, and that down there is our monastery, the Order of Science. As for the walls – allow me to give you a little background. It involves a short folk tale. During the ancient times, this land was plagued by strange happenings until a group of nomadic monks who were passing through made a deal with the local lord. If he walled the land, they'd ensure the mysterious occurrences were contained. The lord agreed and walled those peaks, that lake and the surrounding woods.'

'Interesting tale,' said Tiny, 'but you don't expect us to—'

'I know it's not that believable. And, well, it's a tale that has changed over time. The truth is that this is a place that time forgot. Hidden within the woods, we've been living here in plain sight. Occasionally travellers stumbled across us, and more recently we have begun to reach out and help, working with the authorities by helping troubled youths – which is what has brought you here, right?'

Tiny didn't look happy with the answers, and began to interrogate the monk in his police manner – politely yet with an air of ownership. What were the other children here for? What did the monks do to help them? But slowly he slipped questions of personal interest into the conversation.

'Aren't such gates normally in cities like the Marble Arch is? This one must be the largest I have seen.'

Laksha answered all the queries, usually providing more information than was necessary. He explained how he'd mistaken their arrival for a children's pickup ride he was expecting, and David was glad to learn that other children were leaving.

Satisfied with the answers, Tiny said with delight.

'Thank you Shikshi. I like the title – shikshi. You see I'm also an amateur historian, still studying, so you could say I am also a shikshi.'

Laksha placed his hand on David's shoulder and said in his peaceful manner, 'We're all students and can learn from anyone and everyone.'

The police officers made more small talk asking about the monks' brown robes and the monastery. David looked on, engrossed; when Laksha happily explained that the monastery had links across the world and helped solve behavioural issues using science.

A doorbell chimed, interrupting their conversation.

'Ah, that must be the ride now. Come, we have a few minutes before it arrives. Let's get the paperwork completed. I'm sure you'll want to return before the storm,' said Laksha.

Muscles glanced at the blue sky. 'Storm? Isn't that going to blow into the sea? That's what the experts said. How can you tell it'll make landfall? Is that like a monk thing?'

'Oh no!' Laksha smiled. 'We have our own weather station.'

'You do?' Tiny looked around.

'Yes, down there.' Laksha pointed at the monastery down by the lake.

'And in here?' asked Tiny.

'Here we have a library, a banqueting hall, a presentation hall and living quarters. All in there.' Laksha pointed at the building on their right, then gestured to the one on the left. 'There we have a gym, smaller classrooms, an auditorium and the monks' living quarters.'

'An auditorium? Do you have that many children?' Tiny asked.

'No, that's for visiting monks who lecture other shikshis. Now come this way; let me offer you a drink while we complete the paperwork.'

'A drink? Good, saves us stopping for coffee,' Muscles said.

'It's not coffee but no less delicious. A special brew made according to an ancient recipe – most refreshing.' Laksha opened the door labelled 'Reception' to the right of the tunnel behind them.

'Refreshing; good, good,' Muscles said rubbing his palms together in anticipation.

****

After the officers left, Laksha turned to David, handed him his rucksack and said in a friendly voice, 'Young David, Shikshi Virath, our head shikshi, would like to meet you before you get started.'

David nodded, trying hard to control his gaze, which kept diverting towards Laksha's coarse robe. He'd read about monks wearing these, but this was the first he had seen one and didn't want to be rude. Laksha was tanned with a weathered face and close-cropped hair, almost bald. The lines on his face were deep, a testimony to the harsh environment he'd endured at some point in his life. One could have easily mistaken him for a sailor in his mid-forties but David was certain he looked younger than he really was.

Laksha headed back out to the high platform, and David followed leisurely, hooking his rucksack over his left shoulder. As he went David studied the walls snaking around the land, recalling Tiny's description: 'Our own Great Wall of China'. It was the strangest place, and yet his dowsing feeling was at rest, as if he had found water at last. For once he followed obediently.

Laksha continued to speak as he led the way down the winding stone steps towards the grassland and the monastery. 'Normally he does not see children on their first day. You are lucky to have an audience with him.'

'An audience,' David repeated to himself, studying Laksha's disciplined walk: arms folded, one hand inside the sleeve of the other. He followed in silence, choosing to be himself rather than putting on the usual act. It was difficult, but he resisted the urge to hide behind a mask.

A few minutes later, he was breathless from trying to keep up with Laksha's deceptively quick stride. They were only halfway down the steep descent and there was still a fair way to go. A few more turns along the twisting steps, they passed a chubby monk coming up with three teenagers; they appeared fine and normal.

By the time they arrived at the monastery, David was exhausted but Laksha didn't stop. Inside they went through a narrow stone passage, up some steps, past two murals of monks and stopped at a plain wooden door engraved in a language he didn't recognise. Laksha knocked and ushered him in only after a soft yes sounded from within.

The head shikshi's office was a large room unlike any other David had seen. It was empty of all furniture. He'd come to expect such offices to house aluminium cabinets, white shelves, worn files and a cheap desk with a noisy computer and dusty printer. The shikshi's office was big and it was virtually bare. David noticed the silhouette of a monk sitting on the wooden floor at the far end. The image only raised more queries in his mind. Was that the head monk? Was this even an office? None of it was normal although it felt fine. Laksha gently instructed him to remove his shoes, sit down and wait for Shikshi Virath to complete his meditation. Before David could reply, Laksha left, closing the door silently behind him.

Alone with the head monk, David took a minute or two to look around. It was most unusual; whoever had heard of the head of a correctional facility sitting on the floor? And where were the visitors expected to sit? It was a strange room too. The door was in the top corner of the room. The wall opposite the door housed two large windows from which David could see the steep slope they had come down and the top of the imposing gate. He moved deeper into the room. Behind the monk was a large fireplace and on the walls were large paintings of strangely coloured landscapes. A dark grey one with deep red captivated him the most; it looked volcanic.

A well-stocked bookcase stood in the far corner beside the fireplace. In front of the monk sat an empty mat and two strange objects. One was an X-shaped book stand with three worn books on it. The other was a T-shaped object that David couldn't figure out. *A short walking stick, perhaps?*

Soon he'd checked out the whole room and still the monk remained unmoved. He cleared his throat but the monk didn't respond. Tiring, David decided to sit on the empty mat in front of the monk.

He placed his rucksack on the floor and settled down. No response. He waved his hand before the monk's eyes. Nothing! Feeling mischievous, he turned towards the wooden T-shaped object but stopped short of touching it; should he or shouldn't he? It stood on the bottom of the 'T' and David couldn't understand how it remained upright. After the brief hesitation, he tapped it lightly, expecting it to fall. It didn't. He tried again, harder, certain that should do the trick. It remained unmoved. Surprised, David swiped at it and fell. He'd missed. Confused, he sat up to find the monk holding the object. He'd picked it up with surprising swiftness and ease.

'Force isn't always necessary,' he said in a calm, low voice.

Feeling belittled, David wanted to react, but he controlled himself for he was also amazed. Had he just seen an act of alternative science? 'That was stuck. How did you pick it up?' he asked.

'You needed to will it to move.'

'Will? You mean like in frontiers.'

'Frontiers?' asked the shikshi.

'Oh, I mean alternative science. Things that science can't explain yet.'

'Ah, yes. All things have explanations; you simply need to find them. Now, where are my manners? Welcome, young David. I am Virath and your arrival here is timely.'

'Timely?' He studied the monk's kind face. He had a lighter complexion than Laksha and cropped white hair.

'Yes, I've been expecting you, but all will be explained in good time.' His mind seemed to wander for a moment. 'Yes, all in good time ... Now, before we start, know that you're not here for any correctional classes. You don't need them.'

David liked this conversation; it was a nice change from the normal one, where the centre personnel slapped his file on the desk and listed his violations as if he didn't know them already. He hated when adults did that. Why did they repeat things? Did they think children were dumb? And why did they get to decide what an offence was? Why was it an offence if you didn't want to stay with someone they chose for you? Virath's words sent his mind into overdrive, and it occurred to him that it might be some act to throw him off his guard. He decided to test Virath.

'Can I go then? I don't need to stay here, do I?' He put on a cheeky smile.

Shikshi Virath replied calmly, 'You can, but something tells me you won't. I hope you'll stay to develop your abilities.'

Smirking to himself and liking the attention, he asked, 'Abilities like escaping and running? Yeah, I need to develop those more.'

'Getting out of trouble is a useful skill, yes.'

'That's not an ability!'

'Why, of course it is. And what you have is not just luck; some call it a sixth sense. You have that ability, don't you? To sense when something is amiss. You've unknowingly used it all your life and now you can learn more. However ...'

Aha, knew it, David thought. *Here comes the BIG BUT! It's all too good to be true.*

'Improving your skills depends on you.'

'... on me?' David narrowed his eyes.

'Yes. You have to choose to stay.' Virath placed his hand on David's shoulder. 'But before all that, you need to know yourself better. Why don't you start by telling me something about yourself? Anything.'

David slumped a little. 'Something about myself ...' he whispered. It wasn't that he didn't want to interact, but he did not know what to say. He was an expert at staging performances but in response to Virath's genuine interest he was at a loss. His mind was full of thoughts, racing ahead to alternative science and his latest interest – ghosts and spirits.

'Mmm … Ahm …' He searched for an answer but nothing came to mind.

'Why don't you begin by telling me about your parents?' Virath said after a while.

'Didn't know them.'

'So who do you stay with?'

'Fosters!' He paused for a second. 'I mean foster homes. The last one must have been glad when I left.'

'What do you mean?'

'I guess they are good people but not right for me! Always thinking they know what I want? What's best for me? You know: wear this, wear it like this, eat this and not that, eat at this time.'

'And what do you do when you're on the run?'

David sat up, enthusiastic. 'I see if the stories I've read are true.'

'Stories? How?'

'Why, by staking those places—'

'Like where?'

'Promise not to laugh.' Virath looked serious so David continued. 'Mostly places supposed to be haunted. Imagine if ghosts can be proven to be real.'

'And are they?'

David sat back. 'I never got enough time to find out. Always have to keep moving, keep ahead of the authorities and return to the Fosters before money runs out.' David cast his eyes down and saw the 'T' shaped stick. 'That stick – how did you move it?'

Virath didn't answer. He got up with silent agility and moved away to the bookshelf behind. David was amazed by the smooth movement but annoyed that the monk had avoided his question. He knew exactly what Virath was doing; after all, he too was an expert at changing the subject and deflecting questions. Virath was good, perhaps as good as he was, David thought, when he returned with a small leather-bound book.

'This is for you.'

No one had ever given him a gift before and that lightened his mood. Curious and excited at what it may contain, he asked, 'What is it on?'

'It's a diary. Your diary, but I don't want you to open it here,' Virath said, holding it with both hands. 'You must learn to use it properly, Start by recording what you learn here and soon it will answer any questions you have.'

Lost for words, David looked between the monk and the black leather book.

'And one other thing: no one advertises their personal diary, certainly not a—' Virath paused. 'You are known by another name as well, right?'

'You mean my street name?'

'Yes, remind me of it?'

'It's only for my friends.'

Virath smiled, nodding, so David proudly said, 'Wizard or Wiz!'

'Ah, yes. A Wiz doesn't go around advertising his diary, does he now? This must be a secret between us. Agreed?'

David nodded and Virath finally extended the book. He didn't know what to do. And how did Virath know his other name? Of course. His files.

It was then that Virath leaned forward and peered into his eyes. 'Mmm, interesting,' he said.

David was caught off guard. 'What! What was that for?' It had been some time since anyone had been interested in the colour of his eyes.

Virath thrust the book into David's hands, patted it and said, 'Remember – *personal* diary. It will, in time, answer any questions you have, but as a Wiz, you must learn to ask the right questions.'

'I don't understand. What do you mean "as a Wiz"?' David asked, holding the book uncertainly.

'Some things cannot be explained. You alone must discover your journey with the diary.'

David sat back with a tickle in his stomach. So this was how it felt to receive gifts. In his mind it had been ceremonial and magical.

'And that is the end our first meeting. Now for your quarters: we have selected a room in the eastern wing for you. Is the room ready, Shikshi?' David turned to find Laksha standing behind him.

When did he come in? How come I didn't hear him? he thought.

'It is, Shikshi,' Laksha said, coming up to David. 'Come, let's get you settled before the storm.'

David picked up his rucksack, dropped the diary inside it and slipped on his sneakers.

On their way out, David stopped for a second to study one of the paintings. Something about it had changed, but Virath called out from behind him before he could figure out what.

'Remember, your journey has begun. Learn to use the diary and keep it with you at all times; don't leave it lying around.'

David nodded and followed Laksha out.

****

Outside, ascending the steep incline to the Red Gate, David noticed the change in the air. The pressure had dropped and there was an unsettling calm. Panting heavily as he climbed the steps, he looked at the source: dark, swollen clouds rolling menacingly down from the distant mountains.

'This one is going to be bad,' said Laksha. 'It's deteriorating quickly.' David picked up his pace.

At the top, they headed straight to reception, where Laksha led him behind the counter, and into an admin office at the back. They passed a couple of desks with large monitors and swivel chairs and exited through the door at the other end.

Behind that door, David felt another change in the air. The modern furniture gave way to a barren wooden corridor with an overpowering smell of wood polish. In the fading light filtering in from the collage windows, he felt like he was inside an old black-white photograph. The creaks and groans of the wooden floor completed the effect.

At the other end of the corridor was a smallish wooden door, which led to a much larger and grander stone-floor corridor. This one was quieter, colder, brighter and well furnished. Equally interspaced beams gave the high ceiling the mesmerising impression of railway tracks stretching into the distance and never meeting.

David's pace slowed. There was simply too much to see in a glance. He'd been to museums and majestic public buildings but never seen such grandeur, all of which competed for his attention: the large chandeliers hanging all the way down the corridor, the ornate chairs and benches, and the ornate wooden doors. On the walls were armour, weapons and shields on display, along with numerous paintings and sculptures.

David decided to return when he had more time to explore and ran to catch Laksha.

'Is this part a museum?' he asked. He knew it wasn't but hoped the question would function as an excuse to get Laksha to slow down.

'It is many things, but a museum it is not!' Laksha failed to take the bait and carried on walking at the same speed.

'Many things? Like what? And what's behind these doors?' They'd passed four or five heavy doors.

'That one and the last one you passed leads to the throne room.'

'Throne? Is this a palace?'

'Yes, there's a throne but no, it's not a palace. It's a royal retreat with a banqueting hall and a kitchen. We also have a library up ahead.' Laksha said, looking at the other end of the stone hall.

'Royal? Do you mean like kings, queens, princes and princesses?'

'Yes.'

'And a library! What about the classes? Where are those?' He loved libraries but hated classes; they were mental torture.

'It was once a royal retreat, but only recently does it double as a behavioural centre for children, so the classes have been constructed elsewhere.'

At the end of the hallway, Laksha paused before a passage lit by fire torches. The corridor turned into steps that descended rapidly.

'Real torches?' David asked, staring at the nearest roaring flame.

'Yes, this part's still original; a reminder of our past.' He headed down the steps.

'Feels like we're heading back down to where the monastery is.'

'Good guess! The royal lodgings are at the base of the valley, to the east of the gate.'

'In the wall?'

'Yes. The wall continues all around the top of the ridge and sometimes under it.'

Walking down was exhausting, and David was glad when the steps levelled off and led to another richly decorated corridor with doors on one side. By now he was tired and didn't stop to admire anything.

After a little while Laksha opened a wooden door. 'Here we are: one of the royal quarters. I hope it's to your liking.'

The room was large, with two windows. Like the corridor, it boasted paintings, ornate objects, heavy wooden furniture, weapons and two suits of armour. David took slow, deliberate steps, turning this way and that.

'Something wrong?' asked Laksha.

'Yes!' said David, rather loudly. It was the first time he'd lashed out since arriving.

'I don't understand.' Laksha drew closer.

'What a cruel joke to play. Hope you're satisfied. Other places are bad but they never did this. Tease me with such a room.' He spoke quickly, lest he forget the words.

Laksha placed a hand on his shoulder and reassured him that it was indeed for him. David quietened down and ventured further inside. He moved delicately as though he were in a dream that might vanish with any fast movements. He hadn't gone far when Laksha advised him to stay in the room and rest until he returned. Then he turned and left.

Transfixed, David didn't turn to acknowledge Laksha's exit. His gaze darted from one object to another: the massive antique bed, the fruit basket on the desk by the window, the rug between the fireplace and the settee.

Long minutes later, acceptance set in. David wanted to smile and cry at the same time. His eyes were misty, but before they could release their precious cargo, he dumped his rucksack onto the settee by the fireplace and crashed onto it.

He sat staring at the painting above the mantelpiece for some time; it was of an old man with long white hair and a longer walking stick. Slowly his eyes became heavy; he felt the weariness of his early morning adventure and drifted into a deep slumber.

4

FRIEND AND GUARDIAN

The impossible made possible.

Hours later in London, the Mysun family came through their front door just as the debated storm threatened to break. Dad's automation devices had kicked in: the curtains had been drawn, the lights were on and the television was babbling in the background. Outside, the darkness had crept in earlier than normal. The autumn leaves were beginning to blow chaotically, and the first of the large raindrops were starting to splatter. Maya was glad to be home, warm and dry in her magikdom. She'd been eager to speak to Jack about her dream, especially after learning that *No Words* had been removed from display. It was a sign, Maya was certain, but she hadn't managed to tell Jack. Straight after visiting the text section, Mum had surprised her with a visit to the tropical butterfly house, but Maya couldn't enjoy it because she'd been preoccupied with the warning and eager to get back home.

Maya was removing her jacket when Mum said, 'Children, you have five minutes to freshen up.'

'Yes, Mum!' They ran upstairs.

Minutes later, they were back downstairs and Dad was announcing the programme for the evening. Maya's attention was divided; the cake cutting ceremony was her favourite part of their birthday, but today she was keen to get Jack alone. That would have to wait, as Dad had begun his address, like a mayor at a town hall.

'As we're eating in today, we'll be doing things in reverse: first the cake cutting, followed by photographs and then we'll start the movie of your choice while we wait for the takeaway pizza.'

'Can we have a small piece of cake while we wait for pizzas?' Maya asked, trying to distract herself.

'Of course. Mum's been working on it since yesterday.' Dad slipped into the kitchen as if he were going offstage and reappeared moments later with Mum and a cake shaped like an open book. One page was lilac with a dragon while the other was yellow and boasted a large hunting bow. Their names were written underneath each figure. Maya and Jack quickly arranged themselves on one side of the dining table. Dad lit the candles, dimmed the lights and the moment they had all been waiting for arrived: Mr and Mrs Mysun sang Happy Birthday to Maya and Jack. When they finished, Mum's face said it all. She couldn't contain her delight any longer and said, tearfully, 'Make a wish, both of you.'

'And look here,' Dad added, pointing at his camera on the tripod nearby.

Maya and Jack leaned forward for the camera, took a deep breath and blew the candles out. The camera flashed twice and, as the last flame went out, the house was unexpectedly drowned in darkness.

Instinctively Maya reached for Jack's arm.

'I'll get the trip switch, Dad!' Jack called out, but before he could move, the lights flickered back on.

Maya and Jack found themselves alone in the living room; Mum and Dad were gone. They looked at each other, confused.

Outside, the intensity of the storm had increased, and in the silent house they could now hear the rain drumming loudly against the windows. Maya felt a creeping chill; she had a bad feeling but didn't say anything to Jack, for he too looked worried.

With growing dread, they both called out to Mum and Dad.

'Where are you? Mum? Dad? It's not funny; come out now.'

No one responded.

Despairing, they searched the living room, examining all the possible hiding places: underneath the dining table, behind the settee, behind the doors, everywhere. Eventually accepting that Mum and Dad weren't in the living room, they progressed into the hallway. Together, they checked the front and back doors and found both securely bolted from inside.

'They're in the house then,' Maya concluded in a whisper.

With growing alarm, they turned their attention to the stairs. They were uninviting but Jack bravely led the way. In no time, they had gone through the whole house, even Mum and Dad's office in the attic, and came up empty. Their parents were simply nowhere to be found.

All the rooms suddenly felt alien: cold, dark, unrecognisable. Their home was lifeless without Mum and Dad. Maya thought of all the events leading to that point: the warning from the master of Magik Club, the golden glow in the Scribe and the missing *No Words*. She should have heeded them all. Worried, she retreated into her dimly lit room, her den, seeking comfort from Tommy. She picked him up and held him like a small baby. He crunched on a leaf, oblivious.

'Was that me? Did I make Mum and Dad disappear? The ball last year was me but this wasn't me, was it? I didn't mean to. I only blew out the candles,' she said, cuddling the small tortoise.

Jack came into her room but remained quiet, lost in his thoughts. Maya fought hard to hold back the raindrop tears swelling in her eyes. It was a losing battle. She turned away toward the vivarium, trying to be strong.

'M^2, it wasn't us. I don't understand it, but we'll find them soon.' He wandered out into the landing. 'OK, think, Jack, think … We should call Uncle Philbert. Yes!'

Maya nodded without turning, not wanting to show how scared she was, and distracted herself by wandering over to the window. Water ran down the glass, making it opaque and reflective. She could barely see the road below. It was then that she noticed the moving mist. It wasn't outside, but within the reflection in the glass. Then she saw Mum and Dad. Thinking they were behind her, she spun around, but she was alone in her room – no Mum, no Dad, no mist.

'Jack!' Maya yelled.

He rushed in and stopped in disbelief upon seeing the image of Mum and Dad within the window. They stood clutching each other's hands while the mist curled around them like a serpent.

He called out to them and knocked on the glass but neither responded. Not knowing what else to do, he got his phone out and started recording the scene. As Maya watched, holding Tommy close, Mum and Dad turned away, distracted by a disturbance behind them. She held her breath as a fat, hunchbacked figure appeared, moving erratically. Her eyes grew wide until she realised that it wasn't a hunchback but two beings: a woman in rich, ancient clothes, struggling to keep a thin man from collapsing. Mum and Dad rushed to help them and, with Dad's support, the injured man slowly lifted his head and looked straight at them.

'Your Majesty!' cried a woman from inside Maya's room. Startled, Maya dropped Tommy and grabbed Jack's arm.

'Yikes!' the woman cried again.

Something small flew out of the room. Seeing it, Jack instantly placed himself between Maya and the door.

'Stay behind me, M^2,' he whispered, slowly reaching for Maya's pink pillow. 'Who's there?' he called loudly.

There was no response except the hammering rain. Maya braved a quick peek at the window and her face dropped. Mum and Dad weren't there anymore.

'They're gone,' she said, her voice low with despair.

Jack didn't acknowledge her. He called out to the unseen intruder again. 'Whoever you are, show yourself. Or else …'

Maya heard a quaver growing in Jack's voice, and her heart began to gallop.

'Jack, we need to find Tommy. I dropped him. Oh, Tommy …' She searched the floor. Where did he land? With a sickening feeling, she scanned the room.

The house remained silent.

'Stay close,' said Jack, clutching the pillow. He slowly ventured out into the landing when the woman's voice rang out.

'Children, it's me! Tommy! Maya, Jack, it's me.'

It came from downstairs; the woman was in the living room. 'Tommy?'

Jack turned and pointed down. Warily Maya joined him, and together they descended the steps. The door leading to the living room was ajar, as they had left it. All the lights were on inside, but it was spooky nonetheless. Jack crept forward with the pillow raised; Maya hesitated a little before following, avoiding the creaking floorboards.

The woman spoke again, her voice just audible over the sound of the rain splattering against the windows. 'Maya … Jack … Maya. It's me, Tommeee.'

Though the voice sounded friendly, Maya tugged at Jack's arm and whispered, 'If she's done something to Tommy …'

Cautiously they walked into the living room. The presents lay open where they'd left them, Dad's camera sat on its tripod and the uncut cake sat on the table. Next to the cake stood a small creature, part tortoise, part human. It stood erect like a human, with thin arms and legs. It had a shell that was longer than a tortoise's. Its neck was long and its head was a mixture of a human and a tortoise. They were speechless. It was the strangest thing Maya had ever seen.

'Don't be frightened, children. Come forth!' it said.

Maya and Jack exchanged a glance, baffled. And then Maya surprised herself by responding.

'Tommy?'

'Yes, that is what I am called.'

'You're a girl! And different! And you talk!' Maya drew closer.

'Yes, it's me. Don't be frightened now,' Tommy said in a motherly voice.

Maya turned to Jack with a sparkle in her eyes. 'See! I knew it was all true – magical beings do exist.'

'Careful, M^2.' He stepped closer, ready to defend them with the pink pillow.

The tension built as Maya approached Tommy. 'You talk like the little monkey from my dream.'

'There was a monkey in that dream?'

'Yes! Oh, you're so beautiful, with little cute fingers!' Maya said, admiring the sharp features of Tommy's matronly face.

'I can fly too.'

'I don't see any wings!' Jack jumped in, lowering his shield.

'All in good time, child. First allow me to work out what's happened. Did you manage to capture the images on your device – the phone?'

Jack had forgotten all about the phone in his grip. It was still recording. He thumbed it a few times, and they all huddled around the table to watch the video. Maya surreptitiously studied Tommy as she became engrossed in the images. Jack, on the other hand, stared at Tommy with distrust.

'Oh, great!' Tommy exclaimed. 'None of this is supposed to happen! You weren't supposed to even know of me. This was supposed to be a simple task – secretly overseeing two Siantian children. Nothing should have gone wrong.' She watched the images a few times. 'Nope, sorry, I can't tell where they are.'

Jack raised his eyebrows. 'You mean you haven't done this to Mum and Dad?'

'Goodness, not a great Siantian are you? Jumping to conclusions?' Tommy began to pace.

'They talked about that in my dream,' said Maya. 'Scientians. What's that?'

'Those who live in this world – Siantia. Like you.'

'Siantia? You mean science?' Jack asked, watching her pace up and down the table.

'Yes, that's it: Siantia – science.'

Sceptical, Jack bent down and examined Tommy closely. She didn't like that and returned a firm gaze. They glared at each other until Jack finally relaxed his grip on the pillow and began to fiddle with his phone.

'There will be time to capture me on that device later,' Tommy said. 'For now, let's concentrate on what's happened.'

Jack stopped, shocked. 'How'd you know I was thinking that?'

'Logic. Why else would a Siantian start playing with his phone, eh?'

Without any warning, Tommy jumped up and hovered in Jack's face. Maya's eyes grew in wonder as Jack instinctively retreated. Tommy hung silently in mid-air before him, like a giant ladybird. She had transparent wings that were barely visible; only a small hum gave their existence away.

'Hold out your hand,' said Tommy. 'I don't bite.'

Politely obliging, Jack said, 'I think I should make that call to Uncle Philbert. He'll know what to do.'

'Tommy drifted down onto his palm. 'These matters are beyond him. Your parents' disappearance is disturbing and unprecedented, as were the images in the window.'

'Uncle's well read.'

'But will he believe you talked to a tortoise?'

'He would if I video you talking. Anyway, do you know what's happened?'

'No, but I know one who might.'

'Who?'

'An ancient monk: Shikshi Virath. Yes, he'll know.' Tommy paused. 'He's the one who said watching over you two would be simple.'

Tommy sounded dejected as she paced in a tight circle on Jack's palm.

He relaxed and touched her near-invisible wings. Throwing him a disapproving look, Tommy hopped onto Maya's shoulder.

'I think he planned it!' said Tommy.

'What do you mean?' asked Jack.

'I came here to escape the Konjiurian way of life, and he asked me to help him by being your guardian. It would be a quiet task, he said. No konjuring or teaching; a dream assignment. But this changes everything.'

'So you were to watch over us?' said Jack.

'Yes, but I don't know why.' Tommy gave Jack a stern look. 'Stop fiddling with the phone.'

'I need proof!' Jack cheekily took a photo before putting the phone in his pocket.

Tommy seemed about to react but simply turned to Maya and said, 'Tell me more about that dream and the letter that was delivered this morning.'

'Wait, M^2, not so fast,' Jack raised his hand. 'She should explain herself first. I still don't understand most of what she said about conjuring or the watching over us. Do you? Besides, she's a talking tortoise. I mean no disrespect but that's not normal. And if you're our guardian, why haven't you spoken till now?'

When he finished, the room went silent. Tommy elegantly hopped onto the dining table and strode up and down.

'OK, fine. You named me Tommy, and though it isn't my real name, I've grown to like it. So call me Tommy. Now, I come from another realm. Do you know what a realm is?'

'Another world; like ours,' Maya chipped in, pulling up a chair.

'Yes, that is right. There are many, and the one I come from is called Konjiur, where my kind are guardians to young princes and princesses.'

'Princesses in Konjiur!' Maya exclaimed, getting comfortable. 'The wizard was from there.'

'Wizard? What wizard?' asked Jack.

'In my dream.'

'Yes, you mentioned him last night. In Konjiur, wizards are called konjurers. Now think carefully: what name did he go by?'

Maya shook her head. 'I can't remember exactly. It sounded like T-O-C-'

Tommy stopped pacing and faced Maya; she looked troubled. 'Not Torackdan?'

'Yes, that's it. You've heard of him?'

Tommy nodded.

'You mean he's real? The dream's true?' Maya's face went ashen. She'd wanted to tell them both about the dream since morning, but now she wasn't keen.

'I'm afraid so. Go on, child. What did Torackdan do?' Tommy's attention was fully focused on Maya.

Maya slowly described her dream in as much detail as she could remember. Some fifteen minutes later she concluded. 'Torackdan vanished but I heard his voice saying, "In loss lies victory". And then the small warrior said he'd told the monkey to go to Siantia and find his kind there. That's all.'

Maya stopped abruptly; she was scared after talking about the wraith and the mysterious warrior. Most of all she was worried about the warrior looking and speaking like her; she hadn't told them about that. If the dream was true, did it mean that she'd killed the wizard? Was she responsible for the wretched betrayal and the attack?

'The slaying of Torackdan!' said Tommy, her voice loud against the rain beating chaotically on the window. 'He was a sense konjurer, one of the oldest. Surely this is impossible!'

Maya's anxiety rose, but she tried to act normal by resting her chin in her palms. 'Is it that bad?'

'If true, it's worse than bad. I need to consult with Virath, the protector of this realm. He has vast experience. He'll know more.'

'What's a sense konjurer?'

'An older, more powerful wizard, one who can change his surroundings and himself. That must be what you witnessed, little one.'

'So you also think the dream was real?' asked Jack.

'Yes, although I wish it wasn't. Torackdan's demise, the wraith hunting the staff that travels to Siantia, the disappearance of your parents and the appearance of the King of Konjiur in the window – it all spells trouble. I must consult with Virath.'

'Consult how?' asked Maya. 'Do you have other powers? Can you speak telepathically?'

'No, not that!'

'Other abilities then?'

'Hmm, yes. I am a healer; I konjure health,' said Tommy hesitantly. 'Haven't practised it for some time though.'

'And in Konjiur does everyone have powers?'

'That's the last question, children. Yes, we all have powers. They're all different, and some have more than others. It's not like here, where you depend on devices to do things.'

'And have Mum and Dad gone to Konjiur?' asked Maya.

'I couldn't tell. That's another reason why I must see Virath.'

'Where is he? Phone him,' Jack said, fishing his phone out.

'At the Gate, the place from where this realm can be entered,' Tommy stopped pacing.

'The Gate,' Maya murmured.

'Yes, its gateway to other realms, a dangerous place, a protected place that separates Siantia from the other realms.'

'What's the number?' asked Jack, getting ready to key in the digits.

Tommy shook her head. 'Don't know! I must leave soon. It's at least a half a day's flying, and with this storm it'll take much longer.'

'Can we come along?' asked Maya.

'Yes, we should stick together,' agreed Jack. 'Do you know of any train stations near this Gate?'

Maya nodded eagerly but Tommy didn't like the idea. 'No! No train goes there! Besides, it is best if I go alone.'

'But you said you're our guardian!' Maya protested. 'You can't leave us.'

Tommy didn't respond immediately; instead he paced on the dining table for some long seconds. 'Your reasoning is sound, Maya. There is one way you could come with me, but it's tricky.'

'Tricky?' Jack asked.

'Yes, tricky. I will have to ask the custodians to help us.'

'Custodians? Now who are they?' asked Maya.

Tommy shook her head, 'A secretive lot and they may not take kindly to helping Siantians. In fact, one was here earlier.'

'Here?' Jack stood.

Nodding, Tommy said, 'The one who delivered the letter this morning.'

'Her!' Jack exclaimed. 'Someone at the museum had a similar snake tattoo to her, I'm sure. Are they the custodians and is that where we need to go?'

'All I know is that they're in the city.'

'London? Oh, good, we can train it. Where in London?'

'I'll find it once we are over the river.'

'The Thames you mean?' Tommy nodded. 'Good, let's try to catch the next train then. M^2, dress warm and get anything you need.'

****

Twenty minutes later, the children were standing by the front door, hooded and warmly dressed with backpacks full of snacks. Both Tommy and Jack looked unsure. Outside, the rain had eased but it was still miserable. Even so, Maya was pleased about one thing and voiced it.

'Magic exists.'

Jack half-nodded without looking at her. 'As does science. And we'll be using trains and phones – science.'

Laughing timidly, she said, 'Yes, but you agree. Say magic exists.'

Reluctantly, Jack looked at her with a shy smile. 'Magic exists!' he whispered, to Maya's delight.

As soon as Jack opened the door, little raindrops hit their faces. He glanced back. 'Ready? It'll be a brisk walk to the station. Stay close and don't run.'

Holding Tommy, Maya nodded seriously as the reality of their journey dawned on her: venturing out into a stormy night to find a mysterious place and the man who could help them save their parents.

****

David woke abruptly; he'd been asleep in an awkward position on the settee and, in the dim light, struggled to recall where he was until lightning flashed across the room. In that moment, he caught the outlines of the antique furniture and remembered that he was in his own five-star room at the mysterious Red Gate Centre.

Another lightning bolt lit the room, then another in quick succession. Groaning, he got up and made his way to the window. Outside, the storm was raging and through the heavy rain the frequent lightning revealed the monastery in the distance. Lightning flashed from the other side of it at an angle that looked far too low.

What time is it? David looked around for a clock. He didn't find one, but the fruit basket caught his eye. He'd forgotten how hungry he was and picked up an apple before returning to the settee.

Should he run? Thoughts of escaping arose again but this was a good place with good people. Virath was clever and seemed to understand him. No one had told him what he could and could not do, except for leaving this room. And best of all, no one thought he needed to attend classes; that was a big bonus. David decided he liked it here; it felt right and there was no reason to escape, not yet. Even his dowsing feeling was at peace, and so he decided to wait for the monk.

Only minutes later however, David was bored. He checked out the room: the giant four-poster bed, the traditional furniture, the painting of some old man over the fireplace, the various ornaments, armour and medieval weapons mounted all around, and a small door. A small door? Curious, he opened cautiously and discovered a walk-in cupboard. Inside he found a set of hooded robes, similar to the ones the monks wore. Was he expected to wear them too? David thought, feeling the coarseness of the material.

It was then that he remembered the diary. Retrieving it from his rucksack, he sat at the table by the window, flicking through the pages. They were thick and unlined. He closed the book and ran his hand over the dark leather. It contrasted sharply with the yellow paper within. The diary looked and felt old and dated.

Virath had told him to record whatever he learnt and that the diary would answer any questions he had. 'Do I wait here or go out?' he said to himself. 'That's the question I need to answer.'

He opened the diary once more. This time something caught his attention: a page had the word 'Library' written in elegant, curly writing with a left slant. It hadn't been there before. He closed and opened the book few times, but the writing persisted. Well, the library was his favourite place; he didn't need any more convincing. Believing the writing to be a sign, he closed the book and headed for the door. He assumed Laksha would have locked him in but was pleasantly surprised when the wooden door gave way, although it was far heavier than normal ones. When the gap was wide enough, he squeezed through.

Outside, the corridor was dark and uninviting but not cold.

He slipped the book into his back pocket and stepped away from the door into the dark unknown. It was then that one of the huge torches above him sparked on with a roar.

He hadn't expected that and was momentarily startled. It was a long time since something had spooked him, for David was used to dark corridors and rooms from all his escapades. Encouraged by the light, he took more steps and more lamps came on.

'Who'd have thought,' he said, almost laughing at the self-igniting torches.

The corridor was deserted, and David wondered where the other children were. He tried the next door, then the next one and the one after that; none of them budged. Alone beneath the high ceiling, he felt small and lonely but bravely continued down the highly decorated corridor full of armour, weapons and paintings.

A few more doors down, David looked back and saw that the first torch had switched off and from there on, each time a flame fired up, another behind him died. He was cocooned in the light of six flares, three ahead, and three behind. Isolated in the oasis of light, David resisted the urge to stop and study any items. Soon he reached the steps heading up, and began the long climb.

After what seemed like an eternity in suspended oblivion, David sighted the top of the steps. His stride quickened, and in no time he stood before doors with book-shaped handles. He hadn't noticed them earlier. He checked once more to see if his diary had indeed said 'Library'; it did.

He carefully pushed the larger wooden door open and entered without closing it behind him in case he needed to make a quick exit.

Inside, loud clanks sounded and cold, white crystalline lights came on sequentially. They ran down the aisles of a vast hall, and the growing light revealed murals on the ceiling, a rough brownish stone floor, more aisles leading off from the central passage before him and various globe-like devices lining the central aisle.

David began down the central gangway. In some side passages he observed that the stone floor was more worn, an indication that these were the more popular sections. He took care, ensuring his steps were quiet. Looking down each dark passage in between the shelves, David explored deeper. Why had the diary led him here? There were huge leather-bound hardbacks on the lower shelf, some even larger than him. He noticed a wooden wheelbarrow in one aisle, presumably for these colossal volumes.

Further down, he came across a long wooden table on which books of varying sizes lay open. It was as if though those who had been studying had left in a hurry. And then he heard a sound that was alien for a library: running water. Bewildered, he ventured on with caution and soon found the source: a fountain. It was made from black stone and sculpted to look like books piled on top of each other, from large to small. The water trickled from book to book and at the bottom was a plaque that read, 'Fountain of Knowledge (n.)' with a compass rose sign at the end. He suspected this was the centre of the vast library, and he was in the north aisle. The east, west and south passages were all shrouded in darkness. David glanced at a circular stone bench at the base of the fountain and the other aisles before retreating down the passage he'd come up to look at the books that lay on the table. They weren't dusty, meaning that someone had been studying them recently. He needed to be careful, he thought, looking at the larger ones, when something caught his eye. A glow moved within a smaller manuscript further down the table. He blinked and looked intently, but the light had come and gone, like the one inside a photocopier. Puzzled, he reached for it. The book was about the size of his diary with a flame on its cover. Opening it, he was surprised to find it normal and filled with inscriptions. He flicked the pages few time before settling on one with only four lines on it; a short poem. Feeling mischievous, David got up and, pretending to be important, read them out loud with deliberation and care.

Sound slumber thee, condemned.
Awake from thine dreamy prison
If thy friend is worried
Thou shall be too

As the words petered out, he sensed a change. Without any warning, a bright light shot out from within the book.

Dropping the book onto the table, David retreated a few steps before looking up. A small, bright, lemony-yellow flame the size of a cricket ball hovered above him. He instinctively retreated further but it followed. David turned and dashed towards the fountain, and crashed into the circular bench there. It hurt. Groaning, he turned to find the flame floating before him like a miniature UFO, silently glowing. When it didn't move, he blurted out the first question that came to mind.

'Who are you? What do you want from me? Are you some sort of a librarian? Are you annoyed because I disturbed the books?'

This was exactly the type of thing he wanted to read about – things that science had not discovered – but now that one was before him, he was scared.

'I'm neither deaf nor a librarian,' said the flame in a child's voice. 'I'm just a simple fire genie.'

'Is that you? Did you just s-say that?' David managed, despite his fear.

'Well, you don't see anyone else here, do you?' The flame twirled around. 'Friend, what place is this? Where am I? I am indebted to you for freeing me from this.' The flame floated closer, coming right into his face.

David leant back, pressing himself deeper into the bench as the heat grew against his skin. 'A flame genie!' he said in a firmer voice. The flame floated up and down in a nod. 'Does this mean I am your master?' David's heart was pounding.

'I've never heard of such an arrangement! A friend perhaps,' it said. 'Yes, a friend. And you must be a konjurer, yes? I am Achanak. Pleased to make your acquaintance.'

David didn't understand but he didn't need to; he was good at faking conversations and lying. It was a skill he'd acquired to survive on the streets and the different asylums where he was questioned. So he nodded, more confidently this time. 'A genie, you say you are, and Acha-nak is thy name,' he said, being silly. He swiped his hand slowly over the flame, checking to see if there were any strings; there weren't. The genie looked real.

'What are you doing?' asked Achanak, dropping low.

'Oh, nothing.' He folded his arms. 'So Acha-nak is thy name?' he said again.

'It means to come and go suddenly,' it said playfully, flashing on and off. 'And how shall I address you, konjurer?'

'David!' He drew closer. In the centre of the flame was a boy's face, a little older than him. In that one look, David knew Achanak wasn't streetwise; he was naïve.

'David the konjurer. Where are we?'

'Not far from London.'

'London! I haven't heard of this place but there is a lot I haven't heard of. You must be learned and powerful to have freed me. Tell me, are there many like you?'

'Like me?' David wanted to laugh. 'No, no one else has my learning; I have taught myself many a things.'

'And how did you know where I was, David the konjurer? Did someone tell you?'

'Just David; don't say that other bit.'

'You mean, konjurer?'

David nodded. 'What makes you think I am a conjurer?'

'Well, who else but a konjurer could invoke the spell? Only a sorcerer could have freed me.'

David nodded convincingly. Perhaps he was a conjurer? In any case, it was to his advantage not to correct the flame, at least not yet. To change the subject, he extracted his diary from his pocket. He wanted to check if it was really leading him, speaking to him. It had read 'Library'; he'd followed and found Achanak, a fire genie. What would it say now?

Achanak, floated closer and closer like a small child. David opened the diary and found a new word. Achanak read aloud, '"Help!" Help who? Who needs our help? Konjurer, are you on a mission?'

David shrugged. Yep, the diary was talking to him. Was this what Virath meant when he said it would answer any questions he had? He put the book away.

'Help who?' Achanak repeated, bewildered.

Before David could respond, all the crystalline lights blinked off.

Achanak dimmed instantly. 'What's happening? What shall we do, David?'

David didn't answer. He looked around in Achanak's dim glow; nothing looked out of place. He didn't know what had happened or who needed help, but Virath would know.

'Follow me; we need to find a friend of mine,' he said, heading towards the exit.

PM Perry

5

STORM

Beyond the point of no return.

Standing against the blowing wind, Jack pulled and pushed the station's main door, but it didn't budge. Maya stood close by, hugging Tommy like a baby and peering through the large station windows. Inside, the ticket counter was closed, and the screen showing the train schedules said they were all cancelled. Worried, she turned towards Jack, who stood holding his hood against the wind, looking up and down the road. Feeling his nervousness, Maya followed his gaze. She found the road quieter than normal; only the occasional vehicle rushed by.

'What now?'

Maya had barely uttered the words over the whistling wind when something struck Jack. Startled, Maya felt something flapping against her foot. She looked down and saw a large raven fluttering and shrilling on the pavement. It had flown into Jack and crashed to the ground.

'Oh, poor thing,' said Maya, reaching for it.

'DON'T!' Tommy shouted. 'It's possessed! This is bad. Quickly, find shelter, more will—'

On the road, a white van pulled over and screeched to a halt. Its door swung open, nearly knocking them off their feet. Caught between the raven and the van, Maya cowered against her brother. What now?

'It's the same van from this morning,' exclaimed Jack.

Inside, a girl was shouting and waving. 'Hurry, get in! Quickly, get in now!'

'It's her – the letter girl!' Jack cried.

She was the last person Maya had expected to see.

'Hurry, it's calling others,' the girl shouted over the wind, pointing at the raven hobbling and shrieking on the ground.

'The custodian's right!' said Tommy, leaping from Maya's hands. 'Get in now.'

'Tommy!' Maya cried. She reached out to catch her, but Jack pulled her back just as another raven swooped past, narrowly missing her. It crashed into the door behind them.

'Quickly now!' Tommy called from the van.

'Come on, M².' Jack said, gently lifting and bundling her into the van before jumping in. The girl pulled away immediately. 'Wait!' Jack shouted, reaching for the open door.

Ahead, another raven flew at the windscreen. The girl swerved to miss it and the door rolled into Jack's arm. He quickly slammed it shut.

Tommy thanked the girl and asked her name.

'Qidan,' she said, straightening the van and accelerating down the quiet roads.

Qidan, Maya repeated in her mind. She liked her hoarse voice; it sounded honest and matched her large frame.

In those first few minutes, Tommy continued to ask questions but Qidan wasn't able to answer most of them. The only useful thing they learnt was that Virath had asked for someone to keep an eye on them and she'd been chosen.

'Virath?' said Tommy, surprised.

'He must have known.' Quidan looked at the dark sky. 'We've lost the ravens. I wonder what's got them restless.'

'They're vulnerable to vile konjuring and it's strong this evening,' said Tommy 'Head to Castle Fang for safety.'

'Siantians aren't allowed there!' Qidan protested.

'What's Castle Fang?' asked Jack.

Tommy and Qidan exchanged a brief glance.

'It's where custodians live,' said Tommy. She turned to Qidan. 'I'll speak to the elders. Head for it.'

Excited at the mention of a castle, Maya sat quietly in the warm cab, listening to the swooshing wipers and the beating rain, wondering where it could be. She couldn't think of any place in London where a secret castle could be. She studied the custodian: jet-black hair, an oval face, sharp eyes and a muscular build.

'The same tattoo!' Jack observed.

'This?' Qidan raised her arm; it boasted an image of a curled up snake.

'Only custodians who have come of age have that,' Tommy explained. 'It shows which snake clan they are from. She's one of the Flying Fangs.'

'Snake people?' Maya perked up. She'd read of these beings who were supposedly able change into snakes.

'Sounds like a gang,' said Jack

'Gang? I suppose you say that,' said Tommy, 'but I wouldn't because she can transform into a flying snake, and a large one at that.'

'Really? Transform?' He looked bewildered.

Qidan gave him a brief nod but Jack didn't look convinced. Half an hour later, as they neared Thames and the city centre, the traffic began to build. By then they'd become more trusting of each other, except for Jack who remained sceptical.

Outside, the occasional pedestrian dashed through the rain and in between the buildings, heading for the nearest tube entrance or a bus stop. Soon famous and familiar landmarks appeared: a huge railway station, a world renowned PLC and a famous 3D movie centre. Each one emerged silently from the storm and slipped by. Maya knew this part of London well and searched for the aquarium and the huge wheel. It was then that she noticed a black ball moving towards them.

'What's that?' she asked, pointing.

'Ravens! Hang on.' Qidan turned the van into an empty side road and accelerated. She took a few more turns before slowing and looking into the side mirror.

'Can you see them?' she asked.

'No!' Jack shook his head, trying to peer into the falling rain.

'Me neither!' said Tommy.

Across the Thames, lights glimmered like enticing jewels. In the distance, behind the glittering gems, was a strange blue beam. The scene looked surreal.

'What is that?' Maya asked, pointing at the blue beam that reached out into the sky, like some lighthouse.

'It's from the castle we're heading to,' Tommy began, when something crashed into Qidan's window. Startled, they all cried out. Qidan swerved onto the pavement and slammed into a bollard. She recovered from the unexpected jolt and tried reversing, but the van was dead.

Seconds later a raven landed on the bonnet, shrilling. Another flew past Jack's window and something landed on top of the van. There was no sign of anyone around; they were alone in the rain and the wind.

'Stay inside,' said Quidan. 'I'll call for help and then distract them.'

Tommy nodded, but by then Qidan had got out, slammed the door shut and disappeared.

More ravens landed, making an awful noise. Occasionally one banged into the van. Then Maya heard something she'd only read about: a hissing roar.

'A dragon?' she asked, looking unsure.

'That's Qidan's call for help,' said Tommy.

'Qidan?' questioned Jack.

'Yes, in her snake form. Don't be frightened when others arrive. They'll be big serpents with four heads.' Tommy looked towards the blue shaft of light.

'Four-headed snakes?'

'Cobras. And here they come!' Tommy pointed at a missile coming towards them.

The noises around the van increased, a mixture of hissing and shrill.

'She needs help.' Jack opened his door but Tommy stopped him.

'Yes, and here comes one of the elders.'

A large grey snake swooped down and headed to where Qidan was.

'Impossible! That's huge,' said Jack.

'And fast.' said Maya.

Three more snakes landed one by one around the van. The hissing turned into low growls and the shrills intensified. Something banged twice against the van.

'Quickly, they want us to get out,' said Tommy.

Jack stepped out first before tensely urging Maya to do the same. Outside three snakes fought an unkindness of ravens rushing in from all directions, while the remaining two snakes formed a ring around Maya and Jack, hissing and beating their wings. Both towered over them.

'Jump onto their backs and hold on,' said Tommy, translating the hisses. 'Hold onto the armour around their necks. They say they'll have to carry us to the castle.'

With a racing heart, Maya clutched Tommy tighter and edged closer. Beside her, Jack ducked under a snake's four heads, which were big and fanned out, searching in different direction.

'They're telling us to hurry,' said Tommy. 'Look.' She pointed at the growing commotion.

'And you?' asked Maya.

Tommy leaped up and dived into her jacket. 'I'm with you.'

'M^2, put your arms through there and there and hold on tight.' Jack lifted her before climbing onto the other snake. The

Fang Maya was on was big; it felt like being on the high end of a seesaw. The hissing increased.

'They're asking if you're ready,' Tommy said.

Jack gave a thumbs up.

Barely breathing, Maya nodded.

Tommy shouted something and the Fangs took off. It wasn't graceful; their rescuers struggled with the added weight as they rose above the river.

'Hold on; they're going to dive to gain speed,' Tommy shouted.

The snakes banked into a steep plunge. Maya's ears popped and the swollen Thames filled her view: a pure thick blackness, with waves reaching out like hands to welcome them into the abyss. Thrown forward, Maya held her breath with a clenched jaw. Inside her jacket, Tommy wailed.

Gathering speed, the Fangs levelled off, skimming the waves. Water sprayed Maya's face before they rose again. With each beat of their wings, they gained height and were soon flying past the big clock tower across the river, towards the light in the distance. Remembering to breathe, Maya turned around searching for Jack, when they rolled to one side.

'Hold on, more ravens ahead,' Tommy shouted.

Hugging the armour, Maya tried to look, but it was difficult with the wind in her face. The Fangs were fast and shot past the ravens, trying to intercept them, tilting and turning like jets to avoid collision. She hung on anxiously until the larger Fang sped past, after which their flight got a little easier and smoother.

'He's one of the elders – the one clearing our flight path,' Tommy shouted.

Nodding, Maya looked at the passing London skyscape. Between the rain and the snake's beating wings, she spotted the growing beam and a familiar thin spire next to it. It took her a moment to place it: it was next to the Museum of Myth and Mysticism.

'Almost there! Hold tight, he's going to drop down nooow.' Tommy trailed off as the snake nosedived.

They raced towards the ground. A blue haze filled Maya's vision; she could see rooftops, and they were homing in on one.

'Hold. HOLD,' Tommy cried. They shot down a blue vertical tunnel at high speed. 'Nearly there!'

Maya dared not move. It felt like an eternity, but eventually they passed through the blue light and emerged into a cavern. The fangs flattened out to slow their descent until they were flying gently towards a rock shelf. They were inside a massive space, the shaft entrance high above and nothing but darkness below.

They landed on the ledge moments later. Jumping off their saviours, Maya and Jack looked around in a daze. Tommy hovered up from Maya's jacket and began to give instructions.

'Stay here! Don't approach until I call; let me speak to the Elder first.'

They nodded.

'Remember, we aren't supposed to be here. And just because they helped us does not make them any friendlier.' Tommy paused momentarily as the biggest of the snakes floated towards them. 'Just hope the Elder forgives our intrusion and accepts us.'

PM Perry

6

FIRST STRIKE

Going blindly into the unknown.

David's new companion, Achanak, broke the silence once more. 'What about that door? He could be in there.'

'Doubt it; that's the royal hall. Our best chance is the monk's living quarters in the other building. Virath would probably be there or in his office by the lake. Now shh.'

'Why?'

'If we draw attention, they might tell us to return to my room.'

'Not you – you're a konjurer!'

'Aye, and a guest on a mission. Secrecy is vital, yes?'

The genie nodded.

They were crouched by a bench in the vast stone corridor David had intended to revisit. In the darkness, it looked spooky and the objects that had fascinated him earlier now looked different in Achanak's dim glow. Moving shadows played with his mind and for the first time he felt a chill.

After leaving the library, David had moved cautiously and deliberately. Though the corridor was deserted, he chose to scamper from one piece of furniture to the next. His plan was simple: find Virath without being discovered. However, it was proving difficult with Achanak in tow. The fire genie was jumpy and frequently dimmed with fright. He even vanished once, but never stopped talking. David had shushed him twice but, excited to be free after a long time trapped in the book, Achanak continued to chat.

'What's his name? Why would he know who needs help? Whose castle is this?'

David didn't answer, choosing instead to plough on in the low light. When they passed the banqueting hall, he noticed beams of light moving down the corridor.

'Someone's coming.'

Calmly, he searched around for somewhere to hide. Unable to find a good spot, he reached for the door leading to the hall; it opened. Relieved, he stepped inside.

'Konjurer ... sorry, David, look,' called Achanak, rather loudly.

'Shhh!' said David, realising he'd made a grave error. In his haste he'd forgotten to check the hall. With dread, he turned and spotted several things at once: an immense fireplace, the three long dining tables, another table at the top of the hall and few monks dining.

'Monks! Great.' David's heart jumped when Achanak floated towards them at the centre table.

'Something's not right,' said the genie. 'None of them move. They're frozen.'

Frozen? But before he could investigate, voices erupted from the corridor outside.

'Shh,' David instructed the genie. He tried to peer outside, but it was impossible to do without giving away his presence. Changing tactics, he opted to keep the door slightly ajar and tilted his ear near the small gap. His breathing had sped up and he could feel his heart in his ear; an unwelcome interruption. It resonated faster and faster as the voices grew.

'Check those in the banqueting hall,' someone said.

A torch flashed in his direction.

'And hurry back. I'll check the one who came before the storm. Quickly now. Shikshi Virath is leading a party to the woods and needs everyone to help.'

I knew it; Virath needs help, David thought as lights flashed through the gap in the doorway.

'They're coming; hide!' he hissed at Achanak, frantically searching for a place.

He saw two options: one, mimic the frozen monks dining or two, hide underneath the table at their feet. He didn't like either, but with the voices nearly at the door, he forced himself to crawl under the table. Uneasy amongst the lifeless limbs, he was still trying to settle down when the door swung open and two monks rushed in, their loose robes creating the illusion that they were floating. David held his breath, hoping Achanak had heeded his warning.

'It's all fine,' said one of the monks.

'Yes, as expected.'

'First time I've seen anyone petrified.'

'It's best; keeps them safe and saves us having to explain everything. These Siantian children wouldn't believe it anyway.'

'And they'd get in the way.

'Yes. Let's check the kitchen and rush back. Virath will unfreeze them once things return to normal.'

The monks moved away to the table at the top of the hall and exited by a small door there. Hearing the door click shut, David took a deep breath and scrambled out. He warily approached the nearest boy and waved his arms before the boy's eyes; he didn't blink. He was like a wax model, stuck mid-movement, staring ahead and lifting a forkful of food to his mouth.

'David,' said Achanak, snapping him out of his trance.

'Yes!' He turned and caught the genie reappearing by the mural above the huge fireplace, which was big, like a tunnel. It was taller than him and the glowing embers in the grate resembled magma.

'Our mission?' Achanak reminded him, floating towards the small door the monks had exited from. 'They knew where Virath was.'

'Aye,' David nodded, looking at the children one final time before following.

Minutes later they found themselves in the wooden corridor where the collage windows were ablaze with flashes.

'Hurry!' He ran-walked across the wooden floor, his anxiety rising. By the time he arrived at the reception, he was edgy.

'I think I've heard of him.' Achanak floated close behind. 'Virath the Wise. If he's your friend, you must be good.' He glowed brighter.

David didn't answer. The atmosphere in the reception office was tense, and a strange smell hung in the air. He'd only ever smelled it once before, on a dreadful Guy Fawkes Night that he would have preferred to forget. He'd been in a scuffle with a larger kid when he'd tripped and fallen, giving his attacker the advantage. He'd taken a heavy beating and this odour – a mixture of blood, fireworks and soil was a reminder of that. Was it a bad omen? He hesitated, but it was futile to resist the flickering light outside.

The door leading out to the big gate and the platform was buzzing with flashes, luring him like a teenager to a haunted house. Ignoring the smell, David tiptoed to the door and stood beside it, his back against the wall, like a spy about to break into a house. He felt vulnerable and excited at the same time.

Achanak interrupted David: 'I hate wind and I like rain even less,' he whispered into David's ear. 'Friend, you carry on; this is as far as I go.'

David didn't say anything. He simply gave a dimming Achanak the hangdog look he'd mastered on the streets. It never failed.

'Well, perhaps a little further,' said Achanak.

David didn't speak; he simply stepped outside. The leaves were blowing around in tight circles, like mini-tornadoes. Achanak followed like his shadow. Standing in the relative safety of the huge gate, they looked up in the direction of the mountains and the woods and saw the storm for the first time.

In the drumming rain and crackling bangs, one thing captivated them: the rampant lightning. David took a moment to muster his courage and then said with a deep breath. 'Coming?' He moved out onto the open stone platform.

Rain soaked him instantly. He turned, dripping, to look at Achanak. The genie was struggling against the elements, sparking and crackling, but he followed, growing in intensity. Together they made it to the steps at the other end, where the scene in the valley below stopped them in their tracks. 'Oh, boy,' was all David managed, for nothing he'd seen could have prepared him for what was before them.

In the distance, on the open ground between the woods and the lake, was a bluish-white oval of light, sporadically spitting lightning. It looked like a tear in reality itself.

And between them and the strange opening was carnage. Blazing arrows, floating monks, rocks and fireballs filled the sky. On the ground, monks clashed with huge brutes emerging from the oval of light and marching across the open grassland towards the platform. The clatter and crash of metal and wood rang out in concert with the storm, like some chaotic symphony of swords, shields, arrows and axes all clashing together.

'We're under attack,' said Achanak. 'Your friend will need help.'

David nodded, searching for the best way to approach the battlefield, when a monk came running up the steps.

'RUN!' he screamed, a moment before he was slammed against the steps as if pushed. David could not see what had taken the monk down, for there were no arrows or weapons in his back.

'I've seen that before,' Achanak said, floating backwards. 'Only one thing does that. They will need your help, David.'

'What are you doing there? GET BACK!' shouted someone behind them.

David was afraid and frozen to the spot, trying to understand what had flung the monk so violently. He didn't know what to do. Help the fallen monk? Retreat? Or continue and find Virath?

Some monks ran down the steps and a few took to air from the edge. Amazed, David followed their flight and saw another tumble out of the sky as a large dark creature hurtled down towards him.

'Oh, flames! Ooh, flicking flames, run, David!' Achanak cried.

Captivated, David didn't budge.

'Oh, flames, it's an ekoer!' The terror in Achanak's voice grew.

A large leathery beast with black wings and powerful legs landed on the platform with a heavy whump. Rainwater splashed David and yet he stood transfixed. Never in all his reading had he come across such an abomination: a mammoth monster that was a mixture between a dog and a bat.

'Brave David, what are you going to do?' The beast before them reared awkwardly onto its hind legs. 'Quickly, cast a spell before it attacks,' Achanak whispered. The creature rose to its full stature and turned in their direction, its ears erect and eyes glaring. It towered over them, drooling like a rabid dog with a foul stench. They had its full attention. A chill tore through David and for first time he tried to move. The ekoer had its small head pulled back, poised to strike.

'Do anything,' the genie begged.

Impaled by fear, David looked on with leaden legs until an arrow tore through one of the creature's wings and another embedded in its neck. Startled, it staggered and fell back.

Relieved, David felt his legs come to life, tickling as if with pin and needles. Two monks ran past, firing arrows as the beast beat its wings, trying to rise.

'That was a narrow escape,' a monk barked at him. 'Don't just stand there!'

Annoyed, the ekoer let out a cry that threw the monks back. David didn't understand what had happened exactly, but realised that the creature's screams were deadly.

'Now, do it now!' David felt Achanak's warmth by his ear as the creature beat its wings heftily and took off. 'Cast a spell before it gets away.'

David looked at the steps, and then at the gate behind them. He knew he should return to safety but it didn't feel right; his dowsing feeling pulled him down towards the battle.

'No! We find Virath! Come on.' He descended the steps two at a time, but they were treacherous in the wet and he soon slowed. David hadn't gone far when Achanak caught up with him; glad to see him, he smiled and continued. Halfway down, they came across an injured monk and instinctively stopped to help him, but the monk said in a frail voice, 'Child, what are you doing out here? Turn back! Save yourself!'

David kicked himself. He should have known; adults always thought they knew what was best for children. He ran off, leaving the monk calling, 'Turn back, get back …'

'Is that wise to abandon him?' Achanak asked, catching up. 'He's injured.'

'He'll only divert us from our mission to find Virath,' David huffed.

'So it is Virath we seek. What invocations do you plan to use to help?'

'Invocations?'

'Why, yes. Incantations … *spells*.'

'Ah, spells.' It was time to clear up the misunderstanding and tell the genie he wasn't a conjurer or a konjurer as he called him. But honesty didn't come naturally to David and he ended up being confrontational instead. 'You first; which spell will you use, Achanak?'

'Me? Why me?'

'You're a genie! You can cast, right?'

'I am not that kind. Flaming flames!' Achanak brightened, annoyed. 'Stop playing games.'

'Well I'm not that kind of sorcerer.' There; he'd said it and felt better, even though he still wasn't quite telling the truth.

They stared blankly at each other for a moment. It wasn't what either had expected. Achanak looked back up to the platform, David ahead, thinking.

'What now?' asked David eventually.

Achanak glowed furiously. 'Turn back. There's a flaming good chance we'll be hurt or worse.'

David studied the disorder ahead: the strange light, the flying arrows, the monks and the hulking warriors emerging from the portal. It looked scary, but it didn't feel right to turn back either.

'No.' He pulled out the diary; it still read 'Help'. 'You go back. I'm finding Virath.' He dashed across the grass.

'Oh, flames!' Achanak shouted, flying beside him. 'I've warned you; don't tell me I didn't try to help.'

'Noted,' said David.

'Why don't you ask someone where Virath is? What about that monk?' An injured shikshi lay a short distance away.

'No, he'll only tell us to get back.'

'Good – not a bad idea.'

'No!'

'I'll ask then?'

David kept running.

'Wait! We should keep together.'

They cut across the field, stopping and starting, and stumbled across a slain warrior – one of the beasts that had come through the portal. He lay face down, with arrows sticking out of his back. He was massive and muscular, clad in thick, furry armour. David wanted to study him but he stank.

As they neared the blue opening, David slowed, taking care to avoid the combating monks. Arrows flew in different directions and rocks crashed across the field. Above, the ekoers circled like vultures, diving in and picking off the few monks around the opening, trying to stop the emerging army.

'Can you see him?' Achanak whispered as they crouched behind a rock.

David shook his head, eyeing each monk at the portal. All were busy battling the otherworldly creatures, except one.

'That one not fighting,' said Achanak. 'Is that him?'

'No!' David couldn't see Virath anywhere. Was he too late?

'Look, more fighting there.' Achanak gestured towards the woods on the right, and when David turned in that direction he knew that was the right way; he felt it in his stomach. In the sky above the woods was what looked like a mini-tornado. There was a flash and a fireball lit up the sky.

'That's it; come on!' David broke into a run, splashing through puddles, jumping over rocks and weaving around shrubs.

Drawing closer to the tree line, David dropped and crawled closer to the increasingly loud bangs. Cowering behind a bush, he saw a solitary monk battling a mysterious black smoke that was sliding and snaking towards the woods.

'What's that thing he's fighting?'

'I don't know,' said Achanak. 'Never seen anything like that before.'

The smoke curled in on itself and launched fireballs back at the monk. Nimbly moving out of the way, the monk waved a short T-shaped stick and inexplicably pulled the smoke away from the woods.

'That is him, that's Virath,' David said, recognising the T-stick from the office.

'Doesn't look like he needs any help.'

No sooner the genie had uttered the words than the monk collapsed without warning. Moments later, two ekoers whooshed by. And then the escaping smoke turned and snaked back towards the motionless Virath.

'Get up!' Achanak urged, as the approaching mass began to morph into a shadowy hooded figure.

'I know what that is,' David said. 'A wraith; I've read about them – they're deadly foes that suck the life from their victims. Come on; we have to distract it!'

He broke into a run, shouting and waving. The apparition knelt over Virath and let out a screech that stopped David dead in his tracks. The reality of his situation sank in; he was scared and powerless and alone. Snapping his mind free, he sat down and said wheezily, 'I must do something! Anything.'

He was sizing up stones when a sizzling fireball narrowly skimmed past his ear. Alarmed, he glanced over his shoulder.

'Sorry, out of practice,' said Achanak, floating past.

'Not bad! My turn.' David flung a heavy stone but it fell short. 'Your turn!'

Achanak floated closer, brightened and released two tennis-ball-sized fireballs. The first missed when the wraith stooped down at the last moment. Disturbed, it caught the second and flung it back faster.

'Duck!'

David dropped just in time. 'That was close!' He scrambled to recover, knowing they now had the wraith's undivided attention. He gathered a few stones and let them loose one after the other.

The wraith diffused into smoke and the rocks passed straight through. Then it materialised again and approached them.

'Run!' David yelled, scampering. There was no shame in retreating; he'd done it many times on the streets. But he didn't get far before something knocked him off his feet. He landed heavily and water, mud and grass filled in his mouth. Winded, he struggled onto his back and lay staring into the falling rain, gasping for air and gargling rainwater. Above him the ekoers circled, scavengers awaiting their turn at the carcass. He was done for.

'Get up, David!' Achanak said. 'We've won! Look, it's collapsing. The portal's closing! See, the light's fading.'

It became darker. The ekoers dove away, towards the fading blue light.

'Oh, flaming fumes! Run, David! The wraith is still coming! Wake UP! Up, up!'

But David slipped into growing darkness.

PM Perry

7

CASTLE FANG

A river less travelled.

Deep beneath London, Maya and Jack stood uneasily on the outcrop. It had been some time since the two custodians they'd flown with had transformed into human teenagers and joined the third one at back of the ridge, close to a circular carving there. Meanwhile, Qidan had circled once before joining the elder and Tommy at the edge. They'd been standing there talking ever since.

'Sounds like a heated discussion,' Jack said, glancing in their direction. An occasional coarse whisper floated across.

Maya nodded, looking at Qidan.

'And don't stare!'

Maya sighed and turned away.

'It's still hard to believe it all,' Jack continued. 'The custodians, this cave ...'

'And a castle! Tommy called it Fang.'

'Yes, now *that* is a tall tale. Impossible, that's what it is.' Jack removed his backpack.

Maya shook her head. 'I think it's down below.'

'Maybe! Should really take some snaps – proof.' Jack reached for his phone.

'I wouldn't, Jack.'

Maya wished she had something to do to distract herself from her growing anxiety. They should have been enjoying their birthday with Mum and Dad, not running around on some quest.

Jack interrupted her thoughts. 'Look at that carving where the boys are. Isn't it the same as Qidan's tattoo?'

Maya snuck a peek; she didn't want to look at the three teenagers directly. 'Yes! Must be their symbol; just see how big it is.'

Minutes later, Tommy finally flew back to them. 'The Elder, Tehari, is really annoyed.' She glanced at the huge serpent waiting some distance away.

'Why?' the twins asked at the same time.

Tommy took another peep. 'Because now you know of this place and of Castle Fang. Siantians aren't supposed to—.'

'But where is the castle?' Maya asked impatiently, looking around the vast cave.

'First you must promise to keep their home, Castle Fang, a secret.' Tommy gave the Elder another glimpse. 'It's the largest snake castle in this world and you cannot reveal anything you see.'

'I promise,' Maya said hurriedly.

Jack looked at Tehari. 'Didn't you explain that we didn't intend any of this to happen? So what now?'

'Don't stare,' whispered Tommy, sneaking another look. 'Just give me your promise first … He might grant us passage. There is another route, through the castle. But first your word.'

'Of course we promise,' said Jack, looking at Maya.

'Not to me, to him. He wants to meet both of you. Remember: don't stare at him. Be polite and brave.'

'Where's the castle?' Maya asked again, but Tommy didn't answer for Tehari was slithering towards them, his four tongues flicking.

He was big and much taller than Jack. All four of his hoods were open, like satellite dishes, and his folded wings were like collapsed sails.

Frightened, she stepped behind Jack, but in a blink the snake vanished and a tall warrior in long armour appeared. He had a military bearing and advanced with confidence, as though coming to inspect a parade.

'Sorry if I frightened you.' His voice was hoarse but calm. 'We don't get any visitors down here, which is why I'd forgotten to change into this form. Now you must be Jack, and you Maya. Welcome to our underground abode. I am Tehari.' He extended his arm. The children were taken aback by his friendliness. 'Young man.' He shook Jack's hand first, then reached towards Maya. 'And young lady. I am told that you're on your way to seek an audience with the great monk himself.'

They nodded, eager not to disappoint.

'And you promise to guard our secret?'

They nodded again.

'I was certain of that; Virath wouldn't have asked us to watch over normal Siantians, but I had to confirm.'

Maya nodded but wondered what he meant by 'normal Siantians.'

'Qidan was right to help you when she did; something stirs tonight, something that only the monk can explain. Come.' He walked towards the three teenagers at the back.

Jack was first to react. He picked up his backpack and was ready, clearly captivated by the intricate golden–silver design of Tehari's armour and the knives that were carefully interwoven around his chest plate. Two long, thin swords protruded above his shoulder.

'Come along, Maya; hurry,' Tommy urged, settling on her shoulder.

'To the castle?' She was being sarcastic and didn't expect Tommy to nod, but she did.

Maya's heart leapt but, like Jack, she remained sceptical. She wasn't sure if a secret castle could exist beneath London but hurried along nevertheless. Drawing closer to the teenagers and the carving, Maya traced the image with her eyes: a coiled serpent with its heart-shaped head at the centre. The carving was large and intimidating. Maya felt as though they were sacrificial lambs approaching an altar, but she bravely followed Jack, taking deep breaths. On her third gasp, they reached the rock face. Tehari swung the heart-shaped python head sideways to reveal a small hole.

'A snake lock?' Maya whispered in excitement. It was a myth she'd read about and pondered many times. She couldn't believe she was seeing one.

'Right you are.' Tehari turned towards her. 'What do you know about it?'

'Oh, it's one of the hardest locks to break. Only appointed snakes can open it with their tails.'

'Why, that's right!' Tehari smiled.

'Well done, Maya,' said Tommy at her ear.

'I'll use my tail, as you've said. Don't be alarmed now.' Tehari's big white tail appeared silently from beneath his armour. He slithered it into the lock and gave a twist. Clicks sounded and turned into groans as the rock face began to move. The snake coils spiralled outwards from the centre and, with heavy grinding, a tunnel opened up before them.

'Welcome, once more.' Tehari walked into the darkness.

'Come, Jack,' said Tommy encouragingly. Maya grabbed Jack's arm and they ventured inside. Her anxiety rose when the tunnel became darker. Qidan and the three boys followed, hissing and talking amongst themselves. Luckily it was a short tunnel, and when they emerged on the other side, they found Tehari standing aside in a much smaller cavern to present the castle.

'Our humble abode, little ones.'

Maya could never have imagined the sight before them: a castle carved out of the rock. It was easily twice as tall as their house, with three spires. Around it was an enormous snake statue that spiralled from the tallest central spire, curling around and around all the way to the ground. And its mouth lay wide open right in front of them.

'Is that the entrance?' Maya asked. The mouth had four fangs, two above and two below, poised to bite.

'It's just a carving,' said Tommy. 'Come.'

Tehari began down the path. Jack followed when Maya tightened her grip on his arm and pulled.

'What's the matter, M^2?'

Except for their echoes, it was quiet and empty and sounded hollow. 'So silent,' Maya whispered. 'Are we the only ones here?'

'Today we are, little one.' Maya was surprised that Tehari had heard her, but he continued, obliviously. 'Normally it's bustling, but today the families have instructions to keep to their quarters until the four Elders and the warriors return from the Gate.'

'The Gate?' She and Jack exchanged a brief look.

'Yes, where you're heading. Their absence is why these young ones were lucky to help me. Come now.' Tehari continued into the gaping mouth.

Staring at the thigh-high fangs, Maya and Jack slowly ventured inside and found Tehari at a junction where the tunnel split three ways.

Maya and Jack stared into each one in turn: left, right and straight ahead. The three boys filed past them and headed into the shaft on their left. Watching them disappear, Maya felt uneasy; she didn't think it was right to let them leave without showing her gratitude, so she called out. Her thin voice echoed in the silent tunnel and her thanks put everyone at ease. The boys turned, smiled and bowed respectfully before disappearing into the tunnel, laughing amongst themselves.

'Are we under the Museum of Myths and Mysticism?' Jack asked unexpectedly.

'I was going to ask that,' said Maya. 'We flew past that church tower on the way.'

'Why do you think we're under the museum?' Tehari asked Jack.

'I noticed that symbol… on a museum guard.'

'Yes, we are under the museum. Well deduced, both of you.' Tehari waved Qidan closer. 'Please remind everyone to be more discreet,' he told her.

Pleased with himself, Jack grinned. 'What is this place, really, apart from your home, of course? And how has it gone undetected till now?'

'All good questions, but best left for when we have more time. For now, just know that we are deep underneath the museum.' Tehari turned to Qidan and gave her instructions in another tongue before explaining that they were to proceed down to the harbour with Qidan and wait there while he and Tommy took a detour to complete an important task. With that, he jerked his head at Tommy, swung around and began down the tunnel to their right.

Alarmed by the sudden separation, Maya and Jack both turned to Tommy.

'Where are you going?' asked Maya.

'I need to do something.' Tommy's tone was stern and motherly. 'I'll join you soon. Now go with Qidan, have a bite to eat, rest and be ready to leave.'

Maya's eyes misted up and she wanted to ask more, but didn't. Jack gave her shoulder a squeeze that made her feel stronger, and she smiled and nodded, allowing Tommy to fly away after Tehari.

'The harbour's this way,' Qidan said, walking down the tunnel directly ahead of the one they'd emerged from. Maya imagined the tunnel would be dark, damp and smelly, like a mine shaft, and was pleasantly surprised to find it dry and warm, with a finely ridged floor, and lit by an orange-yellow glow from strange crystals.

Qidan was friendly and gave them constant guidance. Having another girl with them was nice and in no time they all were talking and laughing. Jack asked many questions, which Qidan happily answered in between pointing out the turns and steps ahead as the passageway wound down into the earth. She explained that the ridges on the floor helped the snakes move better and that the glowing crystals were actually diamonds with lava flow behind them. Jack found this the hardest to believe and kept on admiring each radiant diamond as they walked by. Qidan also revealed that she and the three boys had only recently earned their tattoos; it was a rite of passage to becoming warriors, which also explained her earlier hasty actions. Maya was happy to listen, and only after Jack's lengthy questioning did she muster the courage to ask about the letter.

'Qidan, the message you sent me said it'd be safe at home, in my magikdom. But my parents disappeared from there. Did the magik club get it wrong?'

This time Qidan did not have an answer. 'Only Shikshi Virath can answer that for you,' she said, before explaining how she had been chosen to deliver the note and that she was pleased to have been of help, despite breaking some rules.

'Will you be in trouble?' Maya asked, struggling to keep up. She was growing tired and thirsty in the heat. The tunnel had narrowed and was descending steeply. Maya wanted to collapse onto the floor for some respite but, encouraged by the Jack, she had kept moving. He was much fitter than her and she admired his ability to keep going.

'We're nearly there,' Qidan announced, ignoring Maya's question.

A few steps later they heard gushing water. Maya couldn't quite believe her ears and continued with a spring in her steps. The last few bends were the steepest and tightest, but Maya was petit enough to manoeuvre easily, with a little help from Qidan. Jack, being larger, struggled to scrape through.

The tunnel ended abruptly as the ribbed floor turned into pebbles and the low ceiling opened up into another underground cavity. Before them lay a milky turquoise body of water. Captivated, Maya stood beside Jack on the pebbled beach, simply taking it all in. Water poured into the sleepy pastel pool from a small chute in the ceiling. A trail of mist slowly rose from an opening at the other end of the cave as if it were the mouth of a sleeping volcano. A serpentine vessel was moored at a pinewood pier. Maya turned in all directions, absorbing the spectacular sights.

Suddenly Tommy floated up from the vessel.

Delighted, Maya called out and ran to her across the pebbles and up the wooden walkway.

'How do I look?' Tommy asked. She wore a delicate pink cloak and held a small staff with a white chalky stone caged at the top. She twirled and the cloak floated lazily in the air, giving her a mystical look. 'Well?'

'Out of this world!' Maya blurted, sticking a hand out for her to land on. 'Truly Kon … Konjiu-rian.' They giggled as Tommy hovered down onto her hand and Jack walked up with Qidan. 'Look!' Maya presented Tommy.

'Perfect!' said Qidan.

'Wow, is this your normal outfit? I mean, the stuff you wear?' Jack asked.

Tommy nodded.

Jack smiled and turned his attention to the pier. 'Just look at this place. Who would have thought? Is this our ride?'

Tehari was lighting a torch at the bow of the craft. 'Yes. It'll take you up the secret river, where you'll be safe,' he explained. 'Young Jack, let me show you how to operate this vessel.'

The beige wooden boat looked simple and sturdy but sat dangerously low in the water. A single large sail and snake-head canopy at the back gave it the look of a serpent.

Jack removed his bag and stepped on board. While Tehari showed him how to operate the boat, Maya again turned her attention to the cave. Qidan stood at the end of the walkway staring at the opening where mist floated in.

'Rdita!' Tehari called.

'What's he saying?' Maya asked.

'That's the name they know me by,' Tommy responded and flew over to the boat.

Alone, Maya joined Qidan, admiring the stillness of the blue lake, the small waterfall to her left and the mysterious misty tunnel ahead. 'Incredible,' she said, staring at the opening at the far end. 'What's there?'

'Every Fang's dream … It's an ancient underground river called Kontra, and it leads to the Gate. I thought today I'd be allowed to go but …'

'Dream?'

'Yes, to travel to the Gate and learn the ancient ways from the shikshis.'

'Wow!' Maya stared at opening. 'It looks scary.'

'It can be. It's a river of steam flowing uphill, hence its name.'

'Isn't the steam dangerous?'

'Yes, but you'll be safe as long you're in the boat.'

'Doesn't it get hot?'

'Only warm; the boat's made of special wood—' Qidan explained, when Tehari called to Maya; it was time to leave.

Maya gave Qidan a warm embrace and bid her an emotional farewell. She boarded the vessel with teary eyes. By the time she had found a place for her rucksack, Tehari had untethered the boat from the pier and pushed them out. Smiling, she thanked him as the boat moved out. They were on their way, moving towards the misty gap at the end of pool and the river of steam that would take them to the Gate.

'Remember your promise, Rdita,' Tehari reminded Tommy. 'Avoid the lagoon; get off before the bend. Safe sailing!' Jack and Maya waved until a current took control of the boat. Jack busied himself with the oars, while still waving to Qidan.

'What promise?' Maya asked.

'Yeah, what pool and bend?' Jack added, manoeuvring the oars.

'First things first,' said Tommy in her motherly voice. 'Let's get going and join the river flow.'

Neither twin argued as the boat wobbled, picking up speed.

8

ENCHANTED POOL

Nothing is accidental.

Floating on the Kontra was amazing. There was a lot of oohing and ahing as the hot vapour carried them upstream. Maya and Jack couldn't quite understand how the steam rolled along the ground like water without rising up. Jack had asked but Tommy admitted she didn't know.

'All thermal rivers are like this,' she said. 'They flow along the ground to the base of the mountains.'

Light from the boat's torch reflected off glass-like rocks dotted around the river, illuminating the almost alien settings they were silently drifting past. At first the children found it unreal and unnatural. Jack in particular couldn't understand how such structures remained undiscovered. Stunned, he stood at the back while Maya sat in the middle, smiling and enjoying the passing scenes.

The deep gorges with their steep rock faces and barren cliffs occasionally opened into small bays with abandoned buildings, and they also steered through a field of rocks that rose from the moving mist like anthills. The oars weren't needed so Jack secured them and sat quietly, making small adjustments with his tiller as the ghostly current pulled them up.

Seated on the warm deck, Maya watched Jack with proud admiration. Joining the faster flowing river of vapour had been a challenge; he'd had to ease the boat through the opening where the lagoon bubbled and turned into steam, and he'd managed.

A gentle breeze picked up, offering a welcome change in the warm canal. It brought Maya back from her thoughts to Tommy in her lap.

'Will this get any hotter?' she asked, pointing at the deck. Tommy shook her head.

They were moving along gently, at just the right speed, with an occasional sway. As the journey became easier, Jack began recording the passing scenes on his phone and posing questions as if he were a scientist collecting evidence. 'When was this created?' he asked, pointing his phone at a passing settlement that boasted a wreck – a strange vessel that looked like a chariot. 'Who stayed here? Where did they go?'

'No one's ever asked me before,' Tommy admitted. 'They were probably created by the first Konjiurians who came to Siantia, to protect and hide powerful mythical objects.'

'Like that staff that's coming here,' Maya added.

'Yes, and many more items such as books and weapons, many of which are held at the Fang castle.'

'Do you have anything besides your sceptre?' Maya asked.

Tommy patted her shell.

'Really? I don't believe you.' Maya found it impossible that she could carry anything in her shell.

'No, really; in this humanoid form you'd be surprised how much space there is.'

Jack turned his phone in her direction with a hopeful look, but Tommy wouldn't indulge him. Instead she pointed at the rudder. 'Tie that down and come over here. You don't need to steer until we arrive. The current will carry us. Come, eat and rest. I'll tell you when it's time.'

Soon they were seated on the deck, enjoying snacks and watching the eerie landscape float by. Maya was happy with crisps, Jack with a runny bar of chocolate and Tommy nibbled on a wilted cabbage leaf.

Maya reminded Tommy of the promise she'd made to Tehari. 'You said you'd tell us about it later. What was it?'

'Yes, about some pool?' Jack added, licking the melted chocolate bar.

Tommy sighed. 'The pool is a forbidden place – only the monks are allowed there—'

'What's there?' Maya cut in, excited.

'No one knows.'

'You must know,' she said, getting closer.

'Sorry, Maya, I only know that we mustn't go there.'

Disappointed, Maya sat back. 'And the promise?'

'The promise is to return to meet the council for breaking the rules by revealing their presence.'

'But we won't tell anyone,' Maya insisted.

'I know you won't. Now rest,' Tommy insisted.

Unwilling to sleep, Maya and Jack debated ways to defend Tommy before the council, and only after some time did Maya lie down on the wooden deck. It was warm and peaceful and the easy sway of the boat was soothing. Her mind calmed as she began to follow the strange formations above, while Jack continued with his questions.

'Did the Fangs come from the same place as you? From Konjiur?'

'No they're from another realm, but their alliance is to Konjiur. Rest now.' Tommy said again.

'Just one more question. This gate, how does it allow travel from other realms?'

'Mmm, that's a difficult one, Jack. Some things have to be seen to be understood, but I guess it works by controlling *where* a portal to other realms can be opened in Siantia. And portals can only be opened behind the Gate.' Tommy paused. 'You look doubtful, but you will see it soon enough. Rest now.'

Maya couldn't resist lazily teasing her brother. 'You can't deny magical things any more, Jack, but you're still trying to figure out the science of magic.'

'Spot on, M^2. The magic of science is easy, so I'm trying to understand the science of magic ...'

Those were the last words Maya heard Jack say before she succumbed to sleep.

****

Maya awoke just in time to catch the scream building in her throat. Relieved, she pretended to be asleep for a bit longer, enjoying the warm deck and the soft swing of the boat. She had relived the dream and could still hear all the voices, including the one that sounded like her own.

'... jumped to another world with the staff! ... hunt it down ... He told the monkey to go to Siantia ...'

Thump.

Thump, thump.

What was that noise?

Thump.

Maya opened her eyes to a kaleidoscope of sparkling lights. *We're lost!* She sat up instantly. They were in a gorge, and the boat had come to a stop in clear water at the edge of a small underground beach. All around it were glowing oblong rocks half-submerged between larger boulders. The glowing rocks were all the same size.

'Wow ...' Maya knelt on the deck and tied up her brown curls. Each stone radiated a different warm colour that sparkled off the gentle water, creating a magical display. Captivated by the glittering treasures, Maya thought they had sailed into an enchanted bay and hoped it was the place that led to Virath and the Gate.

Thump!

The knock brought her back to their boat: it was bumping against a boulder, Tommy was asleep beside her and Jack was dozing by the tiller at the back.

Thump!

Maya looked at the inlet they had come through, and beyond it she saw Kontra's steam current. 'There you are …' She inhaled the warm air with its hint of smokiness as she tried to see where it turned into water.

Tommy suddenly hovered up into the air like a possessed bee. Startled, Maya nearly fell, but Tommy continued her crazy dance, spinning around and around. It looked funny and alarming at the same time; Maya felt butterflies in her stomach and couldn't decide whether to laugh or not. For a few seconds, she oscillated between tight lips and giggling before biting her lips with concern. She hadn't seen Tommy so spooked; her eyes were feverish and she whizzed around, searching for something.

'What is it, Tommy?' Maya whispered.

'Shh.' Tommy shot her a sharp glance and dashed off towards the beach. She flew erratically, stopping and starting like a squirrel on a mission.

'Ja-ack …' Maya shook Jack gently while trying to see what had unsettled Tommy. The shoreline was small and pebbled, with larger boulders here and there, some of which rose to meet a steep cliff behind the beach. She followed the cliff face: it rose straight up, facing an opposing rock wall behind them, like two giants having a stand-off.

'What's the matter? Are we there?' Jack asked, sitting up.

'Shh!' Tommy returned in a rush.

'What's up?'

'Shh!' she said again. 'This isn't the Gate. We've arrived at the forbidden pool. Come on, come on, quickly now. We need to go before we are discovered. Quietly help Maya and follow me. Don't step in the water; it will be hot. And don't touch the stones! The glowing ones!'

'Hot?' Maya looked at the water.

Jack turned towards the inlet behind them. 'Can't we just head back?' he asked.

'No, the flow's too fast. Besides, it'll create disturbance and noise!'

Jack stood looking at the moving steam for a second longer before nodding and collecting their backpacks.

'Careful, don't slip, and be quiet,' Tommy said, hovering over the water.

'Why?' Jack asked, hopping from one rock to another before helping Maya. Luckily she hadn't frozen with fear and found the hopping doable. The rocks were warm, dry and safe to grip, making the task easier. Tommy flew back and forth, and with her encouragement and guidance, it didn't take them long to get to the shore and their next hurdle: crossing the pebbles silently.

It took Jack only half a step to realise that it was nearly impossible without making a clatter. They were stuck. Tommy landed on Maya's shoulder and called a small meeting to discuss their options. Together they settled on the only option: to hop across more rocks and scale two boulders to reach the rock face at the back.

'Why do we need to be quiet?' Maya asked.

Tommy hesitated. 'Believe me, with such large gems' she pointed at the glowing rocks 'there must be a guardian close by.'

'What kind of a guardian?' asked Jack.

Tommy shrugged, studying the lagoon. 'Something strong enough to protect such gems. Probably something that lives in water.'

The children didn't need any more explanation.

'Come on, M^2, Jack hopped over to the nearest rock.

Working together, they reached the first boulder. A longer jump was required for the next. Landing on large stone, Jack steadied himself and whispered.

'Come on. Big jump; I'll catch you.'

Tommy hovered close by. With a deep breath, Maya leapt and just made it. She teetered on the edge of the stone when Jack grabbed her arm. Relieved, she searched for a better foothold … and slipped onto the gravel.

Loose pebbles rolled down the steep bank towards the waterline. In a second, the silence had been completely shattered.

Maya clenched her teeth and shut her eyes tight with disgust. 'Sorry,' she murmured.

'Just run!' Tommy cried. 'Get to the cliff face. Run!'

A second later, a thunderous grumble sounded out, and the ground between them and the cliff began to rise.

Jack and Maya hadn't moved. 'RUN!' Tommy shouted.

Maya felt the tremor underneath her feet. A dull growl mixed with crashing and popping sounds filled the underground canyon as loose rocks bounced and tumbled towards them. It wasn't an earthquake but a rockslide. Small stones and rocks rolled down towards Maya and Jack, gathering momentum, turning round and round like a giant washing machine churning wildly out of control. It looked like the whole incline was collapsing.

Jack was first to move. Shielding Maya, he herded her towards a rock at the water's edge. It wasn't easy. Their feet slid and shifted and sunk as pebbles gave way. They reached the water cowering. It was hot but bearable; they waded in. Rushing, Maya lost her footing and stumbled, but caught herself in time by doing the one thing she shouldn't have, holding onto a nearby glowing gem. Instantly, a spark flashed through the stone and travelled around it like an ember working through cotton wool until it was spent. Alarmed, she looked to Jack, and then they both snapped around to see if Tommy had noticed.

Behind them, the air was hazy with dust and smoke, and they couldn't spot Tommy. A whole section of the steep bank had risen, and when the rockslide ceased near the shoreline and as last of the pebbles came to a halt, the twins saw something neither had expected.

'Is that a dinosaur?'

'It's a dragon, Jack!' Maya cried with more curiosity than fear.

'Of course, it is.' Jack rolled his eyes.

'Of course; what else protects such gems?' Tommy dropped onto Maya's shoulder as they watched the massive creature flex and uncoil before them. It was much larger than Tehari and its scales were the colour of earth and rust.

All the books Maya had read described dragons as heavily built beasts, with lengthy necks and wings that ran from their shoulders towards their tails, but this one was longer and thinner than she'd expected. It had leaf-shaped scales that moved in unison, like dominoes, and the rows of tendrils that ran down from its shoulders to the tip of its tail stood on their ends. When its small head snaked forward to them, it smiled and revealed multiple rows of teeth.

'Emerald-flecked,' said Maya, looking at its unblinking eyes and the three leathery frills underneath is jaw.

'Woah!' Jack pointed at its tail, poised like a scorpion's.

'A silver belly,' Tommy added. 'Great, that means she's an ancient one.'

Muscles shifted underneath the dragon's scaly armour as it moved in for a confrontation. Maya surprised herself by stepping forward to take a closer look. Perhaps all the books she'd read had made her braver. 'Matriarch ... it is a matriarch, isn't it?'

Tommy flew up. 'We mean no disrespect or harm, n-nor did we intend to trespass here.'

'Grr-mmm.' The dragon let out a deep sound that vibrated through them as wisps of smoke rose in twirls from its nose, like a volcano awakening.

Tommy floated closer. 'Matriarch, c-can I e-explain—'

She was almost within its striking distance when the dragon spoke. It wasn't a roar but an elegantly delicate, feminine voice that did not incite fear.

'Mistakes committed unintentionally still have consequences and are punishable.'

'Please allow me to—'

'And what is this stink of Siantia? Do you mean to desecrate this nest with that foul smell? Do harm to this brood?' The dragon's voice was calm and relaxed, but her words were serious.

Tommy hovered closer with her staff in hand and her cape fluttering behind her. She was minute but spoke out loudly.

'If you must punish someone, then it should be me. It's entirely my fault, not my wards'. They don't mean any harm; it's a genuine mistake.'

The dragon looked at them all for a long time, fumes rising from her nostrils. The silence was awkward. The dust had begun to settle and they could see the dragon better. No one moved, except Tommy, who bobbed up and down.

'That cape,' it began with growing billows of smoke. 'I recall your kind from a long time ago. You're one of the Maandadi: healers and minders to royals. Not many survived; you must be one of the last few.'

Tommy nodded. 'I am the last of the royal minders!'

'That must make these two, a prince and a princess.

Tommy didn't respond; she simply hovered. Maya narrowed her eyes, wondering why Tommy hadn't corrected the beast. Jack inched closer, gave Maya's arm a gentle squeeze and whispered, 'Princess Maya.' She smiled as royally as she could.

'Well, this is a rare surprise: royalty!' the dragon said with a smile. Her voice was different: meeker and smoother though still loud. 'I am afraid I don't have anywhere to entertain, but let's not spoil the moment. There will be time for formalities later. Tell me, where do you hail from? What brings you here and why?'

Tommy collapsed on a nearby rock. Jack and Maya exchanged a worried glance but before they could respond the dragon continued.

'Call me Loivissa! Now come forward, young ones; don't be afraid. Let me have a look at you. My sight isn't the same.'

Confused by the dragon's sudden change of attitude, they stepped forward at the same time. Astonished at Maya's bravery, Jack whispered. 'That's great going!' Maya nodded with excitement.

Tommy recovered and flew over to make the introductions. 'I am Tommy and, er, this here is Maya and that's Jack.'

'You mean Princess Maya and Prince Jack.'

'Yes, but here in Siantia it's necessary to drop the titles, you realise, of course.' She paused and then added, 'We humbly apologise if the stink of Siantia offends you. It's the smell of those Siantian contraptions we were forced to use.'

Instinctively, Jack reached for his phone; the movement didn't go unnoticed. Loivissa twitched and snaked forward towards his hand as he produced the device.

'Please …' Tommy jumped in. 'This device has proved useful for us to blend in, really. We are not trying to desecrate your dwelling.'

'I should hope not.' Losing interest, Loivissa turned away towards the crystalline rocks. 'Now let me see, they all look fine; all my dears are glowing. Good! All the eggs are fine.'

Smiling nervously, Maya looked at the glowing one she'd touched, relieved that it hadn't cracked. Eager to move away, she slowly crept out of the water as Tommy began to explain.

'We wouldn't wish that Siantian stink on anyone, least of all here. As to what brings us here: we seek an audience with the Great Shikshi, but I am afraid I cannot divulge why.' She paused for a second and then added, with a deep breath, 'Not because we don't want to, but because it is a royal matter. I hope you understand.'

Maya and Jack shared a bewildered glance. Why did Tommy continue lying?

Ignoring Tommy, Loivissa began to study Maya. With the dragon's large eyes fixed on her, Maya felt alive and excited. She could see Tommy hovering and feel Jack inching closer.

'You're so small and delicate and innocent ... Silly me; forgive me, your highnesses.' Puzzled, the children looked at each other and then at Tommy. 'On this first memorable meeting, I do not have much to give but here is something small for each of you. I hope you will accept my gifts.'

Loivissa, took a deep breath, plucked a shiny silver scale from her underbelly and offered it to Jack with both hands.

'For you, prince. It will protect you against most weapons and konjuring. Use it wisely; make a shield or a piece of armour, perhaps.'

Jack turned to Tommy for guidance and only accepted the gift at her nod. He examined the scale; it was nearly as large as his backpack.

Loivissa raised her hind leg, looking for something. The muscular limb ended in four curved claws and filled Maya's vision for a few moments, after which Loivissa produced a fragment of glowing rock. She turned and set about snapping and chipping the fragment before curing the piece by finally doing what they'd wanted to see, breathing hot flame. She worked fast, then reached over and dipped her hand into the warm water. The white-hot fragment shimmered, the heat dissipated and from within the rising steam she produced a kite-shaped armlet.

'A little glitter for the princess. See if it fits.'

Maya accepted the glass-like crystalline jewellery with a shy smile. It looked magical, and she couldn't take her eyes off the ornate, still-warm piece.

'It will glow green if danger is close by.'

Maya place her arm through the warm curl. It was big for her, but fitted snugly when worn over her jacket. It sparkled and looked expensive. When she was older, she thought, it would be a perfect fit.

'Children, what do you say when someone gives you something?' Tommy interrupted.

'Thank you,' both chorused.

After that Tommy explained that they needed to be on their way. Maya glanced at Jack, annoyed with Tommy for rushing. She wanted to spend more time with Loivissa; it wasn't every day you met a dragon. But she also knew Tommy was right, and they needed to move on.

Loivissa guided them to the steps they needed to take at the back by the cliff face. 'It's what the monks use. Halfway up is a platform called 'Dragon's Perch'. When you get there, take the narrow steps and not the sloping tunnel. The steps will lead you to the Gate.'

'Where does the slope go?'

'That's the tunnel for us. It leads to a secret exit by the edge of the woods where outcasts, runaways and exiles have taken refuge. You don't want to be going that way with these young ones, for not everyone you encounter will be friendly.'

And with that Tommy started the normal formalities. Maya had seen her parents do the same at many birthday parties: thanking people, laughing, joking and waving goodbye while herding them onward. Tommy looked happy to be on their way until Loivissa stretched her neck past Jack and stared at his phone with unblinking jade eyes.

'JACK!' Tommy said in a stern whisper, but it was too late.

'What does this Siantian abomination do?' Loivissa asked.

After a momentary pause, Jack shyly showed her photos of Tehari, then took a few snaps of Maya and Tommy to prove how harmless it was. Tommy was unhappy and eager to leave, but with Loivissa's growing interest they couldn't go anywhere. Jack took a couple of photos of her, then asked if she wanted to be videoed.

'No, no. Absolutely not,' Tommy said, but it was futile.

A full five minutes later, they were deaf and hot and smoky. Jack had captured Loivissa in full form, breathing fire with a war cry. Another five minutes and several replays later, they left with ringing ears. Waving goodbye to a delighted Loivissa, they began to climb the steps. Maya hoped nothing would happen, but she knew from Tommy's look that they were about to have their first telling off.

PM Perry

9

WOODS

Look before you ...

'Look – light ahead!' said Jack.

His words signalled the end of their arduous climb and the intense darkness. Perched on Maya's shoulder, Tommy had guided them with her glowing staff and the children had persevered. They'd walked, staggered, stopped and walked some more, but for how long none of them knew, because the soot-filled tunnel consumed everything: light, time, warmth, sound and even the disagreement Maya had expected.

She knew from Tommy's look that she wanted to address the time-wasting, especially with Siantian shenanigans like photographs and evidence, but she never got the chance, because they'd been beset by another turn of events.

Huddling together in the dim light from Tommy's staff, they had arrived at Dragon's Perch, where they were to take the narrower steps to the Gate, only to find that the tunnel had collapsed. It was a huge disappointment. Standing in the dark on the crumbling perch, Tommy hesitantly decided upon the option Loivissa had warned against: taking the larger tunnel leading up to the woods. Though slippery and smoky, the soot-stricken tunnel was bearable and they had pushed on in silence.

Now, with the end in sight, their pace quickened and they arrived at the mouth of a big cave, facing the freshness of a misty grey morning. Maya and Jack were ready to collapse but chose to hold on a little longer when Tommy observed that something was amiss.

'I can't feel the air cold and clean against my face,' she said.

Awash with light, Maya and Jack looked each other, all soiled with grime.

Jack laughed. 'Mum won't approve.'

Remembering home, Maya beamed. 'Hmm, I can just see it. Dad standing in the front room having tea …' She paused for a second, pointed outside and added, 'It's exactly like that.'

'Like what, M^2?'

'Being indoors! Don't you see? It's cold out there but not in here.'

'Why, of course, why didn't I remember it before?' cried Tommy, hovering off Maya's shoulder. 'Don't move. It must be somewhere here,' she said, with some concern, landing on the floor.

'What?'

'The Veil!'

'The what?' Jack asked.

'The Veil of Siantia. It's what separates this realm from all the others.' Tommy carefully prodded the empty space with her staff.

'What are you doing?' Jack asked.

'Why?' Maya asked at the same time.

'Why what? Separate? Because that's what was decided a long, long time ago.'

'Decided? Why?'

'Well, those who dwelt here at the time began to abandon the art of konjuring in favour of something new – a 'Siantian' way of thinking. They were seen as rebels, and they and their new art have been despised ever since. The Veil was needed to prevent the spread of this new art. Also, the outcasts here have grown weak over time and forgotten their konjuring skills, and now the Veil serves to protect them too.'

The children stood absorbing the information for some time. It explained a lot about their world and raised many more questions. Was this the reason why there were magical myths in the world? Perhaps this could also explain why mysterious things occurred to them on their birthdays? It certainly justified their debates about science and magic.

After some time, Jack bent down and rummaged about on the cave floor. 'What does it look like, this Veil?'

'It's near invisible, like glass,' Tommy explained without glancing back as she continued to poke around.

'Aha, this will do,' Jack said, sizing a small rounded stone in his palm.

'What are you doing?' asked Maya.

'Just checking its shape, M^2, making sure it'll go the distance.' He studied the clear space before them and then gently rolled the stone across the floor. As they watched it go, something happened.

'Did you see that?' Maya cried, astonished. 'It was just like when we pause a video for a second. It stopped before carrying on, as if something held the stone for a moment.'

'Well done, Siantian,' said Tommy, delightfully.

Only a meter away, at the point where the stone had paused, they'd seen the world outside wobble. All the trees, the bushes and the mist: everything vibrated a little. Slowly and carefully, they approached that point and discovered a clear, thin membrane stretched over the mouth of the tunnel. Barely visible, it separated them from the woods outside.

'A force field of some sort?' said Jack. 'Can I touch it?'

'Force what? No, that's the Veil."

'Yes, it's like a force field.'

'You can touch it from this side, but first you should know some important things. Out there is the middle ground—'

'You mean that's not Earth?'

'No, no. It is, it's still Siantia – Earth – but it's also where Konjiurians and others roam freely.'

Tommy was animated, pointing with her staff, and pacing and talking.

'Out there we can meet anyone from any realm, and each one will have different abilities and powers.'

'What, even more powers than Loivissa?' asked Maya, looking doubtfully at their little guardian.

'Some, yes! And that is why it is important that I alone speak to anyone we meet and you do exactly what I ask.'

'You make it sound like we aren't liked,' Jack interrupted. Silence befell them for a second.

'Well, Siantians aren't normally welcomed with open arms.'

Everyone was quiet for few more seconds. Maya and Jack looked at each other, the soot on their faces masking their worries.

'And is it big, the woods? Are there many beings here?' asked Maya.

Tommy floated up high. 'Oh, yes, it's vast. How many? Many! Who? Don't know. And that is why the Veil goes all around and stops them all from entering Siantia. What's more is that a massive wall was also erected to prevent Siantians from entering the middle ground.'

'A wall?' Maya and Jack looked at her with narrowed eyes. 'Why? Why don't they like us?' Maya asked.

Tommy frowned. 'Perhaps some feel threatened. Others consider themselves superior. Then there are those who think it's blasphemous to deny the existence of konjuring. I don't know, but after being with both of you I firmly believe that there are many things that non-Siantians can learn from here.'

The children smiled at Tommy, reassured by her belief in them.

'Now who wants to be the first? There is no coming back once you step through.'

'What does it feel like?' Maya asked.

Tommy landed on her shoulder. 'Nothing. No, not quite. Think of when you touch a bubble and it bursts.' Maya and Jack nodded. 'It's just like that, except without the busting part.' Tommy chuckled.

'Fine,' said Jack. 'In that case can I be first? Then Maya and you last, if it's OK.'

'No, can we go all together?' pleaded Maya.

And with that they all stepped through together.

****

'Wake up! Run!'

David sat up abruptly and looked around, Achanak's voice echoing in his ears. He was back in his room, his five-star chamber in the royal quarters. Light came from two sources: the fire-genie, floating up and down above the side cabinet, and the crackling fireplace. How had he gotten here? The last image he had was of the smoky apparition closing in and large deadly beasts circling above. What were they called?

'How did it end?' he asked, his voice croaky. 'Oh, I'm sorry,' he added, when he saw that Achanak had been resting.

The fire genie ignited, brightening instantly, like a car coming to life. 'No need to apologise; we genies don't sleep anyway.'

David was going to say something, but Achanak loved to talk and carried on without pausing until David had to interrupt him to ask about the battle. He got a detailed account. Their distraction was instrumental, a turning point in the fight. The monk was rescued and the strange blue light everyone called 'the gateway' had collapsed.

'But flaming fumes, that smoking one remains,' said Achanak. 'The one you called a wraith,'

'How?'

'They called it the warlord; he's the reason why no one's to venture out into the woods.'

David remained on the bed thinking. He was relieved that their timely interruption had helped, that Virath had been saved, but wondered why he was not at ease. The feeling was like a phantom itch; it niggled, yet there was no exact spot to scratch. He got out of bed and paced, hoping it would jog his memory, but the rising cold was a distraction. He rubbed his arms and threw a couple of logs into the fire, then nibbled on an apple from the table by the window. He hoped it was just cold or hunger that caused his restlessness, but neither the fire nor the apple helped; the feeling was at the core of him and it persisted. In the background, Achanak continued speaking, saying how Laksha had been pleased with their help but annoyed with them for being so reckless.

'Ha! Some things don't change,' David muttered to himself. 'Everyone else still knows what I should and shouldn't do.'

It was then that he realised what he had to do: calm down and let the answer come to him. He cleared his mind by staring outside at the pale morning. The storm had abated, but the ghostly woods were shrouded in a dull grey mist beneath swollen clouds. All existence of the snow-capped mountains, the serene lake and the lush green fields had been replaced by the grey. It looked cold. The only visible object was the solitary monastery suspended in nothingness, a lost ship anchored in a bewitching bay.

David shivered and a moment later the answer presented itself. He searched his pockets and smiled. Slowly and carefully, as though handling a butterfly, he extracted his diary and laid it on the desk.

He stared at it for some time, unsure of what it might say or if it would say anything at all. With a deep breath, he reached over, but hesitated at the last second and turned towards Achanak, tight-lipped.

'What's the matter?' Achanak asked.

'I don't know! It's hard to explain … There's this feeling I have. It's troubling me, but I can't put my finger on it. Do you know what I mean?'

Achanak shook from side to side.

'Last night the diary told us to help. I think it's time to ask it again.'

'Well, what are we waiting for?'

'I'm not sure if it will answer.' David placed his hand on the book. 'And what if it's something we can't do?'

'Hmm, like last night.'

David gave him a mischievous look and opened the book in one swift movement. Achanak floated closer, throwing light onto the page, which simply read, 'Woods'.

Achanak spoke first. 'No flaming way! Laksha won't be pleased. Fuming decisions, this is not a "can't do" but a "mustn't do" situation. Only the hunting party is allowed.'

David was already gazing outside at the uninviting dark woods. The grey mist shifted continuously, silently revealing one thing and consuming another, like an illusionist performing tricks.

'Looks fine. Spooky but fine,' he said.

Achanak joined him. Spellbound, they watched as something emerged at the edge of the trees. Its movement was erratic, stopping and starting but drawing closer to the monastery. Both watched, hypnotised, until a dark void in the woods disturbed them and the wraith floated out.

'Look! It's after whatever moves in the mist,' David whispered.

The black mist of the wraith rose over the grey, silently searching, then stopped moving, poised to attack.

'Stay still. It's right over you,' whispered David to whatever the wraith was hunting. He peered closer, placing his hand against the cold window. 'I think the book means for us to help.'

'Laksha said no one!' Achanak floated up beside his face.

'Remember last night: did we listen then?'

The wraith dived into the grey murkiness below. Dejected, David looked away.

'Look!' said Achanak.

A dark shape rushed out from the woods and headed for the same spot at great speed. Captivated, they watched, pressed up against the glass. A vortex formed: a mixture of grey and black swirls in the mist, and after a short struggle the wraith jumped up, tore itself away and flew into the forest. The shape chased it.

'What happened? What was that?' said David, throwing his grey hood on. He slipped his diary into his back pocket. By then mist had settled and erased all trace of any commotion. 'Come, let's go.' He patted his back pocket twice and opened the window.

A cold wet breeze rushed in. Achanak lost all his brightness and shook sideways – no.

'Fine, then keep a watch. Back soon,' said David, and he stepped out before Achanak could argue.

Outside, he found himself in waist-high mist. It felt strange, like walking out into the sea, for he was unable to see where he was stepping. Minutes later, morning dew began to seep through his trainers, and his lungs went icy with the damp air.

Uncertain, David paused. For the first time in his life he felt like returning to a centre, but he resisted. With shallow breaths, baby steps and outstretched arms he continued, a solitary figure in a grey sea. He looked around and around, occasionally stumbling, halting or backtracking, but trying to move forward all the time. Soon the grey had leached all warmth from his body. His trousers were damp and stuck to his legs, but he was determined to carry on for the phantom itch was no more. This was the right action; he felt it in his bones and walked on, sliding one leg after another. He planned to pass to the left of the monastery, find the lake, and follow the waterline to the haunting woods on the other side where the attack had occurred in the mist.

****

Traversing the Veil had been as expected, and immediately after Maya, Jack and Tommy, all paused at the mouth of the secret dragon's tunnel, for the world outside felt alien. After being underground for so long, the dull light was bright, the air nauseatingly fresh and the cold unbearably sharp. The twins hugged their jackets and were momentarily light-headed as all their senses returned to life.

The woods were quiet and expectant. Dew lined everything; mist slipped silently from tree to tree and the air was heavy with suspense. To their right was a picture-perfect scene: the trees gave way to a clearing filled with mist and floating in the centre was a single, solitary building, an island of refuge. Steps stretched away from it to a snaking wall with a huge gate in the middle.

It wasn't quite what Maya had expected. 'Is that the Gate?'

'Think that's the gate but looks more like a dam,' said Jack, looking at the structure high up on the incline.

'I can see how it might appear like that,' Tommy said, relief painted all over her face.

'And this other building?' asked Jack, referring to the solitary building suspended in the mist.

'Ah, that's the monastery. Normally we'd find Virath there, but this early he'd still be up there in his quarters.'

119

Maya gently picked Tommy up and sat hugging her, happy that they would meet their protector soon.

Jack, however, was preoccupied, staring at something in the mist just beyond the woods. 'What was that?'

A solitary figure in a grey hood rose up, nearly invisible against the grey mist. Only the opening in his hood gave him away.

'Don't move; that's no monk.' Tommy jumped onto Maya's shoulder, her voice cold and stern.

Jack froze and Maya followed. They studied the figure's odd behaviour: taking deliberate steps, then dropping underneath the blanket of fog, standing up again, turning, walking, and disappearing once more.

'What's he doing?' asked Tommy.

****

Out in the misty field, David had found what he was looking for – the site of the attack. The victim was a small armoured monkey. It looked around in pain and then turned abruptly in his direction, its face contorted with fear.

'Who are you?'

'Shh, I'm here to help!' David reassured it, taking its arm.

'Ah, it's you, konjurer! You shouldn't have come; it's not safe! I have led him here …' It paused, and then asked, 'You're the konjurer? Yes?'

David understood what it meant, but there wasn't any time to clarify the matter. He began to lift the primate when it spoke hurriedly.

'No, master – he will return. Quickly, take this.' It extracted an egg-sized crystal from within its breastplate. 'And my walking stick. And leave!'

'But—' David tried to protest.

'Go now! I am at peace now that you have what's yours. Take it!' David gripped the stone. 'And my stick. Find the monk; he'll tell you more.'

David looked around for the stick just as the monkey began to disappear, fading into nothingness.

'Farewell, master ...'

David sat back, shaken by its disappearance. After few long seconds, he stood up and looked around to confirm that he was alone when something curled around his left foot.

****

Inside the cave, Jack watched as the figure stood up with something in its hands. Whatever it was, it sparkled for a second and then he was pulled beneath the mist. No sparkle and no figure. Both were gone in a blink.

'What happened? Did he fall?' Tommy asked in alarm, when the sound of crashing, cracking wood, and thuds and yells rushed past them.

Frightened, Maya turned to Jack and Tommy. The sudden change in the atmosphere reminded her of her dream. She whimpered, but luckily Tommy masked the sound.

'Someone's being dragged.'

'Yes, it's him,' said Jack. 'The one we saw. Come on, we should help.' He darted out from the cover of the cave.

'Waaiit! Jack!' shouted Tommy.

Reactively, Maya grabbed Tommy from her shoulder and dashed after her brother. 'Jaack!'

He stopped and turned upon hearing Maya.

'That isn't our fight,' Tommy insisted, when she and Maya caught up to him. 'Our mission is to find Virath and save your parents.'

Jack didn't respond; he only stood there, staring at something behind them. Tommy and Maya turned to find themselves in middle of the woods. The cave they'd emerged from was gone, and there were only trees and bushes and the mist.

'The tunnel – where's the tunnel?'

Tommy voiced the answer forming in Maya's mind. 'That's why it's called the secret entrance.' Now that they were out in the open, without any cover, she took charge once more.

'Hurry, we should make for the Gate before we meet anyone else. Remember what Loivissa said.'

There were no arguments; Jack led, while Maya followed with Tommy on her shoulder. She was careful to place her steps in his and avoid being caught by any bushes and low branches. They emerged from the woods and into the open field, where the mist quickly rose to Jack's waist and swallowed Maya up to her chest.

'Should we see what that guy in the grey hood was up to?' Jack asked. 'We'll be passing nearby.'

Without warning, the woods became alive with noise. Birds squawked, branches snapped, a deer and a wolf cried out together and hooves beat a hasty retreat. The three looked at each other wide-eyed.

'Only animals,' whispered Jack. 'Let's move.'

Maya nodded. Her lips twitched to ask a question when a chilling, high-pitched shriek that wasn't quite animal or human sounded out.

'The warlord!' she said, remembering her dream. Her eyes darted across the dark canopies, searching all the shadows to see if they moved; nothing did. 'Can't be, can it? The thing from my dream?'

'Quickly, let's not wait for it,' said Tommy.

Jack nodded, taking hurried steps. Maya followed close behind, and soon they were in no man's land at the halfway mark, too far to turn back and not near enough to the monastery.

Breathless and hare-eyed, Maya was soon flustered, burning hot from the effort of keeping up with Jack, with icy cold nose and fingers as the mist licked away the warmth. Luckily, no one had appeared, and with every step she began to feel a little better until Tommy uttered words that filled her with dread.

'On second thought, we should do a quick search; he did disappear somewhere there.'

'Allow me.' Jack gave Maya a brief look before taking a short deviation and disappearing underneath the mist.

She knew it was the right thing to do. The woods had gone unnaturally quiet and Maya could only hear her own breath. Behind her, the mist had covered their trail.

'Found something! I'll be few more seconds, M^2,' Jack called from somewhere within the grey.

Maya wasn't pleased and kept a nervous vigil with Tommy. They turned and peered in different directions like couple of meerkats.

The mist shifted. The smell of smoke rose, and a coarse scraping sound came from within the grey.

'Jack, is that you scraping?'

He came through the mist holding a small, twisted, wet twig.

'What a strange twig,' said Maya.

'What else? What else did you see?' Tommy asked eagerly.

Jack returned a vacant stare, holding the twig close to his chest. 'I found it. It's mine. Get your own,' he snapped.

Tommy and Maya exchanged a shocked glance.

Jack sliced the air, left and right, as though he were wielding a sword. 'It's perfect. I like it.' His voice was flat and mechanical.

'Jack?' Maya questioned.

Grinning, he held the twig out.

'Jack, what's the matter?'

He turned towards the woods.

'Jack!'

He began to retrace his steps.

'JACK!' Maya and Tommy called in unison.

Uncaring, he continued marching towards the woods.

'After him, Maya.'

She was already running. Fear gripped her heart; something was really wrong. Was this how Jack felt when she was in trouble? She didn't like the feeling.

'Jack! Wait up, Jack. That's the wrong way. The Gate's back there!'

'We can't lose him! F-faster, Maya!' Tommy cried, bouncing on her shoulder.

Ahead, Jack was already re-entering the woods.

****

David stirred with a throbbing headache. Wearily, he tried to focus but couldn't. His head hung in pain and all he could see were his feet on a dark stone platform. He stood motionless for some time, trying to recall how he had gotten there, but all he could remember was something curling around his left foot. After that, all he had done was scream every time something hit or scratched him as he was dragged across the forest floor, over the protruding roots, up and down slopes, through bushes, and around rocks and boulders, until a low branch had knocked him out.

Gingerly, he lifted his head. The pain shifted and his eyes felt heavy, but he forced himself to focus.

'Where am I? What is that?' There was a strange wall of mist some distance away. He was tied to a tree by vines that wrapped around him from his feet to his neck. The vines came through the strange stone altar that went around the massive trunk, and the tree's tangled roots snaked out in all directions from the base of the slab. More vines dangled from the canopy. It felt unreal.

As his mind cleared, something else caught his eye – a ring sparkling by his feet. Not far from it lay a bone. He snapped his gaze away from the roots and vines and noticed armour and bones lay scattered around him, with bits of jewellery glittering in their midst. Scared, he began to turn and twist, trying to break free, but the vines came to life and tightened around him. It was hopeless. He was tied to a sacrificial altar.

His eyes rolled as he struggled and he noticed a strange white vapour within the canopy above. Had it just moved? Or was his mind playing tricks on him? He peered harder, when a ghoulish grey face rushed at him, mouth long and eyes big. Helpless, David stared as it flew at him, then through him, and at that precise moment he felt the chill, as if he had downed a glass of icy slush. He'd read enough to know what that drop in temperature meant.

'A ghost!' he panted, and twisted to see where it'd gone, but the tree was too wide and he was tied too tight.

The air had begun to bite. David twitched for a second, then something began to warm his left palm – the crystal! He tightened his grip. Was it the crystal they wanted? *No, I was given it; it's mine.* They'd have to fight him for it. But who were they? He looked around.

A warrior stood some distance directly ahead of him, his purple cape and silver armour almost consumed by the fog. He blinked a few times but the image persisted; it was real. He should have been delighted to finally discover a ghoul, but he wasn't.

'Why do you hold me? What do you want?' he asked, using all the skills he'd gained from years of talking to the authorities.

The warrior approached him without responding, picking his way through tangled roots with surprising nimbleness. David noticed he left a trail of vapour behind him, and the other faces that had begun to appear within the mist. The air became icier, and by the time the warrior was on the stone platform, it was freezing. David shuddered and clenched his teeth to arrest the trembling but only managed to rattle and clatter them. Embarrassed, he stole a quick glance at the warrior before him. He was princely and had been handsome at some point. Now, long hair draped over his face, masking his sharp, weathered features and battle scars.

David didn't lower his gaze, but he didn't look directly at the towering soldier either. He drew courage from the warmth of the crystal he held, but then the warrior arched back and let out a hoarse war cry, full of hatred and sadness. David tried to be brave, but with little effect; he was scared like never before.

Then in one flash, the warrior drew his sword and stabbed it into a crack in the platform. It took everything David had to stay calm. He took deep, slow breaths and swallowed the scream creeping up his throat. Long seconds passed, and then the wall of mist around the tree began to move, whirling anticlockwise, like a tornado, and he was in the unnatural storm's eye.

****

Jack moved mechanically. Holding the twig before him like a robot on a mission, he ventured deeper into the dense, misty woods. Tommy and Maya tried calling, reasoning and tugging but Jack didn't respond.

'Is he sleepwalking?' asked Maya.

'No, this is something more. He's possessed … by that stick.'

Maya renewed her efforts, but Jack trooped on, oblivious, turning and twisting around bushes, trees and rocks. He ignored the pricking thorns and protruding roots while Maya struggled to keep up.

And then, unexpectedly, he stopped.

Tommy caught up with him. 'What's here? Is this what you wanted to show us?'

He didn't respond but he didn't need to. Tommy and Maya followed his gaze and were dumbfounded by what they saw. A half-dried body of a hare sat on the forest floor, staring calmly as if it had just quietly shrivelled away.

'How's that possible? What happened to it?' said Maya. Her mouth had gone dry.

'We should go!' warned Tommy.

'W-what happened to it? What would do that?'

'Only one thing does that: a wraith.'

'The warlord?' Maya recalled what she'd read. '- sucks the life force, right?'

'A parasite of the worst kind ...' Tommy was still speaking when Jack began to walk away, and they had to again hurry after him.

Deep in the woods, they passed more mummified animals: a mob of deer, a lonely squirrel and a couple of pigeons all stood frozen like weird art against a white canvas. Further on, predators began to appear: a pack of wolves, a large bear. Finally, they sighted their first mystical animal – a unicorn.

Maya turned to Tommy, dismayed.

'I know, I know, this isn't good. We need to snap him out and head bac—'

The twig began to glow. It came to life, jerking and tugging, threatening to break free from Jack's grip, but he held on firmly. The pull grew stronger and began to tow him forward. Maya gripped his jacket just as he broke into a jog.

'Don't let go, Maya!' Tommy jumped up and flew alongside her.

Maya ran and hopped as Jack pulled her onward. She looked for more mystical creatures but there were none; all she saw were weapons, armour and bones. Then Maya noticed a dull glow on her arm; it was her armlet.

'What does this mean?' she asked breathlessly, but Tommy didn't respond.

Jack stopped again. 'What is it?' Maya asked, trying to catch her breath.

Ahead of them, a thick opaque cloud revolved like a haunted merry-go-round.

'I think we're here. Look, the stick's going wild!'

The twig glowed and hauled Jack straight into the cloud. Maya followed, still holding on to his jacket, when the circling cloud parted. They waded into the thick wall of fog, wherein strange light sparked and flew like fireflies.

'Don't let go of Jack,' Tommy whispered.

The cloud continued to give way until they were dragged into a small open space around an eerie tree. The grey hooded figure they'd seen was there, tied to the trunk, next to an armoured warrior.

'Pull, Maya! Pull him back!' Tommy screamed. 'Jack, stop! Wake up! It's a TRAP. We must leave now!'

10

TREE OF VINES

Lifting someone else will lift you.

The warrior bent down and studied David's poker face. Tired, frightened and freezing, David was trying to forget the unnatural moving mist. He'd made a mistake of looking directly at it and now tried to distract himself by focusing on the massive, menacing sword wedged in the stone.

'The tree has chosen its victim poorly,' said the warrior. 'This one is small. It will not like this miniscule meal, but *we* don't mind, do we, boys?'

A thunderous roar sounded out from the mist. David resisted all impulse to turn in its direction. Drawing strength from the crystal, he looked at warrior's silver armour, then slowly met his cold gaze.

'And who might you be?' he asked in his bravest voice.

The warrior's heavy laughter reverberated through David. 'Who am I? You mean to say you haven't heard of DrAgA?'

'DrAgA who?'

'LIAR! For your insolence you shall be whipped. That'll help you remember. I am the great DrAgA, and this here is the fiercest band of warriors you'll ever find. Search all the realms; none are better. Isn't that right, boys?'

A roaring chorus bellowed out from the whirling chaos.

'You shall be whipped, but before that, a small drink is in order – the tree is thirsty.' DrAgA stroked the tree as though it were a faithful pet and began circling the trunk. 'That's the pact.

It catches, we slay and everyone wins. The tree is nourished, and our army has a new member.'

'I ain't afraid, if you're trying to scare me. Fight me like a man, if you dare free me.' David shook himself violently. It was an act; once freed, he could threaten them with the crystal or make a dash.

DrAgA laughed. It echoed all around. David craned his neck both ways trying to spot the warrior. He couldn't.

'Like a man? We're *ghosts*. But I promise you shall have a fair chance once you join us.'

Join them? The thought sank into David's mind like a lead weight. He'd researched a lot about ghouls and ghosts, but he wasn't ready to join them. Luckily he had managed to keep his face calm.

'How do I know your promise is worth anything?' he said haughtily.

DrAgA took the bait and materialised on his left. David held his breath. He hoped to be freed soon, for the crystal was getting hot and vibrating like a perpetually ringing cell phone.

'You'll find out, but as I said, a drink first.' A second later, pain shot through David's left arm, an intense sensation of burning and freezing. It stole his breath and voice.

Returning his dagger to its sheath, DrAgA whispered, 'You'll get a fair chance once you're a ghost but not before. Now, relax and let tree have its fill. And as for that tongue – interrupt me again, lobcock, and I shall have it.'

'How dare you call me a ... lob-what?'

'It's what the silly and blundering are called.'

Unexpectedly lightheaded, David didn't argue. He slumped and saw his blood, dripping on the stone, bright red against the dull grey. It flowed into tiny channels in the stone. He tightened his grip on the vibrating crystal; he didn't want to lose the only thing he could use as a weapon.

'More guests?' he heard DrAgA whisper, as if to an old friend. 'Tree, it's our lucky day – you shall feast.'

****

Maya pulled on Jack's jacket with all her might and momentarily held him in suspension, neither progressing nor retreating. Tommy hovered before Jack's face, trying to get his attention. The flashes within the white wall of fog enclosing the clearing began to fly faster and faster.

'Wake up, Jack,' Tommy cried desperately. 'It's a trap!'

The lights became frantic and the commotion increased. Images began to appear within the haze, coming right to the edge before disappearing into the murk, like piranhas teasing a victim. Tommy hit Jack with her staff. Nothing; the twig held him in its grip, pulling him to the tree. Then, unexpectedly, Jack jolted forward, causing Tommy to speedily flap out of his way as he stumbled.

'Tommy, something's coming; look!' Maya's voice was thin and cracked. A tall, slender form was approaching through the wall of mist, its movement fluid and imposing.

'Stay close, Maya,' said Tommy, drifting past her. 'What now?'

Maya noticed a blue glow on her arm. 'That's good, right?' she asked, pointing at the armlet.

The mist gave way to a figure with a long staff. Tommy called out to it in a loud, confident voice: 'That's close enough! Who are you? Some explanation—'

A monkey taller than Jack walked past them without stopping. 'Keep up, if you want to save them,' he said absently over his shoulder. He had a plummy, youthful voice.

'Who are you?' Tommy insisted, following him with her eyes.

'Really, minder? You think now is a good time for introductions?'

Fascinated, Maya observed him closely. He was just like the talking monkey from her dream, only much taller and better dressed. There was a deep orange gem set in the pommel of his sword, where he rested his free hand.

'A youngster from a powerful clan, I think,' Tommy mused, landing on Maya's shoulder. 'He might our only chance to help Jack.'

Maya didn't need any more encouragement; she fell in line, keeping her eyes on his attire: silky cloth and light armour. His fur was dark grey with the beginnings of a silver mane, and his features were sharp. What captivated her most was the movement of his layered, skirt-like armour, which reached down to his leather greaves. The armour's dark blue shade and silver edges complimented his features. He bore neither helmet nor breastplate; only a half rerebrace that sat snugly under his left shoulder plate, which was attached to his skirt armour with many gold chains that ran across his torso. Maya made a mental note to later count the medallions he wore across his waist and his long layered vambrace.

Staff in one hand and the other resting on his sword, the monkey paused majestically to survey the situation in the clearing. Jack was to their right, his arm outstretched with the pulsating twig pulling him towards the base of the massive tree, where the other warrior stood with his hooded prisoner. Maya took in the tree's dangling vines, the protruding roots and the dark canopy; everything looked menacingly alive. And then the whirling cloud slowed and started to form human shapes.

'What are our plans, warrior?' Tommy asked the monkey.

'Our plans?' The monkey snickered. 'There are none. I have plans, but they don't include you.'

'And the boy with the stick; does it include him?'

'Minder, stop talking! If you want to help, get both boys together and away from these ghosts.'

Ghosts! Maya had suspected as much but dared not voice it. The opening they'd entered through was no more, and they were trapped in the clearing. She turned towards the tree just as the warrior there vanished and rematerialised before them. Studying them, he held out his hand and a sword that had been jammed into the stone altar around the tree flew into his grip.

The monkey stepped forward. 'Get the boys; I'll deal with this one. Go now!'

'Mind the roots and vines,' Tommy cautioned.

'Minder, really!'

'That's a flesh-eater! A healer knows her plants and trees.'

Around them, the number of spectres was growing. Maya wanted to ask about the tree, but her mind went blank with fear.

'Move! Get him away,' the monkey shouted, rushing past them.

The other warrior had turned his attention to Jack, but the monkey intercepted him. Staring at each other, they began to pace, the ghost dragging his sword behind him and their champion with his staff in hand. Maya surprised herself by taking steps towards Jack. Tommy's reassuring voice helped.

A bright light flashed from the stick Jack held. In an instant the twig disappeared and in its place was a long beautifully carved staff. The momentary brilliance triggered the attack, as the ghost took advantage of the distraction and silently launched himself at the monkey.

Roars and shouting erupted as the phantoms cheered their man. Sparks flew in all directions and after long seconds they pushed each other back. The monkey had reacted well, fighting with both his staff and his jewelled sword. Pleased, Maya and Tommy instinctively exchanged a quick glance.

'The legendary Topaz!' the ghost warrior cried, admiring the monkey's sword. 'A ghost-slayer blade! Truly a mystical weapon. Let's see if you're worthy of it.'

The sounds of banging shields rang out, and those in the mist broke into another cheer. The ghost and the monkey clashed with growing ferocity, slicing and swashing, ducking and diving, like two savage lions. Giant sparks flew in all directions.

As Maya watched the battle, she noticed the tree's roots retracting each time a spark landed on them.

'Did you see that?' she asked Tommy, with raised eyebrows.

'Yes,' said Tommy. 'They're the trap. It's a flesh-eater tree, and the roots and vines are its web.'

With the roots pulling back, Maya's path got easier and she moved closer to Jack with growing confidence.

Tommy kept vigil. Their champion was fast but the ghost was faster. Defending against the mythical blade, the spectre mockingly disappeared and reappeared around the monkey. Valiantly, their champion persisted, but he was slowing. Tommy and Maya were only a few steps from Jack when the clatter climaxed and the monkey crash-landed near them.

'Come on, get up,' Maya whispered.

Unchallenged, the ghost floated towards Jack, staring at the glowing, pulsating staff in his grip.

The banging ceased the moment the ghost reached for Jack, and without warning, a light shot out from the staff, through the apparition to the hooded grey figure tied to the tree. The spirit tried to escape, but it was caught in the stream of light. It began to panic, arching back and forth, but the light held it a prisoner.

'Don't move. Let me revive our champion before that ghoul breaks free.' Tommy jumped down onto the monkey and retracted her head and arms into her shell.

Maya found it bizarre seeing a headless, handless tortoise standing on two legs. She wondered again what Tommy carried within her shell but kept getting disturbed by the ghost's agitated cries.

Tommy reappeared with what looked like a grass blade.

'Here, eat this,' Tommy thrust the grass at the monkey's mouth.

'Get off. I'm fine.' He swiped at Tommy with his large hand but she dodged the blow. Looking annoyed, he tried to get up but couldn't.

'Very well, have it your way.' Tommy popped the grass into her mouth and chewed while twisting the top of her staff. A sharp point appeared at the bottom of the staff. Tommy rose up and rushed back down, ramming the point into the monkey's bare shoulder.

'Ouch! What did you do?' he snapped.

'You're welcome. I'm returning a favour, that's all.'

'Don't need favours. I can look after myself,' He got up and retrieved his Topaz.

The trapped ghost thrashed violently as it tried to grab the beam of light. Unable to, he called out to those in the mist, but they simply looked at each other and melted away.

Maya clenched her fists in triumph, just as the light beam pulled back towards Jack and knocked him off his feet. Cold greyness engulfed them, and both the light and the trapped ghost vanished. Stunned, Maya stood for a second before rushing over to Jack. She found him on his back, hands clutching the staff. Only now did Maya recognise it: it was Tabioak, the staff from her dreams. Goosebumps ran across her arms as she recalled the wizard. It was all real.

Tommy swooped down. 'Jack! Jack. Can you hear me? Does anything hurt? Jack?'

Jack opened his eyes. He looked confused but Maya was delighted. She collapsed beside him and gave him a hug.

Happy, she held him for some time until the monkey came rushing to them, carrying the boy in the grey hood.

'He's hurt. I'll take this one and that staff to the Gate. Quickly now, hand it to me.'

'Take it; it's only trouble,' Jack said, handing the staff over before Maya could protest.

Tommy fussed over the boy in the hood. He had scruffy blonde hair and his face was contorted in pain. He was in no state to move. 'Just look at that cut on his arm,' she said, 'and that gash above the eye and these bruises. Set him down. They need tending to.'

The monkey set David down in submission to Tommy's matronly tone. She landed near him and swiftly withdrew into her shell, a sight that made Jack sit up. Just as hurriedly, she stuck one arm out with another grass blade.

'Maya, tear that into three parts. That should be enough to revive you all. Each one chew a piece. Now where is … Ah, here it is.'

Distracted by the thought of Tabioak being real, Maya gingerly tore the grass into three pieces and offered the boy one.

'Here.' She had to repeat herself twice before he took notice; he was very weak. She focused on him in an attempt to keep her attention off the staff, afraid of what its appearance meant. When she placed her tiny bit of the leaf in her mouth, a sweet, lemony taste burst on her tongue and instantly she felt livelier.

Tommy emerged from her shell holding a tiny brown pouch. The look on her face suggested she was holding something nasty.

'Quick, we need to get going,' complained the monkey.

Tommy gave him another firm glance and pointed at David's left sleeve, torn and drenched with blood. 'That there is a cut from an ice-fire blade; a ghost wound. Don't you know anything?' Taking a deep breath, she pinched some powder from the pouch and placed it in her mouth. Her face contorted, her eyes widened and her cheeks bulged. Maya almost jumped with worry, but Tommy gestured she was fine. The stuff probably just tasted awful.

'It's not safe here, healer. I need to be on my way,' the monkey whined. He was examining Tabioak as if it were made of delicate glass.

Ignoring him, Tommy continued to chew. She landed on the boy's arm and spat the mush into the cut. He flinched in disgust and let out a small cry, but Tommy simply continued applying the salve. 'Get me something to dress the wound.'

Maya removed her backpack to check for anything to use as a bandage when the monkey approached with his dagger drawn. She froze, wondering if he was going to threaten them, but instead he cut a thin strip from his silky robes and held it out to Tommy.

'Work faster, healer.'

'Thanks. Maya, can you help me?'

Obediently, Maya assisted, although the sight of a wound filled with spit wasn't appealing. She distracted herself by wondering about the monkey. She liked him. Though abrupt, he clearly cared.

'What's your name, child?' Tommy asked the boy.

'D-David.' The boy turned to Maya. 'Did that tortoise just ask me my name?'

Maya nodded, glad to see he was thinking clearly.

'Hush, child – rest,' Tommy said. 'What you have here is a cut made by ice fire – a ghost blade. It's like a cut, a burn and frostbite all in one.'

He nodded. 'How'd you know that's what it felt like?'

'It's my job; I'm a healer. Now, this will warm the cut but cool the burn. It's what I call a warm freeze – a mixture of chilli and a bitter root. It will halt the bleeding, but be warned – it will hurt as it warms up. Be strong—'

PM Perry

'Healer, you take too long,' the monkey interrupted. 'Follow the trail I leave. It will lead you out of woods. Then head towards the Gate.' He was wrapping a gold chain around the two staffs – Tabioak and his own.

'Look!' Maya pointed excitedly at the Tabioak's crystal.

The monkey stared at her. 'Yes, it's a pretty crystal.' He turned back to Tommy. 'Hurry, something lurks here.'

'No!' Maya insisted. 'See – the ghost's inside the crystal.'

Her statement caught everyone's attention and they approached for a closer look. The monkey studied the staff and burst into a loud laugh.

'Can I see?' Maya asked shyly. The monkey simply adjusted his armour and made to leave. 'Just one look, please?'

'A glance wouldn't do any harm,' Tommy piped up, to Maya's surprise. 'Besides, I want to see as well.'

The monkey sighed and held out the staff. 'Only because you gave me that portion. This is not a game, so make it quick.'

Maya didn't waste any time. She held the staff delicately and tilted the tip towards her, unable to believe Tabioak was in her grasp. But the ghost was no longer there. 'Where is he? I can't see him.'

'Here,' the deep voice spoke.

Startled, everyone turned and found the ghost standing a few feet away, free, with his blade drawn and his eyes on Maya.

The monkey leapt forward, drawing Topaz, ready to battle. Maya's anxiety rose, but then subsided upon seeing her armlet glowing blue.

'Wait! You don't mean to harm, do you?'

The ghost looked meek and held his blade out as though he meant to present it as a gift. He floated past the monkey and knelt before Maya.

'I am yours to command. Who are you, little one? How did you free me? I am indebted to you.'

Maya found all eyes resting on her. Uncomfortable, she shook her head. 'That wasn't me. I don't know how to do that.'

'Perhaps, but it occurred at your touch, so I am yours to command.'

Maya shook her head again.

'I don't understand.' The ghost sounded dismayed. 'Am I not worthy? Many would kill to have my band in their service, and yet you refuse.' Dejected, it lowered the blade and slumped. 'I don't have anything else to offer.'

An uncomfortable silence descended. Unnerved, Maya tried to reassure him. 'You don't need to give me anything. You're free to—'

'No!' Tommy, Jack and the monkey all yelled at once.

'That would be unwise,' the monkey explained, 'without its word and its blade. He will not let us leave.'

Overwhelmed, Maya lowered her gaze. She thought about the times when Mark the bully had trapped her. It wasn't nice, especially when she hadn't done anything to provoke him. Her armlet was blue, so she gambled that the ghost wasn't trying to hurt her.

She looked up at the monkey. 'I know what it is like to be trapped. Besides, I don't think he means us harm any more. So if it's up to me, then I mean to let him go.' She turned to the ghost. 'Go; you're free.'

'Really?' The ghost stood, delighted. The monkey tensed himself for a fight, but the ghost did not attack. 'Your kindness has earned my alliance forever. Here.' He produced a tree-shaped brooch and pinned it to Maya's collar. 'If you ever need help, my men and I are but a shout away. Hold this pin and call my name three times. I am known as DrAgA. Remember: DrAgA, DrAg—' With that, he faded away.

Maya moved her fingers across the single eye-shaped leaf on each branch of the brooch. She wanted to smile but dared not, not with the monkey looking at her in disgust.

'Stop sulking, bearer of the ghost slayer,' they heard DrAgA say to the monkey. 'You've a lot to learn, especially about wielding your blade. I can help, but only if you ask. The kind one's clever indeed. By releasing me from my debt, she's earned my eternal favour.'

The monkey took both the staffs and stomped off in haste. This time Maya didn't mind; perhaps Tabioak was better off in his hands. Tommy burst into activity, flying around to corral the children.

'Jack, will you help our new friend David? He's weak with that cut. Mind the dressing, please. Good, let's keep up and not slow our champion down. Hurry; he leads us to the Gate.'

11

OPENING

Unexpected events aren't always bad.

'Fine, you may come along, but keep the pace up and the noise down!' said the monkey, his voice clear and tone strident. Maya was relieved; the woods were teeming with the slain and the mummified.

'Allow me a moment to get my bearings. We move on my return. Be ready!'

Tommy nodded, but the monkey wasn't even looking at her. He swung both the staffs around, struck the ground and, with a giant leap, vanished into the canopy.

'"Allow me",' Maya repeated with a smile. 'How noble …'

'Noble! Hmph, that language doesn't fool me,' Tommy muttered. 'He didn't even introduce himself,' she added loudly.

Maya began to protest when a commotion broke out behind them.

'I don't need no hand – I'm fine,' said David, nursing his arm. When he saw everyone staring at him, he added, in a more pleasant tone, 'Sorry, much better really, thanks! That paste is working.'

Tommy smiled.

Maya was amazed. She'd found David's reaction odd; surely he wasn't still in shock?

'Jack!' Jack pointed to himself then at Maya. 'That's M^2 – sorry, Maya – my li'l sis, and this here is Tommy.'

'You weren't too surprised to see Tommy talking,' Maya pointed out. She'd expected him to react the way she and Jack had back at home.

'No, not after what I seen here. That might surprise *you*.' David smirked.

'Really?' Excited, Maya wanted to know more, but the monkey descended from the greyish-green canopy. He landed masterfully, stood tall and looked at them all in turn. Maya beamed. She loved his mannerisms and how his layered armour continued to sway over his ninja-style trousers.

'I'm Rgapont, the woodsman,' he said, glancing at Tommy. 'But this isn't the time or place for introductions.' He tapped the staffs on the ground.

Tommy laughed a little. 'And how has a woodsman come to be in Aughurnend army colours? I recognise the dark armour with silver edges and royal chains. You're not who you say you are. You're royalty unless you're a deserter or a thief. Or you could be all of those.'

The monkey stamped the staffs and gave her a cold stare. It looked like he might lash out, but instead he clenched his jaw and moved off. 'Make haste if you are coming. Slow me, and I'll leave you and your brood behind. And remember that something else roams these woods.'

He was annoyed and yet he was helping them; he must be of noble descent, Maya was sure. She repeated his name: 'Rgapont the woodsman, Rgapont.'

'Yes, we know there's something sinister in the wood,' said Tommy. 'We saw the victims.'

'Do you know of the warlord?' asked Rgapont.

David interrupted them. 'The crystal and the staff were entrusted to me. A little monkey asked me to get it to Shikshi Virath.'

'Virath! That's who I—' Rgapont stopped and swiftly drew his blade.

A new voice called out calmly, 'Let's not waste more time, then!'

Startled, everyone turned to find a number of hooded monks silently standing around them.

****

'Laksha!' David had recognised the voice but, worried, he'd be told off for disobeying instructions and venturing into the woods, he decided best not to say more.

He didn't need to. At his exclamation, the monkey swiftly returned his blade to its sheath. One monk stepped forward, taking a particular interest in the girl and the boy.

The tortoise, Tommy, said, 'Shikshi Laksha, I apologise for coming unannounced, but my wards and I seek audience with Shikshi Virath. There are matters I need to discuss.'

David looked on, rubbing his arm. It was OK. Throbbing and tight, but OK. His head, though, was a different matter: it felt light and hazy. Best to speak less then, as the flurry of activity quietly escalated. More monks approached to help him, while others appeared leading large deer saddled like horses.

Laksha stepped up to the large monkey, the woodsman, who stood meekly. Everyone stood still for a moment as the primate stared down at the monk, fists tight around the staffs.

Then Laksha laughed. 'Your Highness! Good friend Prince Dyathen. It has been a long time.' They shook hands and patted each other on the shoulder.

Tommy slipped off the girl's shoulder. The kid had been right about the monkey's nobility all along. Tommy began to whisper to the girl, something David hated. It made him feel like they were talking about him. Luckily he caught the odd word and relaxed.

'Prince? Great …'

'I knew he …'

'… best go over with an olive branch.'

With that, Tommy flapped over to Laksha and the prince. David concentrated on their conversation; it was animated with fingers pointing into the woods and Dyathen stabbing the staffs on the ground. Occasionally the word 'warlord' was used. He gravitated closer until two monks disturbed him. They wanted him to mount a deer, a large beast with long antlers. Unable to ride, he wasn't keen.

'I'm not riding that; it don't look right. Looks girly—' He stopped abruptly when he saw the girl and the boy staring at him. He'd done it again, drawn attention to himself. Best to cooperate even if he didn't know how, he thought, hoping his outburst didn't invite any kind of reprimand for venturing into the woods. So David respectfully allowed the monks to help him onto the animal without throwing any tantrums. The deer was warm and gentle beneath him, and its fur was soft. Feeling strange and awkward, and with his arm hurting, David looked around while hugging his steed for balance. The girl and the boy looked comfortable on their mounts. Of course they knew how to ride; all rich kids would. He shifted into a more upright posture and pulled on the reins. Uneasy with the taut leash, his deer moved forward and allowed David to catch the end of Laksha's conversation.

'The staff Tabioak mustn't fall into its grasp. If everyone is ready, let's make haste and get back.'

****

Maya didn't know how long they had travelled when Laksha signalled for a halt. They had arrived at the edge of the woods, where something had spooked the deer. She'd ridden uneasily at the heart of the convoy, safe but lonely. The forest was abnormally silent. In the fading light, the shadows darted about and every crackle and snap sounded loud and suspect. Led by

Laksha and Tommy, they trekked in a single file, occasionally swapping positions. The prince was on foot at the back, for he was too big to ride the deer.

Riding alone, Maya was plagued by thoughts of her dream and of Mum and Dad. She was trying to determine how it was all connected, but her steed was a continual distraction. It was agile but nothing like a horse. It instinctively knew where to step, how to jump over bushes with ease and tread through the dense vegetation with the utmost discretion, but riding the animal was difficult and Maya battled to remain in the saddle. When Laksha called the halt, it pulled her from her thoughts. Jack and David drew alongside her, and Tommy returned from the front of the convoy and perched on her shoulder.

In between the trees, she spotted a familiar blue flash.

'Jack!' Maya called with nervous excitement. She was about to remind him of the portal when a painful shriek sounded from the forest. Maya recognised the cry. 'Aldrr!'

Everyone had frozen, and only after long seconds, when nothing emerged from the darkening woods, did they turn their attention to the blue light ahead.

Prince Dyathen had rushed to Laksha's side and now stood quietly pleading with the monk. Occasionally he pointed at them and then at the staff. Eventually, a few words from Laksha stopped the discussion. Dyathen stopped unexpectedly and stared down dejectedly.

'Oh no,' said Tommy.

'What happened?' asked Maya, but before Tommy could respond the prince returned, glaring at them with a wrinkled nose. Maya didn't dare speak.

'Curse Siantia! And this!' He raised Tabioak. 'I can't accompany the monks to battle because I have to deliver this and escort your wards to the Gate! I'm missing all the fun! Aah!' He paused to compose himself. 'Healer, those two monks will lead. You go next with the girl. Boys, ride in the middle

145

behind her. I'll be last. On my mark, we make for the Gate. Follow the two monks. Ride hard. Don't look back. Trust the beasts; they travel in herds following one leader.' He grabbed their reins and looked at each of their faces, like a commander scrutinising his troops before a battle. 'The others leave first, for the battle. Then we go.'

He spoke not a moment too soon, for hooves began to thunder past them. Their excited deer kicked and pranced, bleating to the racing herd, but Dyathen wouldn't let them follow, holding the three animals steady.

Following Laksha, the monks rode out into the opening and galloped towards the blue flashes. Maya was tight-lipped, nervously wondering how she would cope with the deer for the rest of the ride if they had to go that fast.

A momentary lull followed the last monk, and in it Maya could hear her own heart racing. Then the prince released their reins.

'Go! Go!'

The two lead monks kicked their deer into action and darted towards the open grassland.

Tommy was at her ear. 'Now, Maya. Kick now.'

She glanced at Jack, then tapped the deer's flanks with her heels. It sprang forward.

'Hold tight!' Tommy shouted.

The animal hopped over low bushes, heading for the clearing. Maya held her breath for a big jump, and they landed in the open field.

'Yikes!'

There was an immediate change in atmosphere. The air was dense and blustery, and though Maya wanted to look at the blue flashes, her buck snapped the other way, following the two monks.

'Woah!' she heard Jack shout from behind.

Maya held on as the animal gathered speed, jumping and swerving. The open grassland wasn't as perfect as it looked from afar: half-buried rocks, bushes and ditches rushed past. Maya was constantly battling to stay in the saddle. And then she spotted the solitary monastery in the distance, appearing and disappearing as the ground rose and dipped.

****

David tried to ignore the pain in his arm, but the jerky ride didn't help. The crazy beasts were racing each other. When the other boy's larger deer shot ahead, his own sped up, yanking his arm as it hauled on the reins. Despite his best efforts, he began to lean heavily. The girl was yelling something when he drew alongside her, but he was hanging too precariously to make out her words. He could see the ground rushing by; the fall would be bad. Then someone helped him sit up – the prince, sprinting alongside them.

'How are you running so fast?' David gasped.

A raindrop splashed onto his head. The expectant clouds had burst, and large drops began to lash at everything. The ground quickly became treacherous, and the unthinking deer began to slip and slide. Luckily the monastery was looming straight ahead. David knew he couldn't take much more. Just then the lead monks up ahead turned left and galloped up the steps to the Gate.

'Great! Not up the steps.' David had forgotten about the Gate and looked on blankly as the herd followed. The boy was first, then the girl, who nearly missed the almost hidden steps. Suddenly his deer skidded. He bit hard, thinking he wasn't going to make it, but his mount defied all odds, righted itself and began to climb clumsily.

At the top, in the stone courtyard, monks stood blocking his way. David was certain he was going to crash. The beast dug its feet in but kept sliding, and he lurched forward and over the animal's head. He expected a hard landing and the slam of the deer's body as it hit him, but Dyathen's hands grabbed him again. A moment later he found himself standing next to the prince, the boy and the girl, who were all fixated on the distant blue flashes. It was the second time he found himself watching the lights. It was further away this time, in the distant clearing between the lake and the forest.

'What is that?' the boy asked.

David was about to answer when the girl did. 'That's the portal I dreamt of; it's a tear between two worlds. Remember?'

It expanded and contracted as it ate the fabric of their world. *Nothing to get thrilled about,* David thought.

'That's right, they call it the gateway,' he told them. 'I like to think of it as the crack, and it isn't a good thing! Bad things came from that yesterday.'

'Yesterday?' Tommy said, still huffing from her flight.

'Yes, there was another opening yesterday,' the prince answered. 'That's how I came here, so it's not all bad. Luckily this one's smaller – much smaller.'

Drenched by the waves of rain, David didn't respond. Laksha's riders had formed a defence position just before the portal. In the distance, above the woods, a familiar black figure appeared: the smokey wraith.

'The warlord!' the prince called, a split second before the sound of fireworks launching behind them distracted him.

'The Fangs!' the girl cried.

'Fangs?' David turned to see glowing four-headed snakes hovering above them. Two of them shot towards the portal like luminous arrows. His eyes darted between the portal, Laksha's riders, the wraith and the Fangs.

The warlord was heading for the growing blue portal when a rider and then another and another emerged from within.

'Here they come! I should be there!' the prince said eagerly, placing his hand on his sword.

A small party of riders now galloped to attack Laksha and his monks. The warlord wailed in anticipation. The monks fired arrows, which did nothing to stop it joining the riders.

'Great,' the prince spat in disgust. 'Now it's got a unit fighting with it.' His hand twitched on the hilt of his blade.

But then the approaching riders formed a 'V', lit their arrows and fired at the wraith.

'They're attacking it!' cried Jack. 'I thought they were together.'

The prince didn't respond. Meanwhile the blue gateway collapsed like an old TV flatlining. Darkness enveloped everything.

'What happened?' the girl asked.

'Seems like the riders I assumed to be fighting with the warlord have defected to our side.' The prince peered at the dark landscape, 'A welcomed change; for once the wind of treachery blows in our favour.'

'Meaning?' the tortoise asked.

'Meaning they were our enemies but now they are friendly. But who are they and why are they here now? That's the question.'

'Come, let's head inside,' said the tortoise, trying to round them up. David didn't need any encouragement; he longed to be warm and dry in front of the fire in his room, but then the tortoise said, with some urgency, 'We must meet Shikshi Virath. Come now, quickly.'

David wasn't interested; the light and warmth pouring from inside was too welcoming. Suddenly three blasts of warm air hit them from behind in quick succession.

'Prince Dyathen!' someone hissed. David turned to find four-headed snakes sliding towards them.

149

'Prince,' one of the heads shouted. 'A message from Shikshi Laksha.'

The sight of the large serpent was intimidating, but in a blink it shifted into the form of a young human soldier, who stopped before the prince. David was amazed, but neither the girl nor the boy seemed bothered. For the first time, he wondered exactly who they were.

'Dispense with the formalities and speak up,' Dyathen told the snake.

David didn't like his abruptness. The prince was proud and full of himself, a bit like himself.

'Sire, the shikshi has requested that your party remain out of sight until he sends for you.'

'Out of sight; wouldn't have expected any less with Siantians about.' The prince nodded just as a monk called from the tunnel.

'This way, Your Majesty.' A monk was holding open a door to the Centre.

12

CATCH UP

The magic of science.

Two monks led Maya and her party at a fast pace, turning left and right through doors and corridors. Maya struggled to keep up, and every time she slowed, Prince Dyathen softly nudged her backpack. Occasionally, she caught dribs and drabs of the two monks' conversation.

'Prince ... safest place ... science dwellers ... Royal Quarters ...'

After the short walk, the monks pushed opened a pair of heavy doors marked '2'. Maya had been expecting to see the Royal Quarters and was somewhat disappointed by the hall they all stood in. The rows of tiered seats, a large screen, two whiteboards and a projector reminded her of an auditorium, only it wasn't. It also had spacious worktops before each row of seats, large windows along the opposite wall, a rostrum and a long table with a white washbasin at its far end. It looked like a mix between an auditorium and a laboratory. A 'laboratorium', she mused.

'Sire, we apologise for housing you here,' one of the monks told Dyathen. 'It's only temporary, while we prepare more appropriate quarters for you.'

The prince nodded. 'Can you store this safely?' He held out Tabioak. 'Perhaps in your armoury, with the other weapons?'

'Yes, sire; only the shikshis have access to it, so the staff should be secure there. What of your blade and the other staff?'

'I'll keep these for now, if that's OK.'

'As Your Highness wishes.' The monks left with Tabioak.

The little group stood studying the lecture hall before dispersing. It was an awkward moment; they'd been thrown together with no time for proper introductions. Prince Dyathen was the first to move, climbing over the worktops and seats on all fours. *How odd for a prince,* Maya thought. His sword and staff knocked against each worktop as he made his way to the very top bench, where he sat alone. Secretly, she was happy that the Tabioak she'd dreamt of was safe but also worried that her vision was real.

Nursing his arm, David walked past the long desk at the front and stood by the lowest of the five large windows that ran along the opposite wall. Tommy flew over to the long table and began to pace. Seeing how everyone had gravitated in different directions for solace, Maya set her backpack down to look around the room. It had a mix of old and new furniture with a wooden floor that was well-oiled. Large speakers were positioned at the rear and the rostrum at the front came with a screen and control console.

Maya was still observing everything when the double doors swung open and the monks entered with a tray of fruit, packets of crisps and biscuits, and cans of drinks. They laid everything out on the bottom worktop before turning to the prince.

'Sire, our apologies for these meagre refreshments. With the arrival of the others, we are unable to cook and can only muster these snacks for you and the children.'

The prince nodded, allowing the monks to leave.

No one moved to eat, descending instead into their own thoughts. Maya tapped Jack's arm and they exchanged a glance; no words were needed for him to know what she meant. He gave her a bear hug. Happy he was back to his old self, Maya smiled to herself. They held their embrace for some time, and when they parted everyone was smiling at them. The atmosphere had lightened.

152

Jack wasted no time doing what he was good at: mingling and making friends. He grabbed drinks, crisps and biscuits and started handing them out.

'Try these, Your Highness,' he said carefully to Dyathen, offering him the packet of biscuits. The prince frowned, so Jack took a biscuit, bit into it and extended the packet again.

'Jack! He won't take—' said Tommy sharply, when the prince took one.

Everyone stopped. The prince sniffed and then licked the rusk. Everyone waited. He smiled and popped the whole piece into his mouth before reaching for another. Jack, Tommy and Maya shared a glance.

'I'm Jack; that's Maya over there. Tommy you know and …'

'David,' reminded David.

'Yes, and David, who you saved, Your Highness.' He gave Dyathen a packet of crisps. 'Like this, sire,' he said, opening his packet slowly to demonstrate.

The prince raised his hand. 'This isn't my realm of Aughurnend, so let's dispense with the formalities. Here I am only another friend, so address me simply by my name, Dyathen.'

Jack grinned and placed a crisp in his mouth, but Dyathen was hesitant. He licked one, testing the flavour; then his eyes widened and he shoved a handful into his mouth. Maya giggled.

'The prince – sorry, Dyathen – likes the chicken flavour,' Jack announced.

Next was a drink. Jack opened a can; the sound startled the prince ever so slightly. He raised the can to his lips. 'Just take a small sip, see if you like it.'

The prince opened his can, sniffed, and took a small sip. They waited as he let the soda wash over his tongue. Then he placed the can to his lips again and gulped it dry.

Everyone laughed. The prince burped. 'Siantian food is different but good!'

'Siantian?' asked David.

'Yes, Siantia is what they call our realm, instead of Earth,' Maya explained, surprised at her own boldness.

Meanwhile, Tommy took the opportunity to apologise to Dyathen for her earlier behaviour. 'Forgive me, Dyathen, for my earlier accusations.' She bowed, hovering before the prince.

The prince didn't speak; he simply looked into her eyes, closed both his eyes and nodded once. Tommy apologised again, this time for stabbing him with her staff. The prince gave her a peculiar look. 'Why didn't you use your staff the way other healers do?'

Tommy settled on a worktop, looking a bit dejected. '… out of practice, a result of my long stay here in Siantia. As you know, spells and even potions are forbidden here.'

With that, Tommy explained how they arrived at the Gate: the Mysun parents' disappearance, the encounter with the Fangs, meeting Loivissa and their mission to get Shikshi Virath's advice. By the time Tommy concluded, the prince was on his fourth packet and third drink can.

'That's us, Dyathen. Now pray, reveal what brings you to Siantia.'

He reached for another packet and a drink. 'I … no, *we* came to deliver something.'

'The staff,' Maya interrupted, only to receive a sharp glance from Tommy. She blushed. Luckily she'd not called the staff by its name, for Tommy had not mentioned her dream.

The prince dashed a handful of salt and vinegar crisps into his mouth and cringed. It made Maya giggle, earning her an intense stare from the prince. Jack tensed, but the Dyathen gleefully repeated, 'Different but good.'

His jovial, carefree manner made everyone laugh. Devouring the crisps, he began his tale, explaining how, only a night before, the qwrks had caused disturbances in his woods.

'Qwrks?' Maya interrupted shyly.

'Aye, the malicious and aggressive brutes of Vykrutz.'

'Vykrutz!' Maya sat up suddenly. Everyone turned in her direction. Caught in the unexpected attention, she simply shrugged and bit her lip. She needed to be more careful. With her newfound boldness, she might reveal more than Tommy had mentioned to the others.

Dyathen continued. 'There were qwrks everywhere, combing the woods for something, when a gateway opened up and one of my kind, a small one, rushed through. The light from the portal must have blinded him momentarily, for he rushed straight into the path of a qwrk.'

'What happened?' Maya asked, eager to learn more but trying not to look *too* interested, lest it seem suspicious. Dyathen's story sounded like the follow-up to her vision: what happened to the little monkey after it left Torackdan.

'Only one thing happened. I wasn't going to sit that fight out, not after it came to my woods and certainly not when it involved one of my kind. I jumped in and battled the brute ...'

'Then?' Maya leaned forward.

'I won, of course. We escaped and hid before more qwrks arrived. It was then that I realised who the little one was, and I instantly knew what he carried.'

'So who was it?' asked David, beating Maya to it.

'A good friend by the name of Hopper. He was an aide to the legendary wizard allied to my father's kingdom. And as for what Hopper carried ...' Dyathen took a deep breath. 'One of the most powerful staffs ever known, the Tabioak. I knew then what had occurred and what I had to do.'

'What?' David jumped in once more.

'Something had happened to his wizard, Torackdan. That's the only reason Hopper would have come to me, the Keeper of the Woods. I had never seen him like that. He was eager for an opportunity to use his last charm to open a gateway to escape to here, but the qwrks were everywhere. Unable to gain the upper hand, we kept moving until something unheard of occurred: the crystal fell off the staff. Worried, Hopper used his last charm. I tried to stop him, knowing the gateway would give us away, but it was too late. We barely escaped but led the qwrks here in the process. And their master, the warlord, followed. I thought we were done for but the monks came to our aid.'

'I saw that; they were trying to close the opening, weren't they?' said David.

'You were there?'

'Yes, I was. But why didn't you join the monks, especially if you know Laksha?'

'I wanted to, but Hopper didn't trust anyone. Before I could do anything, he fled into those woods for cover. Then, this morning ... I don't know what got into him; he nearly gave the staff to the warlord. As I slept, he slipped out into the open, heading towards the house by the lake. I awoke in time to see the warlord attack. Without thinking, I rushed in to battle the wraith. I thought we'd lost the staff when the warlord unexpectedly retreated into the woods' Dyathen turned to Jack. 'By the time I returned, all I spotted was the staff in your grip, so I began to trail you.'

A momentary silence fell, until David broke it.

'Virath was trying to stop that smokey thing from following you into the woods.'

The prince nodded. 'Yes, I didn't know what to do: help the Virath or follow Hopper? It seemed right to follow Hopper – at least until those dastardly ekoers attacked.'

Suddenly a new voice sounded out of nowhere. 'Why, those flying screamers, they make me fume—'

Startled, everyone jumped up. The prince even had his blade drawn when David said, delightfully, 'Achanak, is that you?'

'Come out, whoever you are!' demanded the prince.

'That's my friend, a fire genie called Achanak,' said David, trying to spot him. A faint flame appeared timidly, by the ceiling.

David was overjoyed. Maya and Jack looked on in silent amazement, for neither had expected such a sight: a small flame floating in mid-air. It descended slowly, with a nervous expression on its face, and began to complain to David. It was clear they were friends and worried about each other. It was some time before they settled down.

'Why is the warlord still here?' Maya asked, once Achanak and David were ready to return to the earlier conversation.

'I saw what happened,' Achanak answered. 'He simply got left behind. In fact, he was caught in the collapsing gateway.'

'Hmm, that explains many things: why he didn't fight this morning, why he fled and the petrified beings in the forest,' said Dyathen. 'He's been weakened by the collapsing gateway and has been feeding and trying to regain his strength. He's waiting to strike, waiting to complete his task – capture the staff. The question we need to ask is, what now?'

He trailed off, searching for more crisps and cans, but all that was left was fruit. Meanwhile, Maya was more confused than ever. Her dream was true and she had more information, but none of it explained why Mum and Dad had disappeared. They needed to see Virath soon to shed light on that.

'David,' said Tommy, breaking the growing silence. 'Tell us how you came to be here. And why.'

****

Everyone turned to David, who sat quietly. For the second time he had the rare feeling of not knowing what to say. He could weave a story but didn't have the heart to. They were all looking at him with such keenness that he couldn't speak. He sat staring at space for some time, thinking there were very few people to whom he owed anything, and now he owed Dyathen for saving him and Tommy for her care. He decided to start by thanking them, not as a formality, but with heartfelt words, which were much more difficult to utter. With a lump in his throat, he held them in a steady gaze and hoped they understood how difficult it was.

Then he described the morning when the cops had caught him in London, his arrival at the Red Gate Centre, the previous night's battle and, finally, his encounter with Hopper earlier that day. He recounted Aldrr's gutless attack and what Hopper had said as he'd thrust the crystal into his palm.

'"Find the monk; he'll tell you more," he told me. And then he began to fade away. That was the last I saw of him. I got up, looked around, and then something yanked at my leg. Next thing I knew I was tied to the tree.'

Silence descended on the group again. David looked around and found each of them lost in their own thoughts.

'Siantian food is good,' the prince said finally. 'And the folks too.' Everyone smiled. 'You're weak but good, certainly not worthy of hate, as many had me believe.' He studied them each in turn, then he wrinkled his nose and added, 'But the Siantian smell is not natural.'

'The smell?' David frowned. He caught Maya glancing at the projector above them before looking at Jack.

'Smell? What smell? I wish I could smell' Achanak sparked up, looking around.

Seeing David's quizzical looks, Tommy floated up to explain. 'The smell Dyathen speaks of is that of new devices. It represents Siantia.'

Really? The smell of new gadgets? How can someone not like that? David thought.

Tommy continued. 'You see, the devices created here in Siantia have made Siantians forget their natural abilities and knowledge of konjuring. Over time, Siantians drove out konjuring ways in favour of Siantian life. They've persecuted those who practice konjuring, like shamans, witches and others.'

'And dragons?' Maya pitched in.

'Yes. They were hunted to death or hiding. Things like that have earned Siantia everyone's hatred.'

Just then, a blue light filled the room. Everyone spun towards the window. A large bang rattled the glass, followed by a small tremor.

Dyathen ran down to the bottom window. The others followed. In the distance, a new gateway was opening. This one was bigger, with more violent lightning. Two 'V' shapes appeared in the expanding tear.

'Another portal,' said Maya.

'And worse – ekoers!' cried Achanak, going faint with dread.

Maya turned away from the window, making Jack pat her shoulder for comfort. 'That's the second time you've mentioned them,' he said. 'What are ekoers?'

David liked Jack. He asked logical questions, unlike Maya. She'd made one irrational decision already, when she freed the ghost. He could see why she'd done it but wasn't sure he'd do the same. It was a clear sign she'd not survive on the streets, where you just couldn't be kind; that could get you killed. He turned back to the distant scene. Four fast-moving figures emerged on the ground, like bugs skittering out from their burrow.

'Riders!' Dyathen stamped his staff, a crisp knock against the wooden floor. The riders scattered in different directions, moving purposely. Within the tear, larger figures began to form.

'And now qwrks.' He started to pace like a caged animal, chains jangling and sword knocking against his armour. David knew what he felt like; he'd paced many a time, trying to plan a way out of whatever centre they'd put him in.

He turned to Maya, who sat cowering against the window, eyes narrowed. It was obvious that she was trying hard to ignore what was going on, but it wasn't working. 'You must face your fears,' he told her.

'That's what Dad says.' She glanced at Achanak, who was describing the Ekoer.

'A hideous creature, an abomination of a bat and a hound that drowns everything with its unbearable silent cry.'

David saw Maya didn't want to hear any more about its fearsome appearance, but, oblivious, Achanak continued with his detailed portrayal: the foul smell, sharp teeth and talons.

'Does it sound like this?' Jack asked. He was beside the microphone at the rostrum.

The next moment a roar filled the hall. It was different from any roar David had heard before: long, guttural and deep but with a high-pitched note.

'Loivissa!' Maya exclaimed. Achanak flickered, startled.

'What was that?' David had barely asked, when Dyathen spun around with excitement.

'Dragons, here?' he asked.

'Jack, this isn't the time!' Tommy scolded. 'Please put your phone away.'

'I was only trying to understand this creature's cry,' Jack began to plead, when Dyathen interrupted.

'Was that a dragon in there? What is that device? Many a strange thing I have seen, but never a trap that small and powerful. What else can it catch?'

Seeing Jack fiddling with his mobile, David laughed.

'Oh! No, it's not a trap,' Jack explained. 'This is a phone. We use it to talk to others. It needs charging actually; where's my bag?'

'Make it scream again. Is it inside?' Dyathen asked, following cautiously as Jack retrieved his rucksack.

'No, no, it's not inside. Well, not the real one.' He plugged the phone in.

David found it strange to see Dyathen, a bold warrior, suddenly treading warily. He spoke softly when Jack showed him the video that the roar came from.

'Strange Siantian konjuring … How have you captured such a majestic beast in there? How do you make it do the same thing again and again? Are you a Siantian sorcerer – a konjurer? Make it scream again.' They watched another replay. 'Siantian magic's strange and powerful. I must acquire this trap before I leave.'

David, Jack and Maya laughed until the windows vibrated once more. The rumble was different this time. Baffled, they hurried to the glass. Another rhythm pulsated through.

'The invasion drums of the yyenas,' said Dyathen. 'The shikshis must be riding out to meet this new challenge! I should go with them,' said Dyathen.

Outside, the gateway held and the band of qwrks and yyena riders grew. In the sky, a gang of ekoers circled like vultures waiting on a carcass. The drums resonated once more.

A door banged open behind them. Two monks stormed into the hall and said hurriedly.

'Sire, forgive the disturbance, but your presence is urgently requested in the banqueting hall.'

'Banqueting hall? Who requests it? Shikshi Virath?'

'Shikshi Laksha, Your Highness; he also sends these for everyone in your party.' The other monk placed a pile of brown robes on a desktop. 'Best if no one stands out. You may all want to freshen up before adorning them.'

161

'Good idea!' Quickly washing his hands and face at the basin, the prince asked, 'Do we ride to meet this challenge?'

'I'm sorry, Your Grace. The Shikshi didn't say.'

'I should come along to the banqueting hall,' Tommy butted in, then added, 'If you approve of course.'

'Sire, only your presence was requested. Perhaps your friend can stay back to care for these young ones,' the monk advised.

Great. David wasn't pleased with that suggestion and was going to make up some excuse to counter it when Dyathen saved him from having to.

'I am sure Shikshi Laksha wouldn't mind my friend coming along. In fact, I insist on her accompanying me.'

'As Your Highness wishes. Kindly hurry.'

Tommy flew to Maya and Jack. 'Wish me luck: this is it. And when I see Shikshi Virath, I'll ask about your mum and dad. Now you two stay here, where you're safe. Freshen up; I need you both at your best when the shikshi asks to see you.'

The siblings nodded. Satisfied, Tommy flew to the prince's shoulder. She gave them one last look before they left.

As soon as the door shut, David leapt into action. Something was happening and he wanted to know what.

'Come on, hurry.'

Maya and Jack gave him a puzzled look.

'Where?' Achanak said, reappearing. He'd disappeared when the monks rushed in, but in the commotion no one had noticed.

'Didn't you hear? The banqueting hall, of course.'

'Remember the last time you disobeyed.' Achanak glowed brighter.

'I agree; we should stay here,' Jack added his support.

'We weren't invited, but that doesn't mean we can't go, does it now? It sounded important. Come on.'

'It's not the right thing to do,' Maya said, moving closer to Jack.

David expected no less from well-off kids; what did they know about surviving? 'That may be, but I thought you wanted to save your parents. If you want to help them, then you've got to take some chances. Never mind; suit yourself. I'm going.'

The mention of their mum and dad changed the looks on their faces. David busied himself, knowing they'd change their minds.

'Fine,' Jack agreed, looking at the Maya.

David was glad for the company, but became increasingly concerned about stealth and began to explain how they needed to be invisible. It was harder to achieve with the three of them together instead of him alone. They both looked lost, so he began to give instructions.

'Clean up. Put these robes on. We can't take those.' He pointed at their backpacks. 'Take whatever you need and hide it inside the robe. We need to blend in. Become like the monks. Walk like them, think like them, just be them. Got it?'

****

Maya washed her face and slipped the robe over her clothes. It was heavy, rough and slightly long, but she didn't mind. She checked her armlet and tree brooch; both were secure. As she tied her hair, she took a moment to study David. She was not one to makes assumptions, and she didn't know what to make of him. Perhaps he was right: waiting wasn't helping, even if what they were doing was wrong. David was a little rough, a liar perhaps, but he could help them find Mum and Dad. And he was right about facing fears; maybe they needed to take chances as well. He turned and caught her staring at him. She smiled and met his stare for a second. His eyes were odd: one was bluer than the other.

She tied her hair into a ponytail, slipped it inside the robes and pulled her hood up. She was ready. Jack retrieved his phone and patted his pockets, checking for his keys and wallet. Satisfied, he emptied his backpack into Maya's, except for Loivissa's scale, and wore the backpack at the front like a harness. He tapped it flat against his chest, and pulled on the robe. It fitted him well. David was the slowest. He dressed slowly, nursing his arm, and continued to give instructions.

'To be invisible, don't speak unless it's an emergency. Don't use names. Use what they use: shikshi. We're all shikshis. Keep the hood up and look down at the ground. Don't look at anyone unless it's necessary, and if you do, be confident. It's about your attitude. Got it?'

'But I'm short and I'm a girl; they'll know I am not a monk, won't they?' asked Maya.

'Good point, but trust me; I've done this before. Only a few look that closely. With any luck we should be fine.'

Maya wasn't so sure but nodded, so he continued.

'I guess both of ya are alright. You can call me Wiz. That's my street name. What are your street names?'

The twins exchanged a glance. 'We're just Jack and Maya.'

13

MEETING

The smell of Siantia.

Maya, Jack and David scurried along the corridors. Achanak guided them, for he knew most passages, having explored them during David's absence. Able to fade out and become invisible, he discretely flew ahead and around bends and called out simple instructions: 'Stop. Wait. Walk. Don't look back. Slow down and be confident.'

Luckily their route was deserted, except when they had to leave the building to cross from one wing to the other where a couple of monks stood guard out in the courtyard. Their presence didn't stop David, who led the way without hesitation. Maya wanted to stop, but Jack encouraged her to keep moving. She tried to act according to David's advice, walking confidently as if she were a monk, not too fast or too slow. Luckily the monks were occupied with the distant drumming and the lightning and missed the three robed figures silently slipping by behind them.

Maya found the experience alien, with her heart running faster than her feet. She didn't know if it was the thrill of the adventure, the fear of being disobedient or a mixture, but she was beginning to like it. 'Face your fears,' she whispered, remembering Dad.

A few more corridors slipped by while Maya was lost in her thoughts, and then Achanak quietly announced, 'The banqueting hall's up here.'

Maya was stunned by the stone passage they'd just entered. Jack had also stopped in awe of everything: the paintings, the sheer size of the place, the armour and the weapons. Everything competed for their attention. For a moment they stood studying their surroundings with the muffled sound of distant drums in the background, until David's voice brought them back to their mission.

'Achanak, could you check if the neighbouring hall's empty? Keep up, guys! We don't want to be out here too long.'

The next hall, the Throne Room, was empty, cold and dark. David led them in with caution and, on entering, he quietly stole away towards a door on the far left. Maya and Jack stopped once more to admire the great hall. The little light that shone through the large windows at the other end revealed a room even more majestic than the corridor. A crystalline chandelier, the large paintings, the shiny armour, the ceiling murals, a thick rug and the lavishly decorated walls: everything pulled at their curiosity, but it was the grand throne that their eyes rested on. It sat imposingly at the top of the hall, with other ornate seats arranged in a circular setting around it, as though ready for a council.

'Psst!' David's hiss brought them back to the task at hand. Soon they were huddled around a richly carved wooden door, eavesdropping on the proceedings inside. David had teased the door open, and they could see one length of a long, stately dining table inside. Jack seemed impressed with David's street skills, which were certainly handy, although not as fascinating as real magic or Loivissa. They made a good team, especially with David beginning to trust them. Settling down, they crouched around the crack in the doorway to observe the meeting.

A heavy debate was already in progress and coarse, stiff voices floated through the gap. Maya took in every detail, starting with the three monks who sat closest to them. A little further down the table were four Fang elders in immaculate attire, seated upright and staring nobly down the hall. At the far end, sprawled on high-backed chairs, sat three brutishly large soldiers.

'Qwrks!' a shiver spread through Maya. They reminded her of the scene in Ebbelle's tower from her dream.

The qwrks dwarfed their seats in their thick, leathery armour. Some poor creatures' matted fur hung from their shoulders, hiding most of their ashen, muscular build, except for their dirty, scabbed, hammer-like arms, which rested on the table. Intimidated, Maya turned away from the gap before plucking up the courage to study them once more.

A few chairs towards the centre of the long table stood untidily, except for the heaviest, biggest and most decorated seat in the middle. It remained untouched. Huge pieces of dirty, broken armour lay on the table, partially hiding refreshments that had been laid out for the guests: a few jugs, deep trays of what looked like bread and bronze cooking pots.

The voices grew louder, and one brute at the far side abruptly jumped to his feet. Instantly, the prince, with Tommy on his shoulder, stepped into view.

'Careful now; Siantians aren't that bad. They are weak, strange and don't understand our ways but are otherwise OK,' Dyathen said, resting one hand on his blade.

Maya smiled, happy for his support, when the rude voices of others sprang up.

'Aughurnendant, you Siantian admirer, you may like their stench but it's repulsive; an alien smell devoid of anything enchanted.'

A foul smell, a mixture of horse manure, wood, burnt meat, vomit, sweat and grass drifted through the gap and into the Royal Throne Room.

'They can complain,' Jack whispered into Maya's ear. David pinched his nose.

'Well, you're in Siantia,' said Laksha. He sounded close but Maya couldn't see him.

The remaining two thugs at the table leapt up, when a thunderous bang and a stentorian voice rang out.

'SILENCE!'

Maya and the boys jumped back, almost hitting each other. A large hand had slammed the table, directly opposite the royal seat.

'Smell!' the new voice continued. 'We aren't here to discuss whiffs. SIT down!' The children looked at each other nervously in the low light. 'SIT.'

The instigators settled down timidly.

Curious, the children tried to see whom the powerful voice belonged to.

'Thank you Lord Vorsulgha,' said Laksha.

Maya's attention perked up at the mention of Vorsulgha: *the one from my dream!*

'I can understand your men's anxiety,' Laksha continued. 'Defecting from Vykrutz and riding to Siantia cannot be easy, and the smells of Siantia need time to get accustomed to. I apologise for having these Siantian devices and those frozen children here, but your arrival was somewhat unexpected.'

'Does he mean us?' Jack whispered in alarm.

Maya gave a quick shake with her head but held her breath in fear. She turned to the boys, who both looked like they expected the door to be shoved open at any second.

'Fate gave us no choice in our arrival!' Lord Vorsulgha bellowed.

His voice snapped Maya from her thoughts, and her heartbeat shot up, thumping so loudly she was certain those around the table could hear it.

'The invasion drums of the yyena are beating, and the enemy bangs at your gate. Time is fast slipping away; I beg an audience with Shikshi Virath.'

Maya and Jack both drew closer to the gap in the door at the mention of Shikshi Virath.

'My lord, forgive me, but I'm afraid Shikshi Virath travels for more help. You can, however, speak openly to the Council of Siantia. If you prefer not to, then it may be best if you excuse us, for we have preparations we must tend to. But without any further explanation, the council sadly cannot trust you nor offer you any refuge here. You will understand, I am sure. Every second we waste weakens us. Prince Dyathen has already brought us the news that Vykrutzians chased something here; if that is the news you bring, then the council is already aware of it.'

Lord Vorsulgha walked around the far end of the table and into the children's view. He was easily the largest and meanest-looking qwrk Maya had seen, but his men had helped Hopper, so he could be trusted. Proudly wearing a slain beast on his shoulder, he slowly treaded behind the three brutes at the table and sat down beside the royal seat. All eyes were on him as he leaned forward, rested his white-bearded chin against his club-like fists and stared straight ahead. Tension rose in the room.

'Shikshi Laksha, do you trust your monks?' he asked.

'My lord! Are you trying to antagonise the council?' Laksha retorted. 'What kind of a question is that?'

Vorsulgha glanced around the room. 'Shikshi, I'll speak to you alone with one Fang Elder and the prince. The healer may stay if she wants. The rest of you, get out!'

Maya, Jack, David and Achanak were glued to the gap as the chairs shifted. One by one, the qwrks, the shikshis and the Fang Elders left. When the door snapped shut at the other end, Laksha, the prince and Tommy came into view as they moved closer to Vorsulgha and the remaining Fang Elder. Tommy hopped onto the tabletop to pace. Vorsulgha lowered his voice, although for someone like him it still wasn't particularly quiet.

'Shikshi, I apologise if my comments were rude. I am sure your monks are all trustworthy. However, I can only vouch for my men, and I need to know if you can do the same for yours.

Powers are once again in flux and treachery will soon run rampant, like a plague. Those once trustworthy are now suspect; question everyone's alliance. Sadly, for my men and me, the choice was made for us, but we don't regret it.'

'Made? What do you mean?' the Fang Elder asked in a noble, contained manner. 'Explain why a Vykrutzian general would betray his own kind. If you can stab them in the back, then what's stopping you from turning on us?'

'Believe it or not, our fate was sealed when my men were discovered helping the Konjurer's friend, one called the Hopper.'

Maya's eyes widened.

'A likely story,' said Dyathen. 'Why would you help an enemy?'

Maya almost blurted out that Vorsulgha was telling the truth but bit her tongue.

'It was an act of trust … I led my men to escape a hateful tyrant.'

'And who is this new oppressor?' Tommy's thin voice rang out, sounding alien amongst the men.

'Not new—'

'Then who? Not Orm-Ra; he was slain in the Great War,' Dyathen added.

'No, another, who calls himself Orm-Ra's identical, Orm-Roth!'

'An identical? A twin? Orm-Roth …'

'Yes, a cruel Vykrutzian who keeps to the shadows and slays blindly. Consumed by the prophecies, he rises, planning a war like none since the Great War.'

'That's a myth! A legend!' interrupted the prince.

'The prophesised ascent of a weaker identical sibling!' Tommy countered. 'It's something all my kind are taught to recognise.'

'And by his side he has another,' Vorsulgha continued. 'A

Hiertan: a changer of hearts.'

'And a controller of thoughts! It gets better,' Dyathen laughed. 'Even if the council were to believe your tale, why do you not fight for this Orm-Roth? Why leave?'

Maya had seen the Hiertan but didn't say anything, for she'd seen her own face in its hood.

'Mockery doesn't befit a prince.' Vorsulgha continued by saying, 'You've a lot to learn in the matters of the state. I have glimpsed Orm-Roth's rule. It brings only darkness and destruction. Many chieftains, kings and konjurers in all realms will be slain, while the few who earn his trust will be rewarded with the power of the wraiths – his new commanders. The one we encountered is called Aldrr – a dwarf king. He is the first of many more to come.'

'And those who resist face the Hiertan right?' said Dyathen.

'Aye, that's right! I'd rather live and die free than be one of Orm-Roth's mindless minions. This is why we followed Hopper to help him. My men heard he escaped Aldrr and brought the konjurer's staff here. Orm-Roth's allies mustn't acquire it, but when I saw the wraith I feared it might be too late.'

In the throne hall, Maya struggled to contain herself. She wanted to rush in and tell them everything. Tension grew as Laksha requested the Fang Elder, Dyathen and Tommy for a quick discussion. They moved away, out of her view down the banqueting hall.

In the growing silence, she began to hear the distant drums; she'd forgotten about the army. With growing anticipation, she looked at Jack. He gave her a smile. David was obliviously nursing his arm. She was going to ask about the cut when Laksha spoke.

Quickly arranging themselves around the opening, they spied Laksha, Tommy, the prince and the Elder coming back into view.

'Lord Vorsulgha, Prince Dyathen confirms parts of your

tale and so the council trusts the news you bring. And of course, your actions to attack the wraith have spoken loudly of your intention to defend the staff. So on behalf of the Siantian council, you and your men are welcomed here at the Red Gate!'

Vorsulgha grunted his assent. The prince began to report on the recent events, with Laksha occasionally offering his input. Exhausted, Maya turned away and sat against the wall to listen.

'Pity the little one didn't survive,' Vorsulgha lamented. 'Still, all is not lost. But Aldrr mustn't gain the staff, or Orm-Roth will gain a big advantage and Konjiur, the seat of pure konjuring, will be lost, for it stands weak without the Master Konjurer. We must protect the staff with our lives.'

Knowing the brutes would be on their side gave Maya a brief smile, but she wondered how all this was connected to her parents. Jack patted her shoulder gently. Comforted, she continued listening to the discussion.

'Last time, they underestimated your strength,' Vorsulgha was saying. 'A stroke of good fortune, if you ask me, but they will not make that error again. We shall know soon enough how many march this time.'

'None of that explains why the staff was sent here, to Siantia,' said the Fang Elder.

'That's obvious,' said Laksha. 'It's for safekeeping. What better place to hide it than here, where magic is frowned upon and hardly practised?'

A loud knock on the door startled the children. Someone entered without waiting and a deep voice said. 'Milord, as you suspected, a strong force arrives. We estimate that over fifteen ekoers, at least eighty yyena riders and over three hundred runners got through before the gateway collapsed.'

'Collapsed?'

'Yes, milord. And *he's* joined them as well.'

'Ah, the battalion has its commander! Does he march or camp?'

'Camp, milord.'

'Tell our men to be prepared; it may change quickly.'

'Yes, milord,' the heavy voice grunted. The footsteps retreated and the door slammed shut, leaving behind a heavy silence.

Vorsulgha's loud voice broke it. 'Shikshi, that's the second misfortune I have had tonight. First we arrived late, now a large force advances on us. Pray that we don't hear of a third before the night is over. A trinity of setbacks would be bad indeed.'

'A large force ...' Laksha mused.

'This one is a deadly battalion of flyers, riders and runners: a complete land-invading unit. Ekoers will blanket-crush our men with their silent cries. Yyena riders are a deadly combination of beast and rider, both skilled in expertly picking off weaknesses. And my fellow qwrks, though slower, are the strongest and will deal heavy blows. We need to be alert this night, lest they attack in the cover of darkness. Now, can you say if Shikshi Virath will return before sunrise?'

'No, not by sunrise. Hopefully by sunset at the earliest.'

Maya turned to Jack in despair as Vorsulgha voiced her thoughts.

'That is unfortunate! It leaves us weaker than I expected.' He sat back contentedly at the table and added, 'But I like a challenge. What do you make of the unit?'

Jack and David observed the battle planning with interest. Worried, Maya sat staring at the throne until a familiar sound disturbed her. It was a phone, ringing in the banqueting hall. She turned to find Vorsulgha ready to strike and smirked as Laksha began to apologise.

'Forgive me, my lord; those are the messages I am expecting. I'd sent a request to all our friends here in Siantia, asking those nearby to come to our aid. Sadly, only a few will arrive tonight. Most can only be here by midday tomorrow. According to my count, this leaves us gravely outnumbered: one to four, perhaps five. Not good news, I fear! We're on our own, a thin line that must make a stand for the staff and this Siantian realm. Our objective will be to hold until help arrives.'

'That's the third setback,' said Vorsulgha. 'What say you, prince?'

Dyathen didn't answer, choosing instead to remain quiet with his hand on the topaz blade. Maya smiled, knowing he was ready to battle.

'Our plan is simple,' said Laksha. 'We will not venture out. We'll wait for them to come to us. Prince Dyathen, you'll assume command of the monks skilled in physical combat and hold the platform.'

'Physical combat?'

'Yes! Unfortunately, not all the monks here have konjuring knowledge, but all are well versed in physical skills. You will be the thin edge of the blade they face. Rdita, you'll be with the prince.'

'In the battle?' Tommy responded in surprise.

'Yes, but not to fight; only to caste your healing spells. The longer you keep everyone fighting, the better. My lord, you and your riders will hold the ground inside the gate itself and continually foil charges by the yyena riders.'

Laksha paused and turned to the Fang Elder. 'The Fangs will hold the position above the gateway and foil any charges by ekoers. The monks versed in the art of konjuring will serve two roles: remotely attacking any advancing units and acting as the last stand in defending the Gate and Siantia. And as for myself, I shall engage with the warlord directly.'

Laksha had barely finished speaking when a loud crash stunned them all. Lord Vorsulgha had brought his big fist down onto the table, making everything on it bounce, including Tommy.

'I CAN'T WAIT!' he boomed. 'And what of the staff? Who protects it?'

'Although we can barely spare anyone,' admitted Laksha, 'two monks will take charge of it.'

Satisfied, Vorsulgha turned to see Tommy land inside the salad tray.

'Eating before a battle, Healer! I like it, even if it's just leaves. You must have a little Vykrutzian in you.' He burst into roaring laughter.

'Not eating, Lord Vorsulgha,' said Tommy stiffly. 'Just extracting essences from these herbs, to use for healing.'

But Vorsulgha didn't seem to be listening as he scooped something from a bucket and stuffed it into his mouth. Maya wasn't sure what it was until he pulled a clean bone from his lips. 'Hmm, this is good even if it's small.'

'I'm glad you like it,' said Laksha. 'Prince Dyathen – you wanted to share something as well?'

'Only that, after being caught in the collapsing gateway, the wraith was weakened. In my earlier encounter with it, it was unable to dissolve into smoke as easily as before, unable to dodge weapons by vaporising, although still powerful.'

'What?' exclaimed Vorsulgha. 'Why have you kept that until now? That is the best news I have heard all evening. You should start with such news; it fuels everyone's fury, makes us stronger. Tomorrow night we start our meeting with how the enemy has been weakened, not what losses we have suffered.' He scoffed more food. 'As we speak, he will be feeding on my kind to gain his strength. That means we face fewer qwrks but a stronger Aldrr. He won't be at his peak, but he will be stronger.'

Laksha poured some drink into four large tumblers and one tiny chalice and handed them out, giving the cute chalice to Tommy. 'For Siantia!' he said, raising his cup.

'And glory!' Vorsulgha bellowed, before downing the contents in one gulp. He made a face as if he were dying, burped loudly and picked up a tray of food. 'Shikshi, Siantian food is small but good.'

Laughter broke out, and he burped just as the Fang Elder placed his hand on Laksha's shoulder and made for the door.

'Wait for me,' Vorsulgha called, helping himself to another platter.

It was then that the door the children were spying through was gently pushed open. David and Jack stumbled back and Maya scrambled out of their way, but it was too late. A shocked Prince Dyathen stood in the doorway. No one said anything until the other door closed behind Vorsulgha.

Maya dared not look up. Laksha had come up to the door and returned to the table without saying anything; she knew it was bad when adults didn't say anything.

Tommy flew to Maya's shoulder. 'How long have you been here?'

Maya didn't answer; it was a long time since she'd done something like this. She kept her gaze down and followed the boys into the banqueting hall. She couldn't tell how long they stood at the long table, but it felt like an awfully long time. No one said a word and that was agonising. She wanted to get it over with.

Tommy began: 'Shikshi Laksha, please accept my apologies for their behaviour. It's unlike them! Children, have you anything to say before I introduce you?'

Laksha raised his right arm. 'Rdita, I know who they are, but a discussion will have to wait for another time. First we must get these youngsters to safety.'

'Of … of course. I understand,' said Tommy in a low voice.

'Great, we'll get them to the Vault immediately,'

'The Vault? Is it that serious?' asked Tommy.

Laksha only nodded, already heading for the exit.

Seeing David fall in line, Maya followed, with Tommy on her shoulder and Jack a step behind. The boys seemed as puzzled as she was. What was the Vault? Had they done something so grave as to be condemned to it?

14

THE VAULT

The Science of magic.

They descended into the labyrinth of tunnels deep beneath the Centre, where even the sound of the yyena drums didn't penetrate. As they walked, Laksha asked Tommy to give him a quick introduction to Maya and Jack, and explain what had prompted her to travel so far with her wards. Tommy recounted the same story she'd told in the auditorium but left out many details, including the specifics of Maya's dream.

Eventually, Laksha stopped before a dusty wooden door.

'Ah, here we are – the Vault!'

David studied the door; it didn't differ from all the others they had passed for what seemed like forever. He didn't want to go to this 'Vault'; he wanted to stay with the monks to help. He had hoped Jack would resist, but he hadn't. *Too much to ask of rich kids who do everything they're told.* David had thought of asking his diary for help, but didn't want to use it with everyone around.

Prince Dyathen, Tommy, Jack and Maya crowded around the door. He looked at them in the gentle glow from Achanak: each wore a blank expression from their blurred trek through the maze of barren tunnels. All David recalled were the spiralling steps where Jack had asked Maya to be careful and the low tunnel where Prince Dyathen had to crouch. Jack took care of Maya all the way. David thought it was nice until he remembered her silly decision to free the ghost.

The noise of the dusty knob turning and the creak of the ancient door swinging open brought David back to the tunnel. Laksha had simply pushed the door; it didn't have any locks. *Not a vault!* Inside was a dark void.

'Interesting! Wait here! I'll get the lamps,' Laksha said, before slipping into the darkness.

Interesting? What did he mean? Something was up. They all waited warily until a warm glow grew slowly and poured into the tunnel. Laksha called their names. Cautiously, they entered one by one, with Prince Dyathen crouching low.

Inside was exactly what David suspected: anything but a vault. It was a longish, dry, dusty cave gouged from grey stone, with a high ceiling. The stagnant air was chilly and made him rub his arms as he looked around.

The cave was devoid of any of the chests or jewels expected in a vault. Along the far wall stretched a table full of bottles, scrolls, books, cups, daggers and odd pieces of armour, all arranged in straight lines. David had barely begun to look around when a commotion broke out.

It was Prince Dyathen. 'So many in one place! May I?' He half ran to a low, sturdy bench where an assortment of weapons rested.

His excitement caught everyone's attention. Achanak flew over to see and even Tommy, who had kept close to Maya, hovered up.

'It's Rytylr the Unstoppable ... and this: this is blazing Zyrmw! These two swords were lost a long time ago. How have they and these others come to be here?' The prince was smiling like a child lost in a toy shop.

'You know your weapons and their history, prince.' Laksha paused for a second. 'But this isn't the time to explore. The staff isn't here and we need to find out why.'

That's what was 'interesting'? David was impressed with Laksha's calmness. Three times now, he had not lost control the way the organisers of normal children's centres would have: first in the forest, then when they were caught spying and now. It was a novel experience to see an authority dealing with issues calmly.

'A brief explanation is in order,' said Laksha and closed the door.

David glanced at the last wall to his left, where an assortment of odd items stood: a chariot, a large floor-standing mirror, a statue, a couple of ornate seats, some shields, what seemed to be a rolled-up rug and two ornate earthen vessels.

'Apart from the monks and a select few, now you can enter the Vault. It cannot be breached by konjuring or weapons. Moreover, none of these objects are detectable outside; a konjuring vault is the safest place from any attack.'

It made sense to store the staff here, but why did they have to be locked up too? Jack and Maya were too nice to ask such awkward questions, but David wanted to be part of everything that was happening. It was all he wanted – to learn of things beyond science – so he mustered the courage to ask.

'But why do we need to stay here? Can't we help in some way? Achanak and I didn't do badly last time!'

'True, you were indeed helpful, but you were also lucky. You're to stay here for your own good, away from all the konjuring out there.'

David was prepared for this. 'But why only us? The other children aren't here. Why us?'

'I thought you'd ask that. The answer's simple: You're … special. I don't know why, exactly, but you are.'

'Special? How so?' David gave Jack and Maya a look.

'The other children were, and still are, petrified, but you weren't. That's why.'

'Petrified?'

'Yes. During such events, Siantians within the Centre are frozen, so to speak, a direct result of a spell that protects the

Konjiurian way of life. It prevents Siantians from learning about Konjiur, but it hasn't affected you, so you must be special … different. And this is why it's best that you are in here. At least until Shikshi Virath can clarify the matter.'

Laksha gave him a brief smile and David lowered his gaze; best not to challenge him too much.

'By the way, we are indebted to you for your timely intervention to help Virath: thank you. However—'

'I knew it – a BUT!' David thought.

'—had I known you'd be unaffected by the spell, I would've stressed upon you even more not to venture out last time; it was reckless, not to mention dangerous. This time, with three of you, it's even more risky.' Laksha looked at each one in turn. 'The best way the three of you can help, is by staying here, safe.'

Normally David would have continued disagreeing, but he didn't have the heart to argue after being told off twice. Silence descended until Laksha spoke once more.

'Rdita, I am pleased to have finally met your wards. Virath told me of his request to the Fangs to keep an eye on you and your twin.'

David listened with growing interest. Twins? And Virath knew of them too.

'It's just a pity the Fangs could not prevent the unexpected disappearance of their parents,' Tommy lamented. 'That is what led us to seek Shikshi Virath's advice. It was most bizarre.' She paused, looked around at everyone, and then added, 'But what was worse was their appearance in the mirror with our King and Queen.'

'What else do you know of the King and Queen of Konjiur?'

The prince sat up at their mention.

'Nothing, Shikshi, but …'

'But what? Speak up, Rdita. The King and Queen have indeed disappeared. It's not common knowledge, but it's true.'

'Well, there is the dream young Maya had; it confirms what Lord Vorsulgha speaks of, but it would be better if Maya tells it in her own words.'

Laksha turned to Maya, who gave a hasty description of her dream. She grew in confidence as she spoke, while the prince grew restless. By the time she concluded, Dyathen was unable to contain his fury. He leapt up and drew his sword.

'If that cowardly wraith crosses my path tomorrow, it will feel the wrath of my topaz blade.'

David pondered Maya's story. It matched Vorsulgha's and provided more information, but what did it all mean?

'These are unprecedented events for Siantia,' said Laksha. 'Unfortunately, only Shikshi Virath can explain this and how to help your parents.'

'Can't we call him?' Jack fished his phone out. 'Oh, of course, no network down here and it's almost out of power. Great!'

'Sadly, no. I wish it were possible ... After much deliberation and against my better judgement, I will share some grave news, so you children know not to leave the safety of the Vault.' He turned to Tommy. 'And to explain why your help with the healing spells is necessary, Rdita.'

This caught everyone's attention.

'Very few know what I am about to tell you, so before I say any more I need your word that this does not leave this cave. You must not speak of this, even amongst yourselves when outside the Vault.'

Everyone nodded.

'Shikshi Virath is here at the Centre, but he won't be fighting because he is injured. Last night, the joint attack by Aldrr and the ekoers placed him in a deep sleep. You must keep this secret—' Laksha looked at the prince and Tommy in turn

'—or else others will lose their confidence. It's also the reason why I've kept aloof from you all, to avoid answering questions about Shikshi Virath.'

Laksha's words had shocked them all into silence. David understood now why he hadn't spoken to them in the forest, and why he had avoided speaking about Shikshi Virath every time Lord Vorsulgha asked.

'Come now, we must leave to see what's keeping the monks from bringing Tabioak here.'

Slowly, Dyathen moved for the door. 'That really is a heavy blow, Shikshi! We'll need all the help we can get. Can't we engage the help of the matriarch, the dragon he has trapped in his Siantian device?'

Everyone turned to Jack.

'You mean the phone – no! That's not how it works. In any case, it's dead,' said Jack, retrieving the phone from his pocket.

'Loivissa?' asked Laksha 'You've met our Loivissa, the dragon?'

Tommy flew over instantly. 'By accident, Shikshi. We made an error and happened to be in her nursery. I had hoped to inform you of our adventures before now.'

'She's too old anyway, way beyond all this.'

'But her presence alone would have a great effect on everyone's morale,' the prince insisted.

'True, her presence on the battlefield would strengthen us, but no. Come, we should leave.'

The prince didn't argue. He followed Laksha and gestured to Tommy, who gave Maya a quick embrace before floating up before them.

'I must go; look after yourselves and of course Tabioak, when it gets here. I'll be back the moment I know what we need to do to find Mum and Dad, promise.' So saying, she flew to the prince's extended arm.

At the door, Laksha looked at each one of them in turn. 'Keep this door closed and stay inside. No repeat of your earlier mischief. Remember. Only a chosen few can come inside. Even if the doors open, they won't be able to enter. So stay—'

'Inside, got it,' David finished, nodding ever so angelically. *Just another glorified way to get us out of their way.*

Then Jack surprised him by erupting with excitement, waving his phone. 'I have an idea! It might not be much, but it is possible for Loivissa to be present.'

The prince's eyes gleamed.

'Explain?' Laksha asked, coming back inside.

'If you recharge my phone, you could use her roar.' Jack handed his phone to Laksha with hopeful puppy-dog eyes. 'Project Loivissa's cry from the speakers, towards the approaching attackers.'

Not bad, David thought. *It might just work!*

'Simple, yet it may just… I wonder! Remind me when we get back above,' Laksha gestured at the prince and Tommy with the phone. 'It seems Siantia may have a part to play. It will be unexpected, and if it works it could have far-reaching implications in all the other realms. Science complementing konjuring art; it's unheard of, but perhaps not after tomorrow.'

David chuckled quietly to himself. *How odd; I am looking for things beyond science and in this other place they don't even know of science.*

'If it works, the possibilities are endless. The yyenas must be susceptible to ultrasonic frequencies, if not more …'

'Yes! We could use ultrasound!' Jack added joyfully, looking at Maya. 'See – the magic of science.'

Maya gave him a look of total boredom; it was clearly a private joke between them, and it made David smile. *I suppose she's OK.*

'Well done, Jack,' Tommy applauded, hovering up over Dyathen. She seemed emotional, but she was so small it was hard to be sure.

The prince was waiting at the open door, eager to leave. 'Your idea helps even the odds, but we must still find the staff. Without it, we won't have anything to defend. Come along now. And children, remember to stay—'

'—inside!' they all chorused. Laksha glanced at them once more and walked into the dark tunnel. Dyathen winked before ducking under the doorway and following.

'I'll be back soon; wait for me!' Tommy said, flying out.

David turned to the twins and before they could move, the prince's long arm reached in and pulled the door shut.

15

BETRAYAL

Hope is a road travelled with faith.

Moments after Prince Dyathen closed the door, David began to explore the cave and Jack joined in. Despite their growing excitement, Maya felt lonely and empty without Tommy, like her first day of nursery school. Cocooned in the Vault but troubled by the hollow feeling, her thoughts turned to Mum, Dad and Virath. How did all this affect them? If only Virath was well, he could advise them. Maya tried to remember all she'd read, wracking her brain for a way to help Virath regain consciousness. It had to be a spell keeping him asleep. Worried, she perched on one of the ornate chairs to think. She smiled at Jack each time he turned in her direction. Soon he and David were holding daggers and challenging each other to lift the larger blades and poles.

'It's heavier than it looks!' Jack commented, holding a spear upright, like a knight.

'Let me see,' said David, carefully taking the lance from him.

Maya thought about seeing her face on the warrior who'd fought Torackdan in her dream. Was she the baddie? The image sent a chill through her being. It was the one thing she did not have the courage to tell anyone, not even Jack.

And what about when the warrior had spoken, in her own voice? He'd said that Torackdan had told the monkey to seek his kind in Siantia. The words haunted Maya. 'His kind' meant wizards. Seek wizards! Could it be that simple?

185

'Yes! Of course it is,' she said aloud, wanting to kick herself for not realising they'd been asking the wrong question. They should have been asking *who* the staff Tabioak was sent for, not why it was in Siantia. Yes! It sought a new master, a new wizard. Could it be Virath? She hoped not; he was injured. So who could be the new master? He or she could help in battle and save Virath. And if they saved Virath, then Virath could help them find Mum and Dad.

Immersed in her deductions, Maya didn't notice Achanak until he cried out. 'Help … help!'

She looked up with a start. 'What's the matter?'

'We must not play with these. They're powerful weapons, not toys,' Achanak complained.

Maya glanced at the boys. Jack was engrossed with a rustic bow. It wasn't big and didn't look special, but it held his attention. At the other end of the table, David had a short black rod with something on its end.

'Even that?' Maya asked.

'Fiery flames,' Achanak continued. 'Why else would they be here, in the Vault, if they weren't? David thinks what he's got is just a baton, but that could be a great mace, capable of causing earthquakes or who knows what. They don't know how to use them. We shouldn't play with them and, if they must, then something safe. Perhaps a book from that table, that too before the monks come… won't be able to once they're here.'

Maya grinned in acknowledgement.

'Coming?' Achanak whizzed across to the table at the far end, where he hovered over the items like an excited dragonfly. His eagerness was infectious. 'Oh flames, would you look at this necklace! And me in all these mirrors, so many of me … Looks magical!'

He'd lit the end of the cave with countless sparkling reflections and Maya momentarily forgot her apprehension. Achanak's glow bounced in all directions, creating a mystical vision. On the table he illuminated sat the most spectacular necklace she'd ever seen. She knew from Mum's necklaces that this was a combination of two different types: a choker and a princess necklace. Her eyes were glued to the many small, diamond-shaped mirrors along its length and the large tear-shaped crystal suspended from its centre.

'Magical!'

Attracted by the sparkles, David and Jack came over with their artefacts.

'That *looks* like it could be magical,' David commented. He held out the two-foot wooden rod in his grip. 'I've always wanted a baton. All policemen have one. Great for defending yourself if you're in trouble. Have you seen one being used?'

Maya shook her head.

'Oh, I'd show you but I need to practise; it's not as easy as the police make it seem. It's also great for keeping people at distance.' David slowly swung it in an arc. 'I thought this one might have some special power. Sadly, it's just a lump of wood. Jack's bow is the same – only a bow.'

'It's a great bow, though,' said Jack. 'It's light, made from some sort of horn; they're strong. I suppose it could have a longer range or faster release than normal, but it's too dangerous to try in here. Besides, I still need to find arrows.'

David pointed at the necklace. 'Would that have any powers?'

'Don't know,' Achanak interrupted, 'until someone tries it on. It could make the wearer stronger or braver … or more beautiful.'

Braver? Maya carefully lifted the necklace of mirrors. Jack leaned his bow against the table and helped her put it on.

Maya felt each small piece settle on her skin, from her shoulders to her neck and chest. Its size and weight made it feel more like armour then a necklace.

'Well, do you feel different? Stronger?' Achanak asked as Maya turned to catch her reflection in the full-length mirror by the other wall.

Maya shook her head. 'Not really except for ...'

'Yes?'

'Except for all the light shining straight into my eyes.'

'M², you really had me going there,' Jack laughed, and turned to Achanak. 'These objects – they might be ancient but they are just that: old. There's nothing different or magical about them.'

David nodded in agreement and Achanak dimmed in dismay. Maya felt his disappointment, but at least she had tried. It would have been nice if something had happened. 'I wish the wizard were here; I'm sure he could teach us how to use these. In fact, he could also help Virath,' she said.

'Who? What are you talking about?' Jack gawked at her.

David came closer; Maya noticed his unblinking blue stare in Achanak's sudden growing glow.

'The new wizard. He could help us understand these and help find Mum and Dad.'

'New wizard? You're not making any sense, M². Rewind a little.'

David nodded and Achanak flew up and down in agreement.

All of a sudden, Maya was hot and red-faced, wondering what if she was wrong.

'Go on, M². What did you mean?'

'OK, I sort of deduced something ...' she began slowly. 'But I'm not sure if it's correct.' Jack nodded. 'I remembered something from the dream, which helped me to understand why the staff might be here.'

Standing by the table and fiddling with the necklace, Maya reminded Jack, David and Achanak about the end part of her dream, the part they'd not concentrated on before. She was careful she did reveal the bit about seeing herself and hearing her own voice. Concluding with the words the warrior had uttered, she asked, 'What do you think?'

Achanak was the first to react, increasing in intensity. 'Fiery flames, it's the only flaming conclusion!'

'"Seek my kind": you are sure that's what this villain said?' Jack asked.

Maya nodded, seeing the scientist in him making queries.

'If that's the case, then your logic is undeniable, M^2. So who? Who is the wizard?'

'That's the bit I was trying to work out, Jack.'

They all descended into their thoughts, trying to resolve the question. Achanak rose towards the ceiling; Jack leaned against the table beside Maya, who toyed with the crystal on the necklace.

David strode up and down the length of the table, patting the baton on his palm. 'Not Virath …'

'Nope,' Jack shook his head.

'Laksha or one of the other monks?' asked Maya. She twisted the crystal in its setting and her heart jumped; she hadn't meant to do that and fiddled with the necklace, trying to right it. Luckily it wasn't difficult and she continued, 'Or someone else yet to come?'

As she spoke she realised something was wrong. Jack and David were both staring at her in shock. Achanak had also stopped his frolicking and hung in mid-air.

Looking down at the necklace she asked, 'What's wrong? Has something happened to the necklace? Did I break it?'

'M^2, don't move. Don't do anything.' Jack reached out to her. He placed his hand on her shoulder and sighed in relief. 'How did you do that? Did it feel any different?'

'Yeah? What did you do?' David chimed in.

'Do what?' She was self-conscious and afraid, like she'd been caught doing something she shouldn't have.

189

'Flames!' Achanak sparked up. 'Maya did it. I knew if someone could it would be you.'

Do what? Confused Maya peered at Jack.

'M², you vanished for a moment. You flickered on and off, like a light. Didn't you feel it? Or sense anything different?'

Maya shook her head.

'The necklace's power is invisibility,' said Achanak, hovering before her face. 'You must have done something. Think; what was it?'

'Invisibility ...' Maya shook her head. 'I accidently twisted the crystal. I thought I'd damaged it, so I quickly turned it back.'

'Twist it again, slowly this time,' Jack said with his hand firmly on Maya's shoulder.

Gripping the necklace with both hands, Maya gently turned the crystal. Everyone's expressions instantly changed to astonishment. 'What do you see?'

'Nothing,' Jack tightened his grip on her shoulder. 'I can see and feel my hand on your shoulder, but I can't see you.'

'You're invisible. That's freaky. How does it do that?' said David, bewildered.

Gradually, their surprise turned into delight and everyone praised Maya for her discovery, even if it was an accident. Jack and David both twisted the crystal themselves and made Maya appear and disappear. Encouraged by her discovery, the boys resumed their efforts in uncovering their weapons' abilities.

'Maybe these have a switch or something as well?' David said, examining his baton.

While Jack and David got busy searching, Maya's thoughts turned back to Mum, Dad and the wizard. She returned to the ornate seats by the chariot and sat there in quiet contemplation. Achanak joined her a little later, and eventually Jack and David straggled over too, frustrated after many attempts to decipher the weapons' magical powers.

David collapsed on the cave floor and placed the baton before him. 'Maya, you're right; if only we knew who the wizard is, he could show us how to use these.'

'Who could it be?' Jack set the bow against the other empty seat and joined Maya.

'It could be someone we don't know, someone yet to arrive,' said Maya.

'Aww, at this rate it could take forever,' Achanak complained. He turned to David. 'Why don't you just ask the book?'

Ask the book? What book? Maya could not quite believe what she'd heard.

Achanak flared briefly. 'Oh flames, what am I saying …' David didn't speak or move, but Achanak carried on. 'Forget what I said. Those pages only lead to trouble. I take it back; sorry.'

Maya couldn't contain her excitement. *It sounds just like the Book of No Words!* 'Achanak, this book you're talking about: is it a small book, leather-bound?' She used her fingers to indicate the size.

Achanak's intensity grew. 'Yes. You know of the troublesome thing then.'

'If it's the one I am thinking of, then yes.'

'Oh, it's quite strange. So far, each time David opened it, a glowing message has appeared. Spooky and mostly trouble.' Achanak turned to David. 'Right?'

'And,' Maya asked eagerly, 'does it have anything else written in it?'

'Not that I've seen. It's David's diary.'

'M^2, that sounds a lot like your favourite.'

'The Book of No Words.'

'Yes! And it wasn't at the exhibition.' Jack turned to David. 'Do you have it?'

191

Good one, Jack. She was pleased he'd asked the question on her mind.

'I should have told you, it was supposed to be a secret,' David said to Achanak as he reached into his back pocket. Apologising, Achanak went faint. David deliberately but reluctantly placed a small dark book on the table. 'It's fine, you weren't to know.' He turned to Maya. 'This is my diary.'

'*No Words*! Achanak, please, can you glow brighter so I may see it better?' Maya let out a long sigh at the sight of the one thing she'd coveted for so long.

'How do you know about it?' David narrowed his eyes.

'M^2 knows everything there is to know about it,' Jack answered. 'Right, M^2?'

Maya nodded, her eyes wide with a smile to match. *No Words* was within her grasp, no glass cabinet in the way. Resisting the urge to reach across and touch it, Maya told David everything she knew about it, from its description and how wizards used it before finally mentioning some rumours on its capabilities. 'That's everything in a nutshell! So does it talk to you?' It was the one question burning in her mind.

'For wizards … really?' David sat on the floor, looking lost.

Maya nodded, looking into his blue gaze and seeing that he found it hard to believe what she'd just said. It was then she recalled something else: Torackdan had eyes like David's, one bluer than the other.

With her attention torn between that blue and the book, she asked once more: 'Has it spoken to you?'

'Well, not spoken really. A word has appeared on the page all by itself. In any case, none of this makes any sense; if what you say is true about wizards, then why was I given it? I ain't one.'

Achanak floated down, right in middle of all of them. 'I knew you were a konjurer from the moment we met. Who else could have freed me? Perhaps you just don't know you are one!'

'Yes, it could be that. You might be the one the staff Tabioak was sent for,' Maya said in a low voice, then added more strongly, 'This may be nothing, just a coincidence from my dream, but Torackdan had eyes just like yours, one bluer than the other.'

'You never mentioned that before,' Jack said, staring at David. 'Who would have thought? I noticed your eyes too, and if that's the case, then it's more evidence that you are a sorcerer.'

David raised his eyebrows. 'My friends do call me 'Wiz,' but that's only because I've managed to escape from these homes.'

'And what about what Hopper said?' Jack reminded him. 'Didn't he call you 'master' before giving you the crystal?'

'Yes, I forgot about him,' said Maya. 'He found you – that was his mission.'

Achanak flew over to David. 'To me it makes sense! You are the one the staff was sent for. You're the—'

'—the new wizard!' Maya finished. She sat back, pleased with her deduction. She'd found the person who could help Virath and save Mum and Dad. Everyone looked at David. His face was still painted with disbelief. Seconds turned into minutes, and slowly a smile began to appear on his face. *A good sign,* Maya hoped.

She was mustering the courage to ask him if she could see the book when, without warning, the door swung open and a monk appeared. He stood there for a moment or two, swaying back and forth.

When he spoke, his voice was broken and filled with pain. 'Betrayed! A fellow shikshi has betrayed us. Laksha must be informed—'

Before anyone moved, he collapsed to his knees and fell face first onto the cold cave floor.

Jack rushed over to help. David shoved *No Words* into his back pocket and followed. In the few seconds it took the boys to drag the shikshi inside, Maya surprised herself by springing into action. She'd jumped off the heavy wooden chair and pushed it towards the boys with all her might. It was heavy and noisy against the stone floor, but Maya heaved it across the room, taking deep breaths. Within seconds the monk was able to sag into the seat, grunting with pain. He was in a bad state and there were crimson drops on his back

David knelt and looked into monk's blurry eyes. 'The staff – where is it? Do you have it?'

'He's hurt; let him rest!' Maya pleaded.

Jack was on David's side. 'M^2, we need to know.'

'Taken by the other shikshi,' the monk managed. 'Taken to the warlord.' He tried to raise his arm.

Do you trust your monks? Lord Vorsulgha's warning flashed through Maya's mind. 'Why?'

'Coward wants to save himself. I must go to inform Lakshhh …' the monk's voice trailed off and his arm fell.

Fearing the worst, Maya asked, 'He's not d-dead, is he?'

They all looked at each other. No one wanted to check, but Jack slowly reached for the monk's wrist. Maya watched him intently as he felt for a pulse.

'He's alive, only passed out.'

David sat back in relief, Maya sighed and Achanak floated away towards the other end of the cave, muttering to himself.

'All's lost … all's lost.'

The words struck Maya. 'What now? The staff is gone.'

'No, it's not! He can't have gone far. And I have this.' David held up his baton. 'Jack, you have the bow; we could stop him. I mean, imagine if they get the staff … Lord Vorsulgha said it mustn't fall in their hands.'

'So,' Jack quickly intervened. 'We could stay here and do nothing, as Laksha instructed or raise the alarm as the monk requested. Or, as you say…'

Ready with his baton, David said, 'I say if we find the betrayer before he gets too far, we have a chance at stopping him. There are four of us and only one of him.'

Maya didn't like that plan, but she didn't like the idea of staying and doing nothing either.

'Whatever you do, don't ask the book,' called Achanak from the other end of the room. 'It's already created trouble twice.'

Of course that's the answer: ask the book. Maya thought.

A moment later, David was reaching for his pocket.

'Don't … don't tell me I didn't warn you,' Achanak cautioned loudly.

Maya moved closer, eager to see *No Words* being used. David set the baton down and took his time opening the book. A glowing script appeared, and Maya's curiosity gave way to bewilderment. At the top of the page were two words: 'Save staff'. Below them were six dots, four blue and two red.

'I knew it would work,' Maya said, pointing at the page. 'But what are the dots supposed to mean?'

'Dunno. Never had them before,' David shrugged.

'Dots?' Achanak flew over.

'Did you see that? The blue dot just moved closer to the other three around the red one,' Maya said pointing.

'Look at that red one; it keeps on zigzagging.' Achanak floated down, illuminating the pages.

'Wait a minute!' said Jack. 'The four blue dots are us. That means the red dot is—'

'—the other monk!' they all cried out.

'Wow, it's a live map!' said Achanak. 'With this, we can track the monk.'

'Jack, it'll soon disappear off the page,' said David, indicating the moving dot. 'We should leave.'

Jack glanced at his bow and nodded. No words were spoken, and yet a plan to recover the staff had been agreed upon. David reached for his baton and Jack hastily removed his robe. He took off the backpack he'd been hiding under it and urged Maya to wear it underneath the front of her robe. 'It'll be your chest armour, just like Loivissa advised.' He turned to David. 'How's your arm?'

He flexed it twice slowly at first before nodding with a smile. 'Much better.'

'Good to see. Let's find few arrows.'

Maya should have been happy. They were going to save the staff and give it to David, the person whom she had concluded could help Virath and ultimately help them find Mum and Dad. But she was apprehensive about disobeying Laksha and venturing out into the dark tunnels. And most of all, she wasn't happy to leave the injured monk alone. It was only when the boys promised they'd send help as soon as they could did she feel bit more at ease.

16

IMAGINATION GAME

Shortcuts are not always pleasant.

In the gloomy tunnel, David and Jack dropped their weapons in annoyance and stared at the four blue dots on the otherwise blank page in despair. They had come to another dead end. The passage they'd hoped would lead them to the traitor monk had unexpectedly ended in solid rock face, and the staff was rapidly moving away.

Maya was breathing hard to recover from their fast pace. They had travelled quickly but warily through the confusing labyrinth of unlit tunnels, stopping briefly at every junction to decide which passage to take. Both Jack and David had been confident of tracking the monk with *No Words*; their strategy was simply to reduce the distance between their four blue dots and the red one on the page. However, navigating blindly with no map had only favoured the traitor. They had ventured up blocked tunnels and wasted precious time backtracking.

Frustrated with their decisions, Maya left Jack and David to evaluate their decreasing options and wandered away to the end of the tunnel, wracking her brain for a solution. In the low light from Achanak, she prodded the walls of the blocked passage for any openings or holes. As she fiddled with a knob of rock, a loud voice said, 'Do you mind? That's my nose.'

Startled, Maya jumped and rushed back to Jack. Alarmed, all four huddled together in the middle of the tunnel looking at the poorly lit dead end. Afraid, Achanak began to disappear.

What a good idea, Maya thought, remembering the necklace she wore.

But as darkness encroached, Jack said in a low, firm voice, 'Achanak, pull yourself together!'

It dislodged the fleeting idea from her mind and made Achanak brighten up.

'Show yourself! Who are you?' Jack called, primed with his bow and one of three arrows David had discovered. David tucked *No Words* away and readied himself, curling his fingers around the baton.

In the dark silence they waited, staring at the shadowy rock ahead until the energetic voice returned.

'Lost ones aren't in any position to make demands. Navigating my tunnels isn't child's play.'

'Who are you?' asked Jack.

'The one you chase retraces his steps, searching for a different route.'

David reached for his diary and checked. It was true; the red dot was heading back.

'How do you know that?' asked Jack, seeing the dot drawing closer.

'I witnessed the ghastly deed myself! A treacherous act that consumes him. Now he runs in fear, stumbles and runs some more. He is in a rush to escape, searching for the mount exit! I can help …'

Jack interrupted. 'Mount exit? What's that? Why would you help us? And how? No, first show yourself. Where are you?'

'Yeah! Come out,' David added.

'My, my, if only you opened your eyes as much as you do your mouths, you would have seen me by now.'

'Where are you?'

'Very well. Look at the rock the little lass leaned against. She pressed my nose and yet offered no apology.'

Achanak brightened and floated closer to the tunnel wall but snapped back like an elastic band when he saw the rock.

One by one, they looked and were astonished, for a young face with soft features protruded from the rock's surface, like the beginnings of a statue.

Jack and David lowered their weapons, while Maya marvelled at the spectacle before them. How did it speak? Where did the sound come out? Did it move? Did it have arms and legs as well, or was it just a face? After everything they'd already seen, she knew she shouldn't be so amazed, but she was. Here they were, lost in a maze and bargaining with a rock to see if it could help.

'Kuts with a K is my name, short for "shortcut"!' the face said, looking at them in turn. 'I've seen fire genies before but the little Siantians – now there's a first. Who are you?'

'Kuts! Fiery flames!' Achanak approached, growing brighter. 'The mischievous lot who control the tunnels; I've heard of you too. You must have a proper name; Kuts isn't your name, is it?'

'You know it?' asked David.

Achanak turned around briefly. 'No, I've only heard of their mischievous doings.'

'Fine,' the face conceded. '"Kuts" is what we are known as to all except our own kind; to them I am "D" but to you I am still Kuts. Now, are you going to introduce yourselves or simply waste time while the thief slips away?'

'Wasting time,' Achanak snapped, 'is what we would do, if we listened to you. Come, let's go everyone. Come on.'

'We are playful, genie, but also known for honour and the integrity of our word. It's been a long time since I have spoken to anyone. Little Siantians – so young and brave, have faith, for I can help you catch the murderer.'

'Murderer?' Maya blurted.

'Well, I was jumping ahead, but he will be soon enough if the injured monk doesn't get help.'

Maya sighed.

'Let's not waste time then, how? How can you help us?' Jack stood tall.

'Why, I thought the clue was in my name: as a Kuts, I can reveal shortcuts.'

'He's wasting time; we should go!' Achanak retreated down the passage and waited.

But Jack continued speaking to Kuts. 'OK, explain what you're going to do, please.'

'Down here there are many rifts and cavities, and the tunnels wind a long way around. Then there are bridges that link the openings and rifts and form shortcuts. However —'

'More time wasting!' Achanak called.

'—only those of worth are able to cross those bridges.'

'If you're the guardian, why can't you just allow us to pass?'

'Good question, but I don't know why. All I know is that a riddle gives access to the secret bridge, and only the worthy are able to cross it successfully.'

'And how do you know if someone is worthy?'

'Oh, there's a challenge and whoever complete it is deemed worthy.'

Maya didn't know what to think. Kuts' offer was tempting but Achanak's concerns were equally important.

Jack turned to the retreating fire genie. 'You're not happy?'

'Don't trust it. It's a time waster.'

'Your quarry is getting further away,' Kuts reminded them. 'He's lost, but still some distance away.'

'Let's go!' Achanak inched back into the tunnel. 'Or ... we could ask the you-know-what?'

They took a peek at *No Words*. It showed the same message, except the red dot was almost off the page. Then it disappeared altogether.

Achanak repeated his warning but this time it wasn't helpful. With no map and no red dot to track, there was nothing they could do. Maya checked the armlet under her robe; it wasn't glowing green, so Kuts probably wasn't a danger to them. Reluctantly, they agreed to accept his help. Jack stepped forward and introduced them all.

'Great to make your acquaintance.' Kuts' lively voice rang out as he looked at each one. 'Remember, you have to answer a riddle for access and complete a challenge to get to your betrayer. Understood?'

'Perfectly,' Jack answered.

A riddle! Maya rubbed her hands in eager anticipation.

'And your question is: What binds two people yet touches only one? I'll give you a little help: it's not a wedding ring I seek.'

'This isn't a trick, is it?' Achanak hovered right in Kuts' face.

'We're playful, not treacherous, fire genie.'

'Like a ring but not …' Maya wondered aloud.

'Think carefully but not for too long,' warned Kuts. 'You have exactly one moment.'

'One moment? How long's that?' Jack asked.

'Oh, ninety seconds to be precise.'

Achanak huffed in annoyance but the children were lost in their thoughts and didn't react. The genie became restless and flew around randomly. 'Any clues?' he asked Kuts.

'Thought you'd never ask,' Kuts sighed. 'The one you chase carries the object used to create them. Yes! That's a good one.'

Everyone turned and looked at each other. 'A staff?' Jack and David said together.

'I think I know!' Maya said eagerly.

Kuts began to count down. 'Time's nearly up, ten, nine, eight, seven, careful now – your first answer—'

'Are you certain?' Jack asked. Maya nodded.

'Hurry,' David prompted.

Achanak rushed in closer as Kuts said 'three'.

'A spell! That's what binds two people but affects only one,' said Maya.

'—one, zero. Time's up!' Kuts stopped with its eyes closed.

Suspense mounted in the silence. Maya began to doubt if she was correct.

'A spell,' said Kuts. 'That's quite …'

They waited and waited.

'RIGHT!'

'Yes! Yes! Yes!' The boys punched the air before high-fiving Maya.

Maya smiled. *Yes.* She took a deep breath and brushed her brown locks back, ready for the next part.

'And now for the challenge! You must play a game – a game one of you knows well. Ready?'

The stone slab holding Kuts' face began to rise with a grinding noise, and they felt a light breeze as the cavity beyond came into view. It was a small passage, just big enough to allow them to enter in single file.

'Aah … feels good to open that doorway after so many years. See you on the inside. The betrayer you seek rests, so be quick.' With that, Kuts disappeared as though someone on the other side of the stone had stepped away.

They hesitated at the entrance to the smaller tunnel. Increasing his intensity, Achanak assumed the lead and flew in. Pulled by his glow, they followed one by one: David went first, gripping his baton, Maya went a step behind and Jack came last.

Inside, the air was cold, stagnant and thick with the recently disturbed dust. Maya traced her hands along the tunnel wall on either side and concentrated on each step she took. She felt safer in this smaller tunnel where Achanak's light wasn't lost. Ahead, David moved cautiously towards an opening from which a brighter light emanated. Occasionally, he waved his baton and picked at his face, but Maya didn't question what he was doing. She already knew the reason for his peculiar behaviour: the near-invisible webs of her greatest phobia were wrapping around his face. *Think of other things.* She distracted herself with what the challenge might be. *Something one of us knows. How does Kuts know that?* Its voice suddenly echoed through the tunnel.

'Quickly now!'

David didn't rush though; he slowly stepped out from the tunnel and immediately called out a warning: 'Careful! The path ends.'

Moments later, all four of them stood on a foot-wide stone ledge. In the bright glow from crystals set higher up in the rock face, they looked on, mesmerised. They had emerged into a vast triangular rift in the earth, where their ledge gave way to a bridge of rope and wooden planks. Looking around, they saw three more bridges to their right, all leading to an opening at the apex of the triangle. Three more bridges intersected these longer ones and connected them to other caves.

'Shortcuts?' questioned David.

Maya shook her head. To her it resembled something else: an abandoned spider web hanging in the blackness. She searched above and below, but the light from the crystals didn't penetrate far in either direction.

'Welcome to the imagination game!' Kuts announced, appearing above the cave at the apex of the triangle. 'A game the lass who answered the riddle likes. Please tell us more about all this. How do you play?'

A game I like! Maya thought. How did Kuts know? Beside her, Jack counted the number of caves aloud. She knew the answer before he finished – eleven. Suddenly self-conscious, she asked, 'Can you read my mind?'

'I wish, little one … Maya, right?'

She nodded.

'You've done all this, and that's why it's called the imagination game. Your thoughts, your imagination has created all this.'

'Flaming flares! Is this one of your tricks?' Achanak flew straight over to Kuts and, without waiting for a response, began interrogating him about all the tunnel entrances.

'Check the bridges themselves: they look old and worn,' David pointed out anxiously. Seeing the rope bridges hanging loosely in the crevasse, Maya understood his unease. 'This is like no game I've seen! You couldn't have imagined something simpler like chess or checkers?'

It was then that Maya realised what the game was. Covering her mouth with both her hands, she slowly said, 'It's like Bagh-Chal, the Nepalese board game. Remember Jack; it's the present I got. Yeah … those intersections where the bridges meet … and the cave entrances are all landing spaces for the pieces.'

'Oh no, not the one with the …' Jack groaned.

'With what?' David asked eagerly.

Reluctantly Maya said, 'Three tigers and fifteen goats.'

'On that? No way!' David laughed.

Maya continued in a calm, low voice, 'Actually, it is similar to checkers. The goats have to stalemate the tigers to win, but if the tigers take five goats, then they win.'

'Sounds simple, except maybe for the tigers,' said David.

'It isn't!' Maya explained the rest of the rules: where the tigers and goats began, and how each piece could only move one junction, except when a tiger was catching a goat.

'And is capturing the goat same as checkers, if the point beyond is free?' asked David.

'Yes; if a goat's unprotected, the tiger can jump two spaces and capture it.' Maya smiled, seeing Jack and David grasp the basics.

Achanak returned after inspecting the bridge. 'I have one question.'

'Yes?'

Looking confused and turning around like a dog chasing its tail, Achanak asked, 'Which exit is the shortcut?'

Kuts fired up like an engine coughing into life. 'Ah, the shortcut I will reveal upon your victory. Don't worry about it; get the pieces in place and start! The quicker you win the quicker you catch the traitor.'

An instant later, coloured lights descended from the darkness above. A luminous red butterfly the size of a dog landed on the nearest intersection. The majestic creature captured all their attention. One by one, butterflies with unreal, vibrant colours descended like fairies and came to rest on the bridge intersections and at the entrances of the caves. Maya was in awe.

'But where are the goats?' asked David. 'Didn't you say there were goats?'

'This is the imagination game,' Kuts explained. 'Both the game and the pieces are from Maya's imagination. It seems she must like butterflies, so we have butterflies instead of goats. Beautiful butterflies, just as you imagined, I am sure.'

'That would mean,' Maya thought out aloud, 'that instead of tigers there'll be something I don't like!'

'That's right!'

'What's that? What don't you like?' Achanak asked, rushing to her.

Maya didn't reply; her eyes were fixed above, searching the abyss. Jack nudged her with his elbow. She followed his gaze and caught movement at the opening beneath Kuts. She dared not breathe as her greatest fear climbed up from the shadows below: a black spider even bigger than the butterflies. It was shiny, with sharp, pointy legs, a dark foe ready for combat.

Instinctively, Maya stepped back, retreating into the tunnel. Jack grabbed her hand and gave it a gentle squeeze. Strengthened by his support, she forced herself to stand and face the spiders.

'Twelve; there're only twelve butterflies. Shouldn't there be more?' asked David, his finger wagging as he counted.

'And the three of you,' said Kuts. 'Now get into your positions.'

Maya took a deep breath. *Be brave. You can do this for Mum and Dad.* Jack turned and looked into her eyes. She didn't wait for him to say anything; instead she forced a smile.

'That's the spirit, M^2; ready to stalemate them.' She nodded, and he wrapped her in a tight hug. Then he and David carefully edged across the thin ledge to the two vacant spots at the adjacent cave entrances.

Maya studied all the players. Everyone was in position: *time to start*. No sooner had she thought it than the spider closest to them got up and skittered to an empty intersection. The mass of pointy legs moved quickly, snapping and tapping on the warped wooden planks of the bridge until the spider arrived at its new position and abruptly settled. The movement left them all unnerved. Breathing hard, Maya watched the bridge bouncing up and down. Each ripple fed her anxiety.

Luckily Achanak jetted back to her and forced her into action. She gave the boys another look and began to study the bridges.

'Just call out the moves, M^2,' Jack said.

'Just like checkers, Maya,' David shouted. 'Come on; let's show them how it's done.'

She smiled nervously, knowing all eyes were on her and conscious of her every move. She stood on tiptoe like a ballerina, struggling to see all the butterflies and study all the intersections. Butterflies covered six of the entrances. Of the remaining five colourful creatures, four were on the first four intersections nearest to them. Only one was on the second intersection, but it was safe for now.

Just make a simple move to start and make sure it's covered.

'You,' she began in a cracking voice, pointing at the bright green butterfly furthest away. 'Move to that junction there.'

The butterfly came to life, flicked its wings and flew the short distance to the junction Maya had pointed to. It was magical sight, but a moment later a *tap-tap-tap* noise distracted her and the bridge began to bounce. One of the spiders was on the move. It came closer until only the royal blue butterfly in front of Maya separated her from the monster.

Invasion of the big spiders: The news headlines flashed across Maya's mind, and she thought of pointy legs, sharp fangs and poisonous darkness. She clenched her fists. She saw Jack calling but didn't hear anything. She turned around and found David waving at her, but she was locked in her own world. *Why don't they come to help me?* She wondered, *Are they stuck to the spot?*

Something rushed at her: It was Achanak. His sudden movement snapped her to attention and sounds rushed back. Jack and David repeatedly called her name. Bravely, she turned and looked at them in turn, realising that they hadn't come to her aid because it would have been interpreted as a move and wasted the turn. Once more, she nodded bravely, smiled and contemplated her next move.

****

A few turns later, Maya had managed to get the junction before her free and courageously stepped onto the bridge. It was an unsettling feeling, like being on a small dinghy, rising and falling on waves of darkness. Jack looked concerned with her bold move, so she explained her plan.

'We need to occupy that entrance underneath Kuts; it's crucial. Need to move everyone that way.' She thought of it as manoeuvring her army, moving them all in a tight formation to capture the opening underneath Kuts. Like a tide, the spiders advanced and retreated, attempting to find weaknesses in her defence. Growing confident, Maya peeked at Jack and David; they seemed pleased with her progress. Soon she had moved them onto the suspended walkways, but with all three on the bridges, the swinging and the bouncing became more pronounced. The continuous movement made her feel sick and she neglected to cover the green butterfly. And she soon regretted her oversight: the closest spider moved in and revealed its two fangs, like the open arms of death.

Maya expected the worst, but at the last moment their foe began to roll the butterfly in silvery white webbing. They watched, helpless, while the spider went about its business, silk dripping like saliva from a rabid dog. It rolled the green butterfly again and again, cocooning it. Maya could see the fear in the delicate creature's eyes increasing with the bridge's bounce. Unable to bear its look, she gripped the ropes for support. Finally the spider finished and lowered the mummified victim into darkness, leaving it to dangle from the bridge before continuing to the next intersection, where it settled down as if nothing had happened.

Maya's heart was jumping; all she wanted to do was stop and sit down, holding her head in shame. She had let the butterfly down. She wanted to give up but she didn't. Fighting hard, she willed herself on. 'Still possible … it's possible!'

'Only one lost so far. Not bad, little one, not bad!' Kuts said, like a coach. 'Conquer your fear. Learn to face adversity.'

That's what Dad would say: face your fears. Maya smiled, took a deep breath and continued.

A few moves later, Maya was one intersection away from the apex entrance but couldn't progress further unless the spider there vacated that spot. She repeated the same move in the hope that the spider would move to another intersection. Engrossed in her plan, she failed to spot another attack and lost the yellow butterfly. Seeing the second cocoon being lowered into the abyss, Maya felt her world go grey. *They trusted me. Oh, I'm so ...*

'The staff, remember, and your parents,' Achanak whispered into her ear.

'Yes!' Maya shook herself from the thoughts, bit her lip and took a deep breath. 'Can you stay here and keep reminding me of that?' And then she said to herself, 'Right, any more losses and this will be a long game. No more!'

With renewed determination, she made her moves, always checking twice before committing. The game soon descended into an intense battle, butterflies, children and spiders, all in the suspended oasis of light. It got increasingly difficult to spot new moves, but Maya persisted. And then, out of nowhere, a solution presented itself.

'That's it.' Maya made a move and with that it was all over.

'Well done, little ones; I believe you've won,' Kuts announced.

Exhausted and relieved, Maya slumped where she stood and caused a panic. The bridge began to wobble wildly. Holding their weapons, Jack and David ran cautiously to reach her. Achanak hung before her for a moment, then called out, 'She's fine!'

Maya didn't respond. The spiders stole away into the black void below. The butterflies flicked their wings a few times and, led by the red one, all rose into the darkness above, like colourful fairies floating to their sky palace.

The spectacle briefly distracted Jack and David, but then they were by her side, fussing and congratulating her.

'Well done once more!' Kuts joined in. 'And now you have a decision to make, Maya. You won, but you lost two butterflies. However, should you want to save them, I will give you one last chance to do so.'

'Save those two?' Maya echoed, peering over the side at the two dangling cocoons.

'Yes, but wait: to save them, you will lose two spaces.'

'More trickery,' Achanak whispered in Maya's ear. Then, loudly, 'What does that even mean? Speak plainly.'

'Genie, learn to trust. Kuts are both honourable and kind. I will keep my word. And offer this rare chance to save the two you lost by trading two tunnels.'

'Meaning?' asked Achanak.

'Meaning if you want to save the butterflies, I will lead you to a point two tunnels behind the monk. Then it is down to you to catch him. Otherwise, I can lead you right to where he rests, but then these two will be lost forever. Hurry now; choose wisely.'

They all looked at each other. Jack and David spoke together: 'Catch the monk!'

'Fiery aye! Get the staff!' Achanak agreed, glowing brightly.

Maya was thankful that the boys had decided, but she had mixed emotions. She wanted to save the staff, but her eyes kept returning to the two cocoons. She was unable to forget the butterflies, especially the green one's look of despair. *She trusted me and I let her down.*

Kuts interrupted her thoughts. 'Sorry, boys; it's only binding if Maya says it.'

Me? Maya's mind battled with the decision. *staff ... Green butterfly ... staff .... Butterflies ...* A few seconds passed, and she realised everyone was glaring at her, waiting for her answer.

'Jack, I'm really sorry but ...'

He was already nodding. Beside him, David rolled his eyes.

'I don't think it's right to not help if we can,' she explained. 'And it's only two tunnels; we could catch up, right? I think, save the two—'

'Wait a flickering second,' Achanak interrupted, flying over to Maya. 'Get the staff first. We can come back and help the butterflies. They'll be here.'

'I agree. You've been kind once and that didn't help us,' said David. 'We aren't a charity that we help everyone we meet. Our mission is finding the staff and your parents, remember?'

Maya knew they were right; but she couldn't bring herself to simply abandon the two butterflies. She turned to Kuts. 'Save them.'

'Right then, all settled! Off they go and you fall back by two tunnels.'

They watched the butterflies emerge from the webbing. Maya gave a little smile of satisfaction but she could see David wasn't pleased.

'More delaying tactics,' Achanak snapped at Kuts.

Unfazed, Kuts said, 'A wise decision, young Maya. Wise indeed. Now quickly, come through the entrance near me, for the traitor grows restless. Follow my voice.'

Annoyed, David moved off without waiting another moment. Maya took one last glance before following, with Jack close behind. The bridge shifted like waves; it was difficult to run but she persisted. Stepping off was different but Maya didn't stop. Led by Achanak, they continued straight into the dark tunnel. Kuts' voice guided them through the tunnels that wound left and right, up spiralling steps and through to a larger tunnel. Maya was breathless by the time they got there, but she didn't complain. They spotted Kuts in a rock by a small cove only two steps deep. It looked like someone had begun to dig and then stopped abruptly.

Kuts whispered, 'Right, on the other side of this cove you'll find a tunnel. Turn left, head straight down, turn right at the next junction and right once more. He's not far!'

They were all keen to move on and did not respond. Maya's mind had already raced ahead to the moment they caught up with the betrayer, but Kuts brought her back to the present.

'Maya, you made good choices. Thinking of others and not just yourself is a strength only a few have. Believe in yourself!'

'Yes, yes,' David muttered.

'Thank you for your help,' Maya added politely.

Fading, Kuts said, 'Slip out once the gap is wide enough. Good luck!'

As the face vanished, a section of the rock within the cove began to move outwards like a door swinging open.

17

MORNING OF THE BATTLE

Sometimes the fight picks you. For Siantia!

Maya stole through the narrow gap without hesitating. She didn't want to cause more delays and let the betrayer escape, along with their chance of saving Mum and Dad. She couldn't bear to imagine it. A few steps away, David was already scouting out the larger tunnel under Achanak's faint glow. Waiting for Jack, she scanned the darkness. She didn't like it; it felt different from the other tunnels. Still, the moment Jack stepped through, she felt guilty for delaying them and forced herself to take deliberate steps after David and Achanak. She caught David at the end of the tunnel, where he stood with his back against the rock wall. Achanak floated dimly by his shoulder.

'OK let's keep moving,' Jack whispered as they drew alongside.

'Wait!' David whispered back sharply. Maya's heart jumped. 'Surprise and caution are our best chance. Plus a lot of luck! Believe me, I've escaped from many homes. We'll need to get as close to the monk as we can. Achanak, you'll have to be invisible.'

Achanak nodded, waning.

'Fly head and come back to warn us if there's any danger or if you spot him. We'll need to be quiet. Wait for your eyes to get used to the darkness and then we go.'

Maya remembered her necklace. *I can be invisible too.* She reached for the crystal.

'I could accompany Achanak,' she suggested timidly. 'Remember this?' She indicated the necklace.

'No, M^2, that monk's dangerous.'

'True, which is why two of us will sneak close by. One looking out while the other grabs the staff …' Maya's night vision adjusted and, turning to Jack, she added, 'Don't you see? I'll be perfect for this. Achanak can't grab the staff but I can. I'll simply walk up to it and take it while he keeps on the lookout.'

'No, M^2, if something happens I won't be able to get to you in time.'

'It's a good plan,' David countered. 'Why didn't I think of it? Jack, all Maya has to do is get the staff and run back this way.' He placed his hand on the baton. 'If he were to follow, we can take care of him, can't we? But don't worry; he won't even realise we've snuck the staff from him.'

Jack didn't look happy, but he was eager to avoid wasting more time.

Maya added hastily, 'If two of you aren't enough, Achanak and I will join in – surely he can't fight all of us.'

'You'll join in, M^2?'

Maya knew he'd say that, knowing she didn't like confrontation. She nodded and said, 'For Mum and Dad!'

'And for Siantia!' Achanak's voice came from above.

'I like the odds: four against one for Siantia,' said David.

Jack reluctantly agreed. 'For Mum and Dad … and Siantia of course.'

****

Minutes later, Maya turned the crystal on her necklace and materialised in the middle of a well-lit tunnel. She was standing before steps leading to an opening at the side of the tunnel. Light and fresh air poured in. Achanak appeared at her shoulder while Jack and David came running, looking for the monk. He was supposed to be here, resting, but it looked like her kindness in saving the butterflies had allowed him time to escape and cost them the staff.

'He may not have gone far. Hurry!' David drew his baton and cautiously headed up the steps. Maya thought he sounded upset.

'He's right; come on. This must be the mount exit.' Jack stopped beside her, ready with an arrow in one hand and the bow in the other.

With a sense of fresh hope, Maya mustered some courage and began up the steps. The rhythmic sound of stamping and the yyena drums hit her, but she clenched her fists and continued.

The light outside was bright and painful to look at. It took a few seconds to get used to. The air drifting in thought the doorway was cold, foul and smokey. At the top of the stairs, it got colder and the stench of the smoke grew stronger, forcing Maya to draw her hood up and cover her nose.

'Another bad smell?' Achanak floated close by, looking all amused and confused at her discomfort.

Resisting the urge to cough, Maya nodded. They had emerged on a slope that gently fell away to meet the grassland. A little to their left was the lake: it was placid and sparkled in the first rays of the low morning sun. Maya didn't dwell on any of that; she went to see what Jack and David were gaping at and was shocked at the devastation before them.

Previously green, gentle grasslands were charred and scarred by dying campfires, hurled rocks and broken trees trunks. Smoke rose in columns, spiralling like mini-tornadoes to meet the scattering clouds above. Hidden in between the swirls, she noticed a new structure with sharp, curved pinnacles.

'Looks worse than any homeless camp I have seen,' David whispered. 'What's that there?' He pointed at the menacing pinnacle.

PM Perry

'Where's the Gate?' Maya added quietly, but a little movement by a campfire below caught their attention before anyone could answer. A short distance down the slope, a tall, hooded monk stood facing the mysterious spires.

'He's got a staff in his hand,' hissed Jack. 'That must be him! Come on.'

'Slowly, one at a time,' said David, head cocked for suspicious sounds. After listening for a few seconds, he said to Jack, 'The commotion sounds distant, but a few of those brutes - the qwrks might be lurking. Be careful. Once we're close, you distract him while I snatch the staff.'

'Flicking flames! You've forgotten how dangerous last time was. We won't be lucky every time,' Achanak warned.

'Achanak!' David shot back. 'Stop scaring us. Let's go quickly now, before he goes too far.' David advanced warily with the baton ready.

Jack followed. Both were tense now that the staff was finally in their sights. With measured steps, Maya ventured out last; she didn't want to be responsible for alerting the monk to their presence.

Outside, the air was crisp; dew began to seep through her shoes. The distant march was loud; roars mingled with banging metal rushed at them. They crouched when a large shadow glided past.

'Ekoers!' David and Achanak whispered in alarm.

Unblinking, Maya watched the creature silently swoop down and scoop up the monk in mid-flight. In a flash, both the monk and the staff were gone.

Disheartened, they gawked at the creature heaving and flapping heavily through the smoke, towards the dark spires. No one uttered a word, but Maya suspected what they thought: if she hadn't insisted on being kind to the butterflies, they might have had the staff by now. Upset, she got up and ran off, past the opening they had emerged from, through shin-high grass to the top of the hillock and towards the growing noise.

'M²!' Jack chased her.

At the top of the mound, Maya froze in disbelief at the scene before her. Jack, David and Achanak all crowded around her in shock. In the morning sun's golden rays, they found the Gate and Centre under siege in the distance. A wide black and grey wave was moving towards a thin brown line of monks who stood defiantly in its path at the base of the platform. High above, ekoers flew in circles like vultures, darting through patches of cloud. The wave was gathering momentum, roaring and rolling forward. It approached the base of the platform. A jagged line of foot soldiers spearheaded the march, while howling and laughing Yyena riders bore down from the flanks.

Entranced, David and Jack began to wander down the little hill. Maya wanted to retreat.

'So few against so many ...' she said as she yanked on her hood.

'M², hope Laksha managed to use my idea?' Jack said, glancing back at her.

It looked as though the wave was within touching distance of the thin line of monks, when a much louder roar tore through the grassland. It was a relaxed growl, deep and heavy. Maya recognised it immediately.

'Loivissa!'

'The dragon!' David moved forward to see the effect.

It was instantaneous: the front of wave came to a crashing halt.

'Science!' Jack punched the air. 'A simple recording played over the speakers has done the trick. See, science is useful.' He turned proudly towards Maya.

'Nice one, Jack.' Maya smiled at him but a moment later he made a horrible face of dread and ran towards her.

'Duck, M²! Get down! There's an ekoer!'

'Duck?' Too late she felt a jolt, next something tightened around her chest; it was a large claw. Then she rose off the ground. Confused, she looked on in terror before screaming, 'Help, Jack!'

Jack leapt, trying to catch her leg, but she was just beyond his reach. She wriggled, turning and twisting, trying to break free. Amongst the chaos, she caught many fleeting images: the large talons that gripped her; David hurling his baton only to have it tumble down without hitting anything; a couple of fireballs from Achanak.

For a moment, the ekoer lost its momentum and its grip loosened as it sank back to the ground. Maya tried to break free and saw Jack grab onto the ekoer's other hind leg.

'Got you! Grab Maya, David! Weigh it down!' Jack shouted.

The beast let out a terrifying cry. Covering her ears, Maya shot Jack a panicked glance; he was struggling to hold on when the creature beat its leathery wings and dived down the mound and towards the Centre. She caught a glimpse of David on the ground as the ekoer passed him.

'Hold on tight!' Jack yelled. The ekoer was trying to gain height, but with their combined weight, it was struggling. Maya felt its powerful wings beating, as it skimmed dangerously low over the ground. With laboured, jerky movements, it slowly gained momentum and height. Maya took a deep breath, almost pleased that the jerky take-off had ended, until she got a hit of its nauseating stench. She pulled her hood tight around her head, hoping it would help.

'Hold on, M^2,' Jack shouted again, trying to gain a better hold. Maya actually didn't have to – the ekoer held her fast – but she couldn't speak with the unnatural stink in the air and simply gave him a thumbs up.

In no time, the monastery and the Gate loomed ahead as they flew over the yyena riders and the hordes of foot soldiers.

Loivissa's roar sounded again, sparking another chain reaction. Other ekoers cried, and the beast carrying them began to ascend. The climb was slow and slowing: they were losing momentum. Despite its strong, wide wings, the ekoer couldn't handle the extra weight. The animal flapped and heaved, trying to reach the clouds above. Exhausted, it screeched at the clouds.

Frightened, Maya looked down. The creature had climbed high; everything looked minute and two-dimensional. She could see the Gate, the monastery and the wall snaking all around the woods and the lake before disappearing into the distance. They floated motionless for a second, hanging in balance like a roller coaster before the plunge. In that split second, Maya noticed that two Fangs had given chase; they were the reason the ekoer had turned up towards the safety of its pack. Now, unable to fly any higher, it turned and dived.

Jack screamed as they began to turn and twist, gathering speed straight towards the ground. It was impossible to look down; Maya's eyes just watered in the rushing air. She held on for dear life as the ground and the Gate raced towards them, catching the flash of the two Fangs as they shot past. Maya snapped her head back and saw them turning like fighter jets, diving back. Behind them, other ekoers come to their abductor's rescue.

Maya turned away in despair, and saw the Gate grow in size. They were descending right above the platform. Scared, she tightened her grip around the beast's claws. Jack yelled something, but she couldn't make out the words. She simply held on, thinking, hoping they wouldn't crash onto the platform. Then, at the last possible minute, the beast extended its wings to their full stretch and began to level off, wailing. They flew dangerously close to everyone's heads. With wide eyes, Maya watched the monks ducking as the beast passed.

Loivissa's roar sounded out once more – much, much louder, now that they were close to the Centre. Maya instantly felt better, but before she could react, they'd sped past the monks and were over the open ground between the two sides. The creature slowed its flight, gliding towards the dark wave ahead with their hill further behind and the strange dark spires in the distance.

Jack shouted, 'Look!'

Ahead, the brutes were converging at the flanks; it was only a matter of time before the excited surge broke. The creature beat its strong wings and gained height as they began to soar over the qwrks. There was growing unrest amongst the brutes below. The front of the wave had stopped, and yet a few large bullies at the back, with spiked armour and large axes, kept driving forward.

Silently they stole past the wave towards the mysterious camp, when a unit of yyena riders passed below, all staring up as they crossed. Maya shuddered at the unnerving sight of them: the heavy-chested beasts looked menacing and reminded her of large monstrous hyenas. Their riders were much smaller and shadowy in their greyish green armour and long black hair that whipped about. Maya was glad they'd gone by when she heard one of the yyenas laugh. It was a disturbing sound that plagued her mind.

The hill they'd emerged from rushed by and the spires in the distance began to grow.

Jack eagerly pulled himself higher up the ekoer's leg and yelled, 'M^2, can you reach the necklace?'

'Yes!' she shouted back, quickly checking her neck to confirm.

'Listen, it might help us,' he began as they flew through columns of smoke and over the charred grassland.

'Look, Jack, it's David!' Maya pointed to where she saw him running around the campfires and debris. 'Where's he going?'

'Concentrate, M^2; you'll need to be brave. Can you do that?'

Brave. Maya's anxiety grew. She knew she wouldn't like what Jack was going say but understood it was the only way.

'Good, we need to escape before it lands,' he told her. 'When it's time, I'm going to jump—'

'*Jump?*'

'Yes! But don't get scared, all you need to do is go invisible. It might trick the beast into opening its claw …'

Maya clutched the crystal. 'OK!'

The beast slowed and the pinnacles slowly grew into tents, like a circus marquee. The largest one with the highest spire was furthest, at the back. Four smaller tents with smaller spires were at the front and formed a large square opening.

'It's landing there,' Jack pointed at the opening. 'Be ready once we pass the first spire.'

Maya nodded, her mouth dry and eyes wide.

'Remember: become invisible.'

They were almost over the first spire. The beast was working hard to hover as it began its descent. Maya kept her eyes on Jack and the approaching spike, with its flag beating crazily in the draught created by the creature. Maya prayed she wouldn't freeze. She was scared, her hands cold and her heart pounding against Jack's backpack.

'Now, M^2!' Jack pulled and punched at the beast's leg. Maya turned the crystal and vanished. Jack punched harder; the spire was directly below them when the beast looked down and squealed.

'OK, M^2, be strong! I'll see you down there.' He let go and fell a short distance onto the curved canvas roof of the tent. Landing on his back, he quickly slid down towards the square opening.

The ekoer wailed and raised the claw that held Maya. Seeing it empty, it yowled again, panicked, and opened the claw to examine it further. Released, Maya quietly fell onto the canvas. It caught her off guard and she landed with a low 'Oof!' She bounced twice before settling on her back and skidding down. She dug her hands into the slippery canvas, desperately trying to correct her slide, but it was no use; her hands couldn't find anything to grip.

'Jack? Jack!' The tent's edge was growing closer.

'Can't see you, M!' she heard Jack calling from below.

'Oops!' She reached for the crystal, the edge almost beneath her.

18

THE DECISION

Acts that shape destiny don't always seem right.

Maya materialised just as she slid off the canopy, and in the split second that she fell she noticed two things: the height of the drop and Jack diving in her direction. And then she crashed into him and lay facing the sky in a tangled mess of arms and legs.

'M^2, are you hurt?' His voice was slow and strained.

Realising he was underneath her, Maya rolled gingerly aside and got onto her knees. She was fine, except for some tenderness and muddy palms and knees.

'Jack, are you OK? Jack?' Ignoring the aches, she wiped the sticky mud off her hands and adjusted her hood.

Jack nodded, his vacant gaze stuck on the light clouds above.

'Sure?' asked Maya, leaning in to examine him.

He nodded once more but continued staring skywards.

'What then?' As she followed his gaze, it dawned on her: the ekoer! It was going to land here.

Jack waited a few more seconds, and only when he was certain it had gone did he sluggishly sit up and look around. The tall tents were deserted, and a pungent smell lingered in the air: a mixture of food, smoke, grass, earth and metal. The ground was all dug up and soggy with smoking tree trunks and uprooted rocks. Maya's eyes darted around, settling briefly on the charred remains of some poor animal. Damaged blades, shields and armour were scattered all around. She felt uneasy and eager to get away.

'I don't like it, M²! It's too quiet. Safer if you remain invisible till we get away.' *Good idea.* Glad to have the necklace, Maya reached for the crystal. 'We should get going, before we're discovered. Turn the crystal and stay close. Whisper, so I know you're there. Quickly now.' He began crawling towards a small stump for cover.

Another thought popped into Maya's mind: *The traitor monk and the staff must be here somewhere.*

'Jack! The staff! Shouldn't we have a look?'

'I know. I might return once you're safe. Besides, I need arrows; lost the two during the flight.' He showed her the empty quiver.

Scared, Maya didn't want to persist, but she was thinking of Mum and Dad, so she forced herself to say, 'It may be too late by then, if … if Aldrr has it, he would flee. We should go now.' She looked around at the debris. 'There must be some arrows lying around, or we'll find some along the way. Besides I'll be invisible and safe, remember.' She turned the crystal, but Jack kept staring in her direction as if nothing had changed. 'What's the matter? You don't like the plan?'

'I can still see you, M².'

See me? No … She carefully twisted the crystal three more times, asking each time if he could see her. Jack didn't have to answer the third time; she knew it wasn't working. Feeling exposed all of a sudden, Maya wanted to hide and inspect the necklace, but knew there wasn't any time for that. She put on a brave face. 'I'm fine. Let's get the staff.'

He remained quiet, which only fuelled Maya's anxiety. Then, looking around the camp, he asked, 'What does your wristband say? Is anything dangerous close by?

'The armlet, you mean,' Maya said, checking inside her robe for Loivissa's gift. She saw the tree brooch sitting on her collar, sparkling in the green glow emanating from her sleeve.

'Green! It's green, Jack.'

'As I suspected. They can't be far off,' Jack muttered, studying the dark tents. 'Best to come back once you're safe.'

'No! Jack, I'll be fine; let's go,' Maya said, fiddling with the brooch. It had given her an idea: call DrAgA. With him here they'd stand a chance. Inside her hood, she closed her eyes in hope that the promise was real, took a deep breath and, with fear dissipating, let out a barely audible whisper: 'DrAgA, DrAgA, DrAgA!'

Rooted to the spot, Maya watched the uninviting darkness of the four tents that led from the opening where they cowered in dread. Just then, green flashes inside one of the tents caught their attention. The unexpected flicker was more disturbing than the darkness. Maya and Jack looked at each other for a second; they knew where the staff would be.

'OK, a quick search before we leave!' said Jack.

Maya forced a slight smile. *DrAgA, where are you?*

'M^2, be alert, stay close and point out any arrow you spot,' Jack said, heading into the dark tent with his bow in hand.

Maya wasn't keen – the smell inside was nauseating – but she followed, sticking close. Quietly, they picked their way towards the flashes and the other opening at the far end. Jack stopped occasionally to examine the odd shafts lying around. They passed weapons, bones and dark piles of muck. The air hung heavy with suspense, and Maya wanted to retreat but bravely continued, losing hope of seeing DrAgA with each step.

Soon it became clear that the other opening was, in fact, a passage leading to the larger tent. Jack stopped to organise the handful of arrows he'd collected. At least now they were armed, not that Maya felt any better. She continued searching for DrAgA in desperation, angry for allowing herself to be so trusting. A sudden grunt from behind startled her. Maya jerked in the direction of the sound, but it wasn't the ghost.

Two qwrks approached them, one large and one small. Hastily, the twins hunted for a hiding place, but there was none. Maya edged closer to Jack, her heart racing, and a knot formed in her stomach.

'Two more shikshi!' declared the larger qwrk in a deep, guttural voice. 'Get them.' Both the brutes skulked forward, playing with their clubs.

'M^2, stay close.' Jack calmly nocked an arrow and drew.

The qwrks stopped. The larger one grunted and signalled with his arm. They immediately separated and began to approach from different directions, predators on the prowl.

Fighting the urge to run down the passage, Maya stood by Jack. He was a picture of concentration, alternating his aim between the two. They stopped a short distance away and an edgy stalemate formed. Jack held the bow's string taut, and Maya held her breath. They had reached a point she knew well: the calm before any exam, that bit of time between writing your name on the paper and beginning the assessment. There was no turning back, ready or not.

Fear-filled, Maya was jumpy and accidentally stepped on something that snapped. Startled, Jack twitched and released the arrow. It shot through the canopy above. The two thugs exchanged a look, snorted and charged. They sank ankle-deep into the mud, but they kept coming, swinging their clubs.

'Come on, Jack!' he said to himself, instantly drawing another arrow.

Smashing and flinging objects out of their path, the two qwrks drew closer, but Jack didn't shoot.

Shoot, Jack! Mud splashed, wood splintered and weapons and stones flew in all directions. Maya ducked instinctively, but Jack stood tall, deciding and aiming. *Soon it'll be too late.* Then Jack released the arrow. The larger qwrk fell back in the thick sludge, groaning and grunting and nursing his thigh. The commotion stopped everyone in their tracks. Maya froze, first in relief and then in panic, for Jack had lowered the bow. Luckily the yowling had confused the smaller qwrk into inactivity, and he kept staring at his companion for direction.

'What's wrong?' asked Maya.

'That was more difficult,' Jack admitted. 'It's not the same as target practice, firing at someone, even if it's them ...'

Maya nodded. It wasn't like him to miss; he was the best mark in their school. He'd chosen to only stop the qwrk, not slay it. 'Perhaps fire a warning shot first?'

Uncertain, the smaller qwrk edged forward, preparing to charge. Jack fired an arrow at its feet. It did the trick; the qwrk flung his club aside and scurried out of the tent.

Maya had barely sighed in relief when the larger brute snapped the shaft buried in his thigh and, shouting and grunting, struggled up using a broken shield that lay nearby.

Jack fired a warning shot at his feet but the qwrk limped forward, uncaring. Jack hesitated, then fired two arrows in quick succession, but the qwrk blocked them with the shield and staggered closer. Jack didn't retreat. A chill passed over Maya when the qwrk raised his club to throw it at them. She wanted to run but her legs were frozen.

'M^2!' Jack jumped back and tackled Maya to the ground. The flying club narrowly missed them. Jack got to his feet and scampered after the bow when something unexpected happened. Two small fireballs slammed into the warrior's back. He growled, struggling to pat out the flames consuming the fur.

'Achanak!' Maya cried, seeing more fireballs light the qwrk's armour. Unable to douse the flames, the brute wobbled in their direction. Maya scuttled backwards until a baton struck the qwrk's knees. It tripped, hit its head against the shield and collapsed with a wet slap, narrowly missing Maya. A breathless David appeared behind the brute.

'Fiery flames! Are you both OK?' The fire genie flew down to Maya.

'That was close.' Jack exhaled.

'A close shave indeed!' David said, catching his breath and looking down the passage.

Maya felt better as they briefly huddled together, readying themselves to move on.

They headed down a small passage to the larger tent. The flashes had ceased. Maya was certain something was wrong, but the boys confidently crept closer, like gladiators on a mission. She looked for DrAgA one last time; there was no one there.

A stench hit them before they entered the tent, and they had to stop to cover their noses. It reeked like nothing Maya had ever smelt, and she was certain that if death and fear had a smell, this was it.

Inside the tent, Aldrr floated with the staff in its grasp. The monk was on his knees before the wraith. The vision of Torackdan being slain flashed through Maya's mind; were they too late?

A familiar screech resonated through the cathedral-like tent. 'What's that smell? Siantians?' Aldrr turned into smoke and, swirling, it turned to face them. 'Fire genie!' it hissed.

Achanak floated down closer to Maya, growing faint. Her heart was thumping; they were facing her nightmare.

'And the meddling apprentice, admirable and imprudent as ever. Come to save the shikshi? Or have you realised that the real prize is the staff?' It set the staff down on a wooden table and floated closer. 'You've meddled for the last time. Twice you've escaped me, but not a third.'

'Twice you say? Reaaally?' David stepped forward.

What's he doing? Maya looked at Achanak for an answer, but he grew fainter with each word Aldrr said.

'Yes, you got away when the gateway collapsed and again this morning, when the walking dead snatched you. Alas, fate now favours me.'

'Walking dead? Oh! The ghosts. They wanted to kill me.'

'Perhaps, but they saved you from my grasp. Now not even Virath or that conspirer Vorsulgha shall come to your aid. And I see you've brought two more to their doom.'

David took another step. 'Really sure of yourself, aren't you? Well I have news for you—'

'You dare mock me?'

'Why not?'

Maya didn't like David's approach and surprised herself by stepping forward to stop him.

Jack stopped her. 'Wait, M², he's trying to distract it; it's working. He's not fleeing with the staff, and that gives us a chance to grab it.'

'You'll pay for your insolence!' Aldrr said, gloating, 'But first you will witness the demise of your friends at the gateway. This realm is indeed frail.'

Aldrr looked up, and within the dark canopy above, images of the unfolding battle gradually appeared, accompanied by loud clashes. Images of qwrks charging towards the thin line of monks came into focus. Maya gaped, temporarily forgetting their own peril. She searched for Tommy and the prince when a dragon roared over the commotion. It had little effect; the hordes continued their onslaught and in the sky, ekoers circled like vultures over a kill.

'Why didn't they retreat?' Maya asked when she saw Loivissa's cry ignored.

'I think they've caught on,' Jack muttered.

'The Siantian dragon has no bite!' Aldrr snickered.

Fearing the worst, Maya watched on, her eyes glued to the images. The qwrk wave was almost upon the thin line of monks.

'Wait, wait,' she heard Jack whisper, as though he were leading the monks. The sunlight flickered for a second as a small cloud of arrows homed in on the charging brutes, who continued undeterred. The shafts found their mark, dampening the approaching surge but failing to stop it.

The charge crashed against the monks, and the grunts and roars were replaced by a symphony of screams, shouts, clashing swords and breaking bones.

The thin line barely held.

'Now!' Jack whispered. More monks ran down from the platform as ekoers dived. Maya held her breath but the image vanished. Startled, she looked around in a daze and discovered that the boys had launched an attack: Jack had fired an arrow and David was swinging his baton. Both weapons simply passed through the smoke; their surprise attack had failed.

Sniggering, Aldrr began to take shape inside its black robe. 'My turn, ignorant Siantians.'

A split second later, smoke tentacles shot out towards all the three of them.

'Jump!' Jack shouted, hurling himself aside.

Both boys lay sprawled with their weapons thrown close by. Maya, however, had only flinched; it happened too fast for her to react. The warlord's misty arm floated right before her.

'What's this? Who defies me? Is it you, genie?'

Inside her hood, Maya looked on, her heart beating wildly; she could feel the wraith's cold presence. Beside her, Achanak flickered.

'Well, genie?' Aldrr seemed to be revelling in their discomfort. 'Well?'

A familiar, heavy voice spoke gently in Maya's ear. 'Does this one bother you? Just nod.'

In a flash, Aldrr's smoke limb retracted. 'Ghouls from the forest! Come forth and speak your business.'

'You came!' Maya blurted. 'I'd given up all hope. What took so long? Where are you?'

'Brr, who you talking to?' Achanak whispered, growing faint.

A second later, a dull scraping noise was heard: the sound of DrAgA dragging his sword against the ground. It was music to her ears.

'He kept his word.' David got up, wide-eyed, as DrAgA materialised nearby.

Jack was already beside Maya and gave her shoulder a reassuring squeeze. Maya smiled, happy that her kindness had proven to be the right choice.

'My men have been eager for an encounter with you, parasite,' DrAgA said to Aldrr. Maya found his gruff voice comforting. 'You've destroyed much of our hunting grounds, sucking the life force from our forest. Now, a simple promise has given us the occasion to repay you.'

Aldrr wailed. 'This is not befitting you; why be slaves to such ignorant, weak Siantians? Join me and be their masters. Orm-Ra will gift you the whole of Siantia.'

Will DrAgA keep his word? Maya wondered.

'DrAgA answers to no one, wraith. We are many things, but betrayers we are not, are we?'

'No!' The chorus of voices made them all jump.

'Nor are we afraid of your master. He may curse us, but do we look afraid? I say, do we look afraid, men?'

'NO!' the warriors boomed again, and one by one the ghosts appeared all around.

Without warning, Aldrr vaporised and shot towards the staff on the table, but the ghosts surrounded him. And then they began to attack like a pack of dogs picking at a larger predator. It was a strange battle: the ghosts threw themselves at the dark smoke, slicing and wrestling and even flying through the wraith. They had the advantage and Aldrr's black smoke was engulfed by grey mist. Light sparked periodically, increasing until a flashing, swirling cloud formed.

The air grew ice cold. Rubbing her arms, Maya's eyes fell on the unattended staff on the table.

'The staff!' she hissed to Jack and David, who stood captivated by the commotion as it gathered speed like some huge turbine.

'Come on, this way!' David picked his way around the spinning turbine to the table.

Maya followed, with Achanak by her side and Jack behind. At the table, David looked at each of the others before ceremoniously picking up the staff.

'Feel anything?' Maya asked anxiously.

David shrugged. 'Do I need to do something, say something?'

'You could ask the book,' said Maya.

'No! It's the reason we are in this mess!' Achanak argued, growing brighter.

Unfortunately, they didn't have the time for a discussion. The otherworldly turbine began to lose momentum. The spinning ghosts slowed and separated to reveal Aldrr kneeling in the centre. The wraith looked tangible, a weak figure slumped on the ground under the weight of its dark robes. The ghosts came to a halt and stood guarding their prisoner. The familiar sound of a sword dragging broke the silence, and DrAgA approached the children.

Aldrr snickered, eyeing David. 'In loss lies victory …'

In loss lies victory? That's what Torackdan said, Maya thought. *Something's wrong.* She chose to be blunt. 'What's so funny?' she asked Aldrr. 'Why did you say that?'

The wraith turned in her direction. One of the ghosts prodded him with his blade.

'Answer her!'

'You sound like another I know. Who are you, little Siantian?' Another ghost kicked it and it fell forward onto its hands.

Maya had turned away in fright. *I sound like another?* She remembered that figure from her dream with her face, her voice. *What does it mean?*

'Explain yourself,' one of the ghosts growled at Aldrr.

He sneered. 'Funny; even in defeat I win. A trick Torackdan himself taught me.'

'Dispense with the riddles!' DrAgA snapped. 'Speak plainly.'

'See for yourself.' Faint images of the battle began to appear in the canopy. 'Despite capturing the staff, your friends will fall. It seems I win after all.' It burst into a coarse laugh.

Everyone gaped. The thin defence line was no more. The solitary building by the lake was overrun by the qwrks and fighting concentrated at the base of the steps leading to the Gate. Slowly the shikshis were retreating up to their last stronghold: the platform. The ekoers dominated the sky, and the Fangs had fallen back to the Gate. It wasn't a loss; it was an annihilation.

'It doesn't matter!' David cried, brandishing the staff. 'We got you and we got this. It wasn't a waste.'

'KILL! KILL! SLAY!' the ghosts yelled, all except DrAgA.

He raised an arm and waited for everyone to go quiet before stooping to Maya. 'Kind one, what is your wish? Do we kill this parasite? Say it and it shall be done. This creature is weak. It has lost all its powers.'

'M^2, it's for the best. Say yes.' Jack stepped closer. 'Either way we suffer, but this way at least we have the staff and can help Virath save Mum and Dad.'

'Listen to him,' David added. 'Don't make one of your posh decisions. One worked out, but the other didn't.'

Achanak descended to her shoulder. 'He didn't show any mercy to us or Virath.'

'Besides, his demise might also save some lives, M^2.'

Maya was in turmoil. They were right; Aldrr hadn't shown Torackdan any mercy either, and killing it could save some lives. But DrAgA could save lives too. She spoke to him in a low voice: 'My friend, can you help those at the Gate?'

'Kind one, if you wish, we will fly at once. But he is still dangerous,' DrAgA said, keeping an eye on Aldrr.

'But weak?' asked Maya.

'Yes, too weak to fly or shift into smoke, but still strong enough to attack you all, I fear,' DrAgA said, gazing at them.

'Not if we have our weapons!' David grabbed his baton and looked at Maya.

Gaining strength from David's confidence, Maya turned to Jack; he stood holding his bow.

It was enough; Maya made her decision. 'Help those at the Gate!'

'Kind one, are you certain?'

She wasn't, but she nodded before she changed her mind.

'So be it. Once more you make the less obvious and more difficult choice. Few are so thoughtful.' He lifted his sword. 'TO THE GATE!'

'TO THE GATE!' the ghosts chorused, fading one by one.

DrAgA disappeared along with them, casting a final glance at Maya.

19

THE LESSON

Nothing teaches like experience.

Alone with Aldrr, the noises of the unfolding battle echoing in the high tent were unsettling. Jack had quickly closed in to cover the kneeling enemy with his bow. David assumed a more relaxed posture and deliberately took his time strolling to Maya and Achanak. It gave the image of confidence; on the streets it was all about being in control, and this was no different. He wasn't happy with the awkward situation Maya had created. When would she get it that you can't be nice all the time? The ghost situation had worked out but now she'd messed it up.

He smiled at Maya and handed her the staff. 'Here! Hang onto this while we keep an eye on Mr Smokey.'

Much to his surprise, she took the staff and said confidently, 'Good point – wouldn't want it falling in the wrong hands.'

As Maya took the staff, Aldrr jerked in their direction. Everyone flinched, and Jack stepped back, pulling the bow's string taut.

David's heart skipped a little. He took a deep breath and composed himself. 'Don't even think about trying anything smart or else.' He had always wanted to say that and paused to savour the moment. He drew the baton and took slow steps to Jack. As he approached, Aldrr directed their attention to the scenes of the battle above.

'Look! See how they scuffle against the might of Vykrutz. Each one will fall, one by one.'

****

Screams and groans muddled with clashes, and clanks of metal against metal intensified to the accompaniment of cracking and battering. The tent was alive with the sounds of death as Aldrr taunted them.

'You who command the ghouls, speak! Who are you? You remind me of—'

'Stop! Stop speaking!' Jack stepped closer.

Unseen inside the hood, Maya was in turmoil from the questioning. Thoughts of seeing herself in her dream plagued her mind, but she suppressed the haunting feelings as she observed the images of the chaos above.

The monks huddled in pockets, brown islands cut off from safety by the surging Vykrutzian tide. Maya searched for the grey mist of DrAgA's ghosts. Unable to spot them, her eyes returned to the few who defended the platform. Heavily outnumbered, the shikshis and Vorsulgha's men fought side by side, trying to keep the circling packs of yyena riders at bay.

In the mangle of metal, flesh and dirt, there was no respect. Maya saw a shikshi slice a qwrk; it fell yowling and only a second later a yyena mauled the monk. He drowned in the dark tide, his arm caught in the beast's jaws.

'See that renegade Vorsulgha struggle,' Aldrr shrieked, sitting up. Close images of battle on the platform appeared. 'Slay him! Kill him!' Aldrr screamed at the image of Lord Vorsulgha, limping as he cut and chopped all around.

'That's enough!' Jack said. Both boys closed in with raised weapons.

Unable to turn away, Maya continued to observe Vorsulgha swinging his heavy axe at everything. Amidst the confusion, a tall, slender figure in distance caught her attention: Prince Dyathen.

Maya's eyes widened in hope as she watched with a deep, held breath. The prince looked tired, his stance lax. Arms drooping, he leaned on his blade to catch a breath when something small whirled by, hitting him twice with a flash.

'Damn a healer!' Aldrr growled. 'Prolonging the inescapable end!'

'Tommy!' Maya said to Achanak. The prince stood a little taller.

She relaxed until she spotted a yyena and its master stealthily launch at Dyathen from behind. The rider dismounted mid-jump, drawing his weapons.

Maya expected the worst but, against all odds, the prince leapt up and over the beast. Somehow he'd sensed the attack. The yyena turned to snap at his heels, but the prince kicked it in the back. It crashed and skidded into the chaos. Its rider and the prince landed dancing in their fighting stances. Their blades clashed, sparks and light flying from the prince's topaz sword. The two warriors locked in a fierce bout, jumping and rolling over dropped weapons and the slain. They carved a path of destruction, jabbing and stabbing others as they went. It was almost inhumanly quick. They stopped abruptly when the rider stumbled and fell. The prince glanced around and then began to hack his way towards Lord Vorsulgha. He hadn't gone far when a Fang crashed down behind him.

'Ekoers! Horrible things,' Maya whispered, feeling a growing knot in her belly.

'Rain your unseen destructions, my flying mutts,' Aldrr cheered weakly.

Images of the sky appeared. The top of the Gate came into view. Arrows, ekoers, Fangs, fireballs and bolts filled the sky.

'Where are your ghastly friends?' Aldrr mocked her. 'Have they been grey with you? Has he duped you? They are known for that!'

'Shh! Quiet,' said Jack. The boys edged forward once more to silence the warlord.

On the makeshift screen, arrows leaving monks' bows were instantly grounded by ekoers' deadly cries. In the confusion, one monk hurled fireballs in multiple directions.

'Laksha,' Achanak said.

Maya nodded as Laksha waved his arms like a master orchestrator. He was overburdened, surrounded and alone. The ekoers were growing bolder and bolder, as were the doubts in her mind; would DrAgA get there in time?

A sickening scream pierced through them all: Aldrr. She turned to him and found the boys smiling. When she followed their eyes back to the canopy, she saw the grey mist rolling in: DrAgA and his gang had engaged. Confusion gave way to panic among the Vykrutzian warriors. Yyena riders turned to flee. With growing confidence and belief in herself, Maya turned, smiling to Jack, only to see him stumble and fall heavily.

Aldrr pounced, wrestling Jack and trying to wrench the bow from his grip. David was already there, carefully swiping his baton at the robe. Maya rushed forward, wielding the staff. She was on her third step when Jack flew free and slid across the ground. She turned in his direction when Achanak caught her attention, faint and floating back towards her. David was retreating slowly as Aldrr rose with Jack's bow drawn.

The warlord had turned the tables on them.

He aimed directly at her. 'Who are you? You're shrewd yet weak.' His voice was soft and calm. 'Those at the Gate were doomed and now so are you. I'll take that staff now!'

****

David was kicking himself. 'Fell for the oldest trick!' He moved slowly sideways to the edge of Aldrr's vision. They had to spread out; the warlord surely couldn't hit them all at the same time. He studied their positions. Maya was to his left with Achanak. Jack was to her left, still on the floor nursing his chest. It was grim; he wasn't sure if Maya would do anything. *Best not to count on her*, he thought. Jack was on his knees now, recovering.

No threats, no warnings; just charge when it's distracted.

'Relinquish it quietly or else!' Aldrr demanded, gloating at Maya. It drew the bow, making an arrow appear. 'Silly Siantian child wasn't even aware of this bow's power.' He relaxed the bow's string and the arrow began to vanish.

'Don't, M^2!' Jack whispered.

'Yes, Maya, move back,' Achanak said, floating before her.

Good! Its attention is divided. David was eager to strike. *Soon. Come on, ignore the pain, Jack. Get ready, buddy!*

****

Clutching the staff, Maya looked around, wondering what to do. Run? *No!* Surprisingly, she wasn't scared until the warlord simply began to walk forward.

'Give it now or …' It drew the bow again.

Maya retreated. At least she hadn't frozen. She was getting better with such situations. Achanak followed, remaining between her and the warlord.

'I don't have time to play games.' Aldrr released the arrow.

It surprised them all. Maya knew, at her core, that Aldrr would act but still couldn't believe he had. Unflinching, she held her breath and looked on. In that second, she saw many things take place: Achanak flew into the path of the missile; David ran, swinging his baton at the warlord's arm; and Jack sprang forward like a lion.

The arrow passed cleanly through Achanak, catching fire as it did so, and filled her vision. 'Duck, Maya!' was the last thing she heard before the flaming arrow hit her in the chest.

For a moment, she lost all sensory perception. Then a rainbow of colour filled her vision, but the expectant pain never arrived. As the colour receded, she began to pat herself, looking for the wound but finding nothing.

Achanak rushed over, glowing brightly. 'How did you do that, the rainbow bubble? Did it absorb the arrow?'

Maya tapped Loivissa's scale with a growing grin. *Of course.* She felt stronger, almost invincible.

'She's good! Maya is unscathed!' Achanak shouted in jubilation.

Maya looked for Jack, eager to tell him of Loivissa's scale, but found him on the ground, wrestling with a dark heap of possessed dark gown. If it wasn't so serious she might have laughed, for it looked like he had brought down a stage curtain. Unable to pin it down, Jack tried to grab the hood and the sleeves but kept slipping. He was struggling when the black mass struck him in the stomach. He sat back, once more trying to catch his breath.

'Off, Siantian!' Aldrr growled in annoyance, only to have David launch himself at the possessed robe. His knees connected with something and the warlord collapsed with a wail. David landed on top and didn't stop. Shouting and roaring, he struck with the baton as many times as he could. It looked as though he were dusting a rug.

The warlord's groans grew louder but David didn't stop. He hit everywhere, his chest heaving with the effort. When he paused to catch his breath, Aldrr grabbed him by the hair. David grappled with its unflinching grip, but he was held fast.

'Enough of this. The staff or I'll kill him.' Aldrr's voice was weaker but intimidating nonetheless. David yelled out in pain, trying to wriggle.

'No, you flaming won't!' Achanak rushed forward, firing small fireballs at the wraith.

It had little effect; the dark gown sat up, wailing, and shoved David into Jack. Both crashed in a tangle.

Achanak flew around, shooting fireballs. 'Take that, and that and that!' The smoking robe caught fire but the wraith rose up, unconcerned.

There was nothing useful in the sparse tent, and nowhere to hide. DrAgA had been right; Aldrr was too strong for them. *I made the wrong decision*, Maya thought. The wraith shrieked once more, getting to its full stature.

'I'll have that staff now, but first let's see who you are. Who sounds like our prince?'

Maya took a deep breath. She wanted to retreat but didn't. A knot formed in her stomach when she saw Jack and David still on the floor.

'Get back!' Achanak yelled at Aldrr, dashing back to her shoulder.

The smell of death and fear grew as the wraith approached. Slowly, it curled its hand around the staff, while brushing her hood back with the other.

Straightway Aldrr stepped back and stared at her for a moment longer, before drawing closer. 'My prince! What trickery or treachery is this?'

It had mistaken her for the small warrior, the one who'd slain Torackdan. She gripped the staff with both hands for support.

'Leave us alone, you … you …' Achanak flew around, glowing bright in fury.

'No! You're not him!' Aldrr cried in realisation. 'You look the same, but there's a kindness about you. Master will be pleased to learn of your existence.' It seized Maya's arm and pulled.

'JACK!' She dropped the staff and instinctively grabbed Aldrr's wrist. Pain shot through her arm like a growing electric shock. She yelped but the sound was drowned out by Aldrr's scream. Maya tried to pull away but her hand wouldn't let go. Aldrr juddered and dropped to one knee. The pain dulled and was replaced by intense sadness and growing darkness. Maya searched for Jack and saw everything moving slowly. The dark robe was shrinking. Jack and David were by her side, trying to release her hand. She couldn't hear their voices; all she saw was the robe convulsing as the pain began to subside. She slumped, tired, and turned once more to the arm she gripped; it had gone ashen and thin. Unable to keep her eyes open. Maya succumbed to growing darkness.

20

THE CIRCLE OF SIANTIA

The end of the beginning.

'Shoo! Let her rest!' Maya heard Tommy's stern voice first and then saw something yellow floating away. *A beautiful butterfly, fluttering* ... She smiled and slowly opened her eyes wider to find Achanak frolicking above her.

'She's awake, everyone!' he shouted and gleefully scooted away.

'M^2!'

'Maya!'

'Your Highness!'

Tommy hovered into view, followed by the smiling faces of Jack and Laksha, both sporting taped cuts. She turned her attention to the canopy above: it wasn't dark with images of the battle but a light cream with rich, golden designs. Confused, she asked groggily, 'The staff? Where is it? Is everyone fine? Mum and Dad?'

Jack took hold of her hand. 'Shh, M^2, the staff's safe! You saved it.'

Trying to sit up, she continued in a cautious whisper. 'Tommy, you're OK? And the prince?'

'Fine, fine! He rests too! Even the injured monk survives, thanks to Kuts.' Tommy said eagerly, floating before her. 'Now lie back.'

'Slowly, Your Highness,' said Laksha, reaching forward to help a relieved Maya.

'Highness?' She settled into a sitting position with Jack's help and studied the room.

She was seated on the largest bed she had ever seen. Above it hung a richly decorated canopy. Directly behind her was a massive headboard, and at the foot of the bed was a cushioned stool. The room was the size of a small hall, and further down was a writing desk, settees in a square formation and a roaring fire under the mantelpiece.

Still feeling woozy, she closed her eyes for a moment, and Tommy's motherly voice soon piped up. 'Maya, here, eat this. Be sure to chew properly.' She'd landed on the bed and held out a small bundle of leaves. 'It's only been a day; she needs more time to recover. Now out with both of you. You have seen she's recovering well; now let her be.'

Feeling her head clear, Maya took the green bundle with renewed curiosity. 'A day? I've been asleep for a day? And wasn't Achanak here? What's happened? Please tell me. Is something wrong? Jack?'

Silence fell. Jack and Laksha turned to Tommy as though to ask her permission.

'Very well.' Tommy gestured to Laksha and Jack. 'But please be brief. Maya really needs to rest if she's to make it this evening.'

Maya couldn't believe they'd waited for Tommy to approve before speaking to her. 'Did you just ask permission to talk to me?' It was bizarre. 'And what's this evening?'

'M^2, Tommy's been especially protective of you. You saved the staff. You were also right; David's the new konjurer. Well, in training. But yes, a konjurer.' Chewing the green leaves, Maya smiled. 'Against all odds, your decisions saved everything: the staff, the Gate, and all of us. Yes, sending DrAgA and his gang saved the Gate and our world. Everyone's eager to meet you.'

Feeling more alert, Maya asked, 'What happened to the warlord? I can remember feeling the sadness and him shrinking—'

'Your Highness—' Laksha interrupted.

'Highness?' Maya repeated.

'Kindly bear with me, I shall reveal all. It has been the most intriguing turn of events indeed. Firstly, I must say everyone will be relieved to learn you are awake; something that Achanak should have seen to by now.' Laksha smiled courteously and carried on. 'About Aldrr, the slaved warlord: You subdued him simply by grabbing his arm. It turned him back to his former self – a dwarf king by the name of Qubegkark. You cured him, removing Orm-Ra's vile konjuring. You freed him from years of being a minion, a slave to Orm-Ra's will.'

'So where is this King Qub ... now?'

'Alas he didn't survive. But, indebted, he left his ring for you.' Laksha presented his closed fist and opened it slowly. At the centre of his palm was a thick, plain gold band with intricate designs. 'A token of his gratitude. In his kingdom, you will always have an ally.'

Gingerly, Maya took the ring. It was too large for her fingers. 'Shikshi Laksha, how did me holding the king's arm turn him back to his old self? All I recall is the pain and the sadness.'

'To understand that, you need to learn who you really are.' Laksha paused. 'Jack told me that Aldrr recognised your voice, saying you sounded like another he knew?'

Maya nodded.

'And when he laid his eyes on you, he called you "my prince". Is that right?'

Nodding, Maya raised her eyebrows.

'The wraith mistook you for the kidnapped Konjiurian prince.'

The small warrior ...

'That only raised more questions until Shikshi Virath awoke and revealed a secret, an elaborate trick—'

'Shikshi Virath?'

'Yes, with the help of Tommy, he too recovers well.' Laksha gave Tommy a quick glance. 'And Shikshi Virath revealed that, thirteen years ago, a pair of twins was born to the king of Konjiur. You, the younger, were brought here to Siantia for your protection. It's a secret known to very few; everyone was duped into thinking only the kidnapped prince was born that night. A trick to keep Your Highness safe. And what better place to hide than here: the world of science?'

'Please call me by my name,' Maya said, staring into space, not knowing what to think of it all.

Laksha hesitated. 'Perhaps behind closed doors … Maya, as I was saying, this means you are a princess, heir to the throne of Konjiur. Shikshi Virath would be the best person to explain more.'

'That's right, enough for now,' said Tommy.

'But I still don't understand. How could I have turned the wraith, Aldrr?' Maya insisted.

Laksha looked to Tommy for approval before continuing. 'Only someone with a very special gift could have done what you did. When you freed the king from the dark influence, you changed his heart, which only a—'

'A heart changer can do!' Maya cried, to everyone's surprise. Her heart was thumping wildly. Suddenly everything made sense: why she'd had the dream, why she'd seen herself in the small warrior's hood, heard her own voice and was able to do what he could.

'Yes, and that's why you were able to help Aldrr. These events have been most intriguing and have raised many questions about Hiertans, about the prophecies and many other myths out there.'

'But Jack's my twin brother, isn't he? And what about Mum and Dad?'

Jack squeezed her hand once more, and Maya threw her arms around him.

'OK, now that is quite enough,' Tommy said, trying to bring the discussion to a close.

'Rest now, M^2; there will be time to talk more,' said Jack, holding her.

'Jack, I want to be with Mum and Dad.'

'About your parents,' said Laksha, 'What we've come to know is that, before he passed, the great Torackdan cast a spell on the kidnapped prince's parents – the King and Queen – to protect them. It somehow affected your parents here.' Tommy was pacing eagerly now and so Laksha concluded. 'Maya, with Virath's help we will find your parents, all of them: your Siantian parents and your Konjiurian parents, the King and Queen. And as for Jack, he'll always remain your twin.'

'M^2, I'm not going anywhere. You're my li'l sis and always will be,' said Jack, slowly getting up.

'Now I insist you rest, Maya.' Tommy flew towards the door, only to have Achanak reappear.

'Everyone's coming,' he said, delighted.

'No! You didn't just bring everyone,' Tommy flew at him, but he was too agile for her and disappeared into the keyhole.

'Rest and we'll see you this evening,' Tommy told Maya.

'What's this evening?' Maya asked.

'A small ceremony in which David will be officially named a konjurer. Now come along, Jack,' said Laksha. He hurried to the door to address those waiting outside.

Jack gave her another quick hug and followed Laksha out. Alone with Tommy, Maya's mind filled with questions. *What will happen in the ceremony? What powers will David have? And how will he or Virath save Mum and Dad? What will Virath be like? And me ... a princess ... really? Do I need to go to school? Or a different school?* Marvelling at the possibilities, Maya began to trouble Tommy for details about the initiation ceremony.

****

By that evening, Maya was much better. She dressed in silky pink robes and made her way to the Throne Room with Tommy. As they neared, however, Maya began to feel unsettled. She'd flown with the Fangs, faced the warlord and braved the spiders, but now her stomach was funny. She knew the sensation well; it occurred every time she'd had to collect a certificate from the school stage.

Before she could turn around, Maya was before the familiar double doors of the Throne Room. She hoped to slip in unnoticed, but two monks standing outside promptly opened the doors for them. The noise inside died instantly.

Great. Maya took a small step inside and found all eyes on her. The hall was decorated and packed.

'Oh dear, silly me,' Tommy whispered floating, closer to her ear. 'I forgot all about the protocol!'

'Protocol?' Maya whispered with some alarm.

'Yes! You're supposed to behave royally. Now, just walk slowly up the red carpet to that seat beside the throne.'

It looked far, and Maya didn't want to walk all the way over there with everyone watching, but she took a deep breath, gave a courteous nod and began for the smaller ornate seat at the far side.

'Just smile, look at everyone and walk slowly.'

The red of the carpet was brilliant, the throne high, and the decorations rich. The hall was packed with Fangs, ghosts, shikshis and qwrks. All were on their feet, following her progress.

Maya took deliberate steps but was relieved when Jack and Achanak rushed down from the far end to escort her. In their company, the parade to the seat felt easier.

At the front, Maya found her friends: Prince Dyathen, David, DrAgA, Lord Vorsulgha, Laksha and an older shikshi holding the staff.

Shikshi Virath, she guessed. Everyone proudly wore bandages, bruises and little cuts.

'Sit; everyone's waiting for you,' Tommy whispered. Maya had been standing before her seat for some time, captivated by David's bluish silver attire. It reminded her of Torackdan.

Snapping herself out of the memory, Maya gracefully scanned the room and sat down; only then did everyone follow suit, except Jack, who remained standing next to her. That didn't feel right, so she quietly asked him to share her seat, but he politely refused. Her little enquiry didn't go unnoticed, however. In no time, another seat was placed besides hers for Jack. He perched on it as though he'd fall off any second. She could tell that something bothered him, but now was not the time to ask about it. Being a princess was nothing like she'd imagined it would be. It was most uncomfortable and Maya hoped there was some mistake.

'Welcome Your Highness, Princess Maya of Konjiur and Siantia!' said Laksha stepping before her. Clapping broke out.

'I speak for everyone here when I say we're all pleased to see you on your feet.'

Again everyone applauded.

Maya smiled as nobly as she could. Everyone was glowing with happiness, and even the qwrks looked harmless.

Laksha continued: 'Today, we witness a very special event – the initiation of a konjurer. But before that, let's remember Torackdan the Gentle, his aide Hopper, who brought the staff to us, and all our friends who aren't with us now. They fought selflessly to protect the staff and our world against those who practice the merciless arts.'

Everyone fell silent for a few minutes. Then Laksha called on Shikshi Virath to begin the initiation ceremony. Virath took a scroll in one hand and a strange stick in the other and began reciting. Maya didn't understand what was being said but watched closely.

When the tune of the recital unexpectedly changed, Maya saw a shikshi enter the hall at the back, carrying Torackdan's twisted staff. Everyone turned and stared at him. The shikshi approached the front and placed the staff on an altar Maya hadn't paid any attention to.

Then Laksha stepped forward with David; he held *No Words* in his grip. As they approached the staff, the crystal at the top began to glow and the staff slowly rose into the air. Virath's recital reached its climax and the staff lazily floated towards David. Maya held her breath as David instinctively raised his hand and allowed it to come to him. Virath stopped chanting and announced, 'I present David, the Siantian konjurer!'

Wild cheers and whistling erupted. Bewildered, David turned to everyone with a smile. For long minutes the noise continued until the crystal's glow began to subside.

As the noise died, Virath addressed David: 'You are a konjurer but will remain here until you've learnt to use your art. Remember that it must be noble, gentle konjuring, not vile and wicked.' David nodded. 'And now for the other reason we've gathered …'

Everyone looked puzzled.

'Princess Maya, the revelation of your existence, the demise of my good friend, Torackdan the Gentle, and the rise of a budding new konjurer have created many ripples, the effects of which cannot yet be fully understood. However, one thing is now certain: the prophecies that spoke of the coming of a twin are true.'

A commotion broke out, and Virath had to wait for silence before continuing. 'There are those who think Orm-Ra is the prophesised one, but I think the prophecies speak of you, Maya. With that in mind, we must form a Circle of Siantia: a small band of chosen ones with a common purpose: to protect you.'

Maya turned to her brother and her friends. *Twins? Prophecies? Chosen few? Circle?* They all looked mystified, but Virath didn't stop.

'Our ally, Prince Dyathen; Tommy, your guardian; Jack the Siantian; Konjurer David and his friend Achanak: they are now the Circle of Siantia. Not too many nor too few – just perfect. This group will protect you, Princess Maya, for in you rests our hope to rise against the might of Orm-Ra. These recent events are but the start; we must prepare—'

'Forgive me, wise shikshi.' The prince stood. 'Surely the princess is safe here in Siantia? If not, then we need stronger beings. I mean no disrespect, but I am not qualified for such a task. Nor is the konjurer, who has yet to master his skills. The healer cannot protect her, nor can the Siantian.'

Virath stood silently for a few more seconds before replying. 'Prince Dyathen, that may be, but we have not all come together by chance. And now that we are united, the circle can only grow in strength. It was the Siantian's art' – he pointed at Jack, then at Tommy – 'the healer's skills and the princess's decisions that turned the battle in our favour and saved us all. It wasn't our might.'

'Then surely DrAgA should be part of the circle, shikshi?' said the prince.

'No.' Virath was stern. 'His destiny lies elsewhere. But your paths will cross before long.' He paused to look at everyone. 'And that brings me to the final matter of this evening.' He paused, and the audience exchanged confused glances. 'I name

Shikshi Laksha as the new head of the Red Gate Centre. He will take my place as my path leads me to Konjiur where, in Torackdan's absence, I must help the King upon his return.' Murmurs broke out across the hall and Virath raised his voice. 'Listen to Laksha as you have me. Under his guardianship, you must safeguard this centre. Now, let's dine for one last time, for I leave tomorrow.'

No one moved.

'Why the long faces? I leave to aid the returning King of Konjiur. Under Laksha's direction, Konjurer David will use his diary and the powerful staff Tabioak to invoke the spirit of gentle Torackdan and undo the spells of safekeeping binding the princess's parents. Let us celebrate the safe arrival of the staff, the coming of our new konjurer, the Konjiurian King's return and the arrival of Princess Maya, the hope of all the realms.'

At the mention of Mum and Dad, Maya clapped, overjoyed, and everyone followed her lead. She stood to ask them to stop but only managed get them onto their feet in a show of respect. She chuckled – how odd to be a princess! The tension broke and smiles appeared on everyone's faces.

Amongst the confusion, Shikshi Virath asked her to lead everyone to the banqueting hall. Maya politely began for the door; it was a most unusual experience for her to lead, but she forced herself to do it. In the banqueting hall, she and Tommy sat next to the large ornate chair at the head of the main table. Jack was beside her, and she insisted that David and Achanak sit beside him. Shikshi Virath, Shikshi Laksha, Lord Vorsulgha, DrAgA and Prince Dyathen all sat with them at the main table.

Once everyone had taken their seats, Virath stood and spoke. 'It's customary for royalty to speak, but as Princess Maya isn't fully recovered, I'll say a few words. We gather to pay a tribute to our friends who cannot be with us today, those who fell in the battle for us and for Siantia, where konjuring is always under persecution.

'Konjurer!' Maya whispered to David, recalling Torackdan's blue robes from her dream.

'Just "Wiz", *Your Highness.*'

'Right! So it's just M^2, then!'

'And you're the Siantian?' David said to Jack.

'I like it!' said Jack. 'You're learning the science of magic; I know the magic of science. So I guess it's only apt?'

They relaxed and enjoyed the evening with Achanak and Tommy, talking, joking and eating a bit of everything.

****

David liked the twins. They were OK, he supposed. His dowsing feeling was at rest, and he didn't feel like running away, although he wasn't sure what was next for him. He was pleased he could be himself: no more putting on acts. Most important of all, he was going to be dabbling in fringe science – or konjuring, as everyone called it. He wasn't sure what to do or if he'd like it, but he had the book and Achanak; it was a great start.

For Maya, it wasn't the best evening she could remember, but she was content. Mum and Dad would be back soon, and she was happy that both Jack and she were right about magic and science.

The banqueting hall remained noisy for a long time, and that was how their thirteenth birthday came to pass, with revelations and adventures, gifts from other worlds and new friends, all united in the Circle of Siantia. Now that's a flaming fine finish!

THE END

Printed in Great Britain
by Amazon